Blood on the Cimarron

No Motive for Murder

Mary Colley
10/2019

Enjoy!

Blood on the Cimarron

No Motive for Murder

An Oklahoma Mystery

Mary Coley

Blood on the Cimarron: An Oklahoma Mystery

Published by Moonglow Books through Create Space
P.O. Box 2517, Tulsa, OK 74101 USA
www.marycoley.com

ISBN: 13: 978-1974475377
ISBN: 10: 1974475379

Dedication

I dedicate this book to my Gamma Phi Beta pledge sisters at Oklahoma State University, Beta Psi Chapter, Stillwater, OK. My years in Stillwater in the 1970s are some of my fondest memories. I drew from that locale in writing this book.

It is because of your support and interest in my mysteries that I keep on writing!

Thank you K.K., Jeri, Kruger, Missy, Mojo, Jan, DO, Connie, Hoppy, Sharon and Carolyn for your sisterly love and special interest!

Chapter 1

Claire Northcutt's RAV-4 bumped down the sloping gravel road toward the Cimarron Valley Ranch complex. She unrolled her window and scanned the pastures, looking for signs of J.B. Floren.

Birds twittered in the damp early morning breeze, lifted from the stalks of grass and dropped to perches only yards away. Another day she might have stopped and enjoyed the 360-degree view of the spring-green fields of central Oklahoma, but not today. The rancher was twenty minutes late.

She neared the central plaza and the grouping of buildings which made up the headquarters complex. Something at the base of the flagpole caught her eye; she slammed on the brakes, turned off the motor and hopped out.

A roaring noise in Claire's head drowned out the fluttering, clucking chickens in the coop fifty yards away.

Surely that wasn't ...

The man's arms were tied to the flagpole. His splayed legs stretched toward her. Beneath him, blood pooled on the rocks, soaking into the rich river bottom soil.

Her vision blurred and her legs folded.

"J.B.?" His name escaped her lips, but she had no hope for a response.

So much blood.

Ten minutes earlier, Claire Northcutt had parked her SUV and glared up the gravel drive into the morning sun. She tapped her short fingernails on the steering wheel.

J. B. Floren, the owner of the Cimarron Valley Rescue Ranch, was a typical seventy-something rancher with smile lines etched around his wide mouth and a perpetually sunburned face. Three weeks ago, when Claire had come out to the ranch for a first interview, his look had taken in her wavy shoulder-length hair. Then he'd checked out the way her jeans fit. She'd stifled the mix of pleasure and anger that flashed in her mind. The muscular man with Paul Newman blue eyes had smiled and winked as if that was all it took for a woman to fall for him.

She wasn't interested.

Claire had met plenty of handsome men in her lifetime. She didn't need or want to get to know another one, especially J.B. Floren. Something about him made her uneasy, and it wasn't because he was a flirt. Despite his friendly banter and twinkling eyes, an undercurrent of something spooked her. She didn't trust him. But right now, she didn't trust men in general when it came right down to it. A few bad apples ...

A scissortail flycatcher flitted down to land on a fencepost. Behind the bird, bright green prairie grass danced in the breeze beneath a dome of turquoise sky. She wiped a finger across her brow. The spring heat was building quickly.

Where was he?

The wealthy rancher more than thirty years her senior now devoted his efforts to saving the lives of wild mustangs and burros. He provided a much-needed refuge for animals removed from western rangelands. She hoped the article she was writing would be picked up by the Associated Press and go nationwide.

Had Floren forgotten their appointment? She pulled out her cell phone. No message. She thought about calling him. At two previous meetings, the rancher had been waiting, parked a few yards inside the gate in his shiny silver pickup. Not today. And none of his rescued mustangs or burros munched the sweet prairie grass nearby. The animals could be anywhere on the 1280-acre ranch, but the rancher should be here.

Claire rolled down her window; moist spring air feathered her cheeks. No choice but to wait. Her editor, Manuel Juarez, expected a polished draft tomorrow, and this was only one of the assignments on her plate for the next two days.

Ask a few more questions about the mustangs and she could finish her in-depth article for *The Stillwater News Press.* Twenty minutes, tops. After editing the article she'd be done with Mr. Floren. But first, he had to show up.

She punched the horn, three rapid honks. Claire's day was booked to the second. She didn't need any delays. If she had to work late, Cade and Denver would have to scrounge for leftovers in the fridge, and there weren't any. Neither would be satisfied with a can of soup or a PB and J sandwich instead of a cooked meal.

Claire slid out of the RAV. Gravel crunched beneath the hard heels of her boots, she felt it in her jaw. *I'm clenching again.* She pulled in a slow breath. *Relax.*

The scent of growing grass and fertile earth tickled her sinuses, and the faint odor of animal manure drifted past on the breeze.

In four long strides, she reached the blood-red pipe gate, grabbed the chain and shook it. The unlatched padlock clunked into greening weeds at the gatepost's base. Claire yanked the chain away from the post and shoved the gate open. It swung 180 degrees and clanged against the fence on the opposite side.

She climbed back into the SUV and mashed the accelerator. The engine roared and the tires spun in the gravel. Chunks of rock rattled in the wheel wells. She steered through the opening, jumped out to push the gate closed, and scooted into the vehicle again.

Before her, a dirt road meandered through the rippling grass and over the ridge to the headquarters, a half-mile away. Even though she kept the speedometer under twenty, her vehicle shimmied on a wash-boarded stretch of road.

The RAV crested a hill; the headquarters complex stretched before her in the river valley. Buildings, barns and paddocks clustered around a plaza where gleaming black river rocks surrounded a centered flagpole. Corrals and holding pens extended behind the barns and the bunkhouse, their fence lines stretching toward the slender willows and tall cottonwoods of the muddy Cimarron River another half-mile further. Above, a turkey vulture soared in a circle. During her previous visits, an American flag at the top of the flagpole had rippled in the constant breeze.

"First thing I do each morning, last thing I do each night, is care for the flag," J.B. Floren had told her proudly that first visit.

Today, J.B. had not run his flag up the pole.

An uncomfortable feeling settled in her stomach.

As the RAV bumped down the sloping gravel road toward the buildings, Claire scanned the ranch complex for movement. A pile of something at the base of the flagpole caught her attention. She slammed on the brakes and hopped out.

A roaring noise in her head drowned out the chickens clucking and fluttering in the coop fifty yards away.

Surely that wasn't ...

The man's arms had been tied to the flagpole. His splayed legs stretched toward her. Floren's handsome face was ruined. Blood streaked his sliced cheeks. Deep, dark red smears splotched his tattered white shirt. Beneath him, blood pooled on the rocks, soaking into the rich river bottom soil.

Gooseflesh raised on her arms. Her vision blurred and her legs folded. She grabbed the SUV's door handle.

"J.B.?" She had no hope that the rancher was alive.

So much blood.
Again.

Chapter 2

Claire bent over the end of the deputy sheriff's smooth vinyl front seat, her head on her knees, legs out the door, eyes closed.

Don't hyperventilate. The chemical scent of carpet cleaner rose from the floor mats.

She didn't want to see the blood or the body again. Everything she knew about J.B. Floren she'd learned during their interviews, but none of it insinuated a motive for someone to kill him so violently.

Older images of another bloody body split her mind open, as if that day had been yesterday and not three years ago. She opened her eyes and focused on the line of trees that defined the distant river. Somewhere, a dog barked furiously.

Two more vehicles rolled into the courtyard which had become a parking lot full of sheriff's department vehicles and an ambulance.

"Claire," a familiar voice called.

Holt Braden slammed the door of his black dually Ford pickup and charged toward her.

Claire groaned and clenched her teeth.

"I heard sirens as I was driving to town. Followed the medical examiner right through the gate and saw your SUV. What happened?" Worry had drawn temporary lines on her neighbor's handsome face, but otherwise he looked as if he could have been on a photo shoot for GQ, prematurely gray hair tousled by the wind, belted khakis recently pressed, golf shirt tucked in to better define his trim muscular upper body.

A deputy held up his hand to stop Holt's progress, his other hand poised above his holstered gun. "Sir, this is a crime scene. You can't be here." The deputy planted himself in Holt's path.

Holt peered at the man's name badge. Towering over the shorter, bulkier deputy, he pointed at the tape ten yards away. "The crime tape is over there."

The men glared at each other.

Claire breathed deeply. Her heart rate slowed. The memory of the other body receded. As much as she didn't want her 'John Wayne' neighbor to be here, he pulled her thoughts away from the body at the base of the flagpole.

"It's okay, Deputy Purdue. This is my neighbor, Holt Braden."

"Ms. Northcutt, I can't allow anyone else at this crime scene." The deputy frowned at Holt. "Stay here. Do not go past the tape."

Holt barreled to her, leaned in, and cupped her shoulders with his hands. His musky aftershave enveloped her.

Claire straightened while Holt rubbed her shoulders lightly. Her tense muscles responded.

"Tell me what happened," he said.

Her half-hearted attempt to smile failed. She didn't want to talk to anyone, but she was certain she'd be asked about finding J.B. Floren's body repeatedly over the next several days. Might as well get used to it. After all, she'd been through a violent death before. She knew the drill.

She tilted her head and squinted at three thin white contrails inching their way across the jewel-blue sky. Her heart hammered wildly.

Her neighbor's presence here wasn't wanted or needed, no matter how upsetting this situation was. Holt had recently joined the short list of men since her divorce who wanted to get her into bed. None of them had been successful.

Holt's look shifted to the flagpole where the sheriff and the medical examiner bent over the body. The wind kicked up and the rope's snap clips clanked against the metal pole.

A snarling black flurry exploded through the just-opened barn door. The growling dog knocked a second deputy sheriff to the ground as he charged across the courtyard toward the professionals at the base of the flagpole.

"Ranger," Claire shouted. She lifted herself out of the deputy's vehicle and yelled the dog's name again, clapping her hands.

The animal turned her way in midstride and skidded to a stop. The long hair along its backbone had bristled. When the dog eyed the men again, they flattened against the deputy's cruiser.

"Ranger, down. Come." Claire extended her hands toward the dog. "Ranger. It's okay, boy. It's okay." The dog's feathered tail dropped, and then jerked from side to side. He trotted to her, sniffed her hands and licked them with a long pink tongue. Ranger sat on his haunches and whined. She knelt beside him.

She slipped her fingers under the big dog's collar and pulled him close. She'd met this animal on that first visit here weeks before. Each time she'd come, he'd sat beside her as she and Floren talked, and trotted next to her truck all the way to the gate when she left.

The animal glanced toward the men again. A growl rumbled low in his throat.

Claire leaned into the dog. "Shhh." She spread her fingers into his fur and felt tense muscles and warmth.

For the moment, with her eyes closed and the morning breeze on her face, the last vestiges of the two bloody images dissolved.

Chapter 3

Later, when Claire opened the SUV's passenger door at her five-acre tract east of Stillwater, Ranger bounded out. The dog raced toward the front porch, his muzzle moving along the ground as he searched for Izzy's scent. Claire scanned the grassy acres, but didn't see her fuzzy white-haired mutt.

"Izzy?"

Ranger charged around the house and loped toward the small barn halfway to her back-property line.

Late morning sun rays filtered through puffy turtle-like clouds and tingled on her skin. She staggered toward the two-stall barn, her legs unsteady and her thoughts spinning.

Floren. Murdered.

She stopped and leaned against the clothesline pole, halfway to the barn. Her breath hitched in her throat.

I'm okay, I'm okay, she repeated.

But Floren wasn't.

The rancher had been a good info source. He'd talked freely and always had a steaming pot of coffee on the stove or lemony ice tea in the fridge. He'd been a perfect host, other than the fact he wouldn't keep his eyes where they belonged.

In her fifteen-year career as a journalist, Claire had encountered men like Floren before. Lots of men over seventy were still hard at work. Many men of that generation still considered a woman's place to be in a kitchen, not the workplace. Not competing beside them. Not thinking or challenging the status quo.

The image of Floren's bloody body and sightless eyes open to the sky flooded her mind as she stepped into the small barn. She was grateful Cade was at school and not at home to see how unsettled she was.

The little tack room was orderly and clean, with saddles, bridles, halters and saddle blankets neatly arranged, thanks to Denver. Her nephew was becoming a great horse trainer. She wasn't sure she and Cade could care for the animals and her five acres without him.

Blaze nickered and poked her head over the half door, tossing her black mane. Claire stepped over to the mustang's stall, glancing into the adjacent one as she passed it. "Hey, girl. Where's your buddy?"

Hooves thudded against the hard-packed dirt floor. A small gray burro plodded into the stall from the adjacent paddock.

"There you are, Smoky." Claire stroked both soft noses. The animals bumped against the wooden slats of their stalls.

"Aunt Claire? Back so soon?"

Denver paused in the doorway, his black cowboy hat low on his forehead but not low enough she couldn't see the question in his brown-black eyes.

"I found J.B. Floren dead this morning," she said. "Murdered at his ranch."

Denver stood at full attention, his slim shoulders straight. His arms hung loose and his fingers twitched. "*You* found him?"

"We were supposed to have our final interview this morning at eight. He'd been killed and left tied to the flagpole at the headquarters."

Denver shuffled across the barn to the tack room, his boots kicking dust. He pulled a rope halter off a peg. "I'm sorry you had to see that."

Why wasn't he sorry the rancher was murdered? She reached for the wall to steady herself.

The heavy smell of hay and horses floated throughout the small barn even though the breeze blew through the structure's open doors. A different kind of heavy air hung around Denver. He was subdued, more so than usual. And his emotionless response to the news of the rancher's murder was as stunning as the death itself.

"I'm going to work with Blaze some more until my appointment with Dr. Rhodes," Denver said. He looked at her. "Are you all right?"

"I will be. I didn't know Mr. Floren well." Claire wrapped her arms around herself.

A muscle jerked in Denver's jaw.

She hoped he'd say more, but doubted that would happen. Nothing ever drew Denver fully into the repartee of conversation, and this topic was no different.

He gathered Blaze's tack and laid it over his arm.

Claire patted Denver's shoulder as he limped past her and into the stall. The horse tossed her head and rolled her huge brown eyes at the sight of the halter, but Denver spoke soothingly until the mare let him slip it over her ears and onto her muzzle.

Denver *was* better in many ways, less antisocial, less hyper-vigilant. The therapist had told her what she personally already knew, *time will heal most wounds.*

"I wonder how Cade will react to the rancher's death," Claire said. "He seemed to like volunteering at the rescue ranch with you on the weekends. Do you supposed the ranch will close?"

Denver buckled the rope halter over Blaze's cheek, pulling it tight. "The man was a jackass. I told Cade last week to help with the hay drops, talk to the animals, and go home. He didn't need to spend any more time than necessary with that man."

Claire watched her nephew pick up a brush and stroke the horse's neck and flank. Her vision fuzzed and then cleared. "Explain."

Denver shrugged. "He wasn't what he appeared to be."

"He was a rancher, saving mustangs. If that's not what he was, what was he?"

The muscle in his jaw tightened again.

"And now he's dead. Why would someone kill him?" she persisted.

What did Denver know about J.B. that she apparently had not uncovered in her research?

Claire's cell phone buzzed. She pulled it out of her jean pocket and glanced at the displayed text. Manny Juarez wondered where she was. He'd have to wait. She needed to be out here where her mind could work through the morning's horror.

The world was still spinning slowly around her. Closing her eyes didn't help. She typed a quick message–be there soon–and pushed *send*.

Blaze nickered as Denver led the horse into the barn's central alley. "Better stay back, Claire. She's still a little goosey with people unless you're at her head. She's got a powerful kick."

"No problem." Claire reached for a shovel from the row of implements propped against the wall and rolled the wheelbarrow into the horse's stall. She scooped fresh manure and straw from the floor into the wheelbarrow.

The former soldier led the horse toward the training ring.

He probably won't say another word about Floren today, if ever. Claire had learned within a week of his arrival that when Denver Streeter didn't want to talk, he didn't.

Lately, when she overheard him talking to Cade, he sounded more like an older brother than a cousin. Her 15-year-old craved attention from a man he respected. He'd certainly never gotten much of it from his father.

Claire finished mucking out the stall and rolled the wheelbarrow into the burro's space. Smoky nibbled at her sleeve and nuzzled her, searching for a treat.

"Nothing for you, fella."

She set to work, but her thoughts lingered on Floren's murder and Denver's reaction. Why hadn't he seemed shocked, or surprised? It was almost as if he already knew. *But that would mean ... No way.*

When she finished cleaning Smoky's stall, she pushed the wheelbarrow of dirty straw outside the barn and over to the compost pile by the back fence. A hawk squawked, circling above the tree line. She lifted her face to the sun and let the breeze tickle her cheek. The world finally straightened and held still.

A dog barked. By the creek that created the north boundary of the neighborhood, Izzy raced through the grass, chased by a bounding Ranger.

What would happen to the big dog? Would he, like the ranch, become someone else's property? The sheriff had wanted to call animal control to pick up the dog since there was no one at the ranch to care for him. But then he'd agreed to her offer to take Ranger home temporarily. Perhaps she could adopt him permanently, if no one came forward to claim him.

Floren hadn't mentioned relatives, no sons or daughters, during their conversations. The purpose of their interview had been strictly business, issues related to free-range animals in the western United States, the problems these ranchers faced with the roaming herds of mustangs and burros, and the need for facilities to provide homes once the animals were captured and removed.

Back in the barn, Claire speared a rectangular hay bale with the pitchfork, broke it apart and tossed fresh hay into the stalls. Finished, she rested against the barn door to watch the training.

Denver worked Blaze in the ring, his voice quiet and calm as he spoke to the horse. She trotted around the ring at one end of his loosely-held rope. He rotated in place as the horse circled.

When Izzy and Ranger raced into the paddock, Blaze shied but Denver kept hold of the rope even as Ranger ran to him, tail wagging. He stooped to pet the dog and reached for Izzy as she danced on her hind legs begging for his attention.

Denver's move from Raleigh to the heart of Oklahoma after he completed his horse trainer education had been exactly what he needed. He seemed to like living here with her and Cade, and he also seemed to love the job. Just as important, he was good at it. Even though Blaze was his first trainee, he worked the horse like a pro. And as far as she knew, he took his PTSD meds and saw the approved Department of Defense psychologist in Stillwater weekly.

Claire wished she could spend the morning watching the horse's progress but her boss was waiting. She waved at Denver and walked to the house, willing her mind to switch gears to the stack of half-finished articles and new assignments cluttering her desk at the *News Press* office.

Mary Coley

Someone else would write both the news article about J.B. Floren's murder and his obituary; she had other assigned pieces to finish. She didn't relish the thought of recounting the discovery of the body to the designated writer. Most likely, Casey Stinson, the newest—but highly experienced—staff writer, would get the assignment. He fit in well in the newsroom, and if she had to talk to anyone about finding the body, she'd as soon talk to Casey.

A terrifying thought came to mind. Would someone reading the story make a connection with her and the man she'd killed three years ago?

Please God, don't let them dig that up again.

But, of course they would.

Chapter 4

Claire parked in the employee's lot of the newspaper office and trudged toward the back entrance. A newsprint delivery truck at the loading dock spewed diesel exhaust into the air. She ducked inside the building. Here, the acrid scent of printing ink replaced the diesel odor. In an enormous room down the hall, with hardly a whoosh and a click, the printed newspapers folded into piles beneath huge computerized printers.

She rounded the corner into the newsroom. Manuel Juarez glanced up from where he stood beside the sports editor's desk. Sally Ferguson, the lifestyles editor, sat at her desk several yards away, typing furiously on her computer keyboard.

"Hey. Thanks for texting the info about Mr. Floren," Manny said. "Casey's written a draft, including the latest info from the sheriff. Look it over and we'll post it to the web edition. What else are you working on today?" Manny's look met hers before shifting back to the sheaf of papers he held.

"I went to the ranch this morning to finish the mustang rescue article. I need a few more facts, I'll have to find another source. I've also got the Sunday feature to finish and a human interest on the bank president and his family."

Manny nodded, pulled a pencil from his pocket protector and initialed the top page of the papers he held.

"I've been distracted since finding the body, but I'll try to get my head on straight. On top of everything else, I dread having to tell my son about his death."

"Your boy knew him?" Manny asked, still occupied with the article drafts in his hands. Like most newspaper editors, he could edit and talk at the same time.

"Cade started volunteering at his ranch after we adopted two animals from there."

Manny passed her the pages he had reviewed. "The man's death will wash over Cade. Kids see people die in the movies and in video games all the time. They don't seem to understand the finality of death unless they've experienced it personally."

Claire cringed.

The editor frowned and ran his fingers through his thick black hair. "Crap, Claire. Sorry." He pulled a wrapped toothpick from his pocket and tore the plastic sleeve open. "I'm a bastard, I know." He stuck the toothpick between his teeth.

She shrugged and glanced at the draft of the news story. "Three years later, and I still have nightmares. Thank God Cade wasn't at the apartment when it happened." She crossed the room to her desk where she dropped her purse and satchel on the floor. "And now I find the rancher dead. I'm glad Cade wasn't there this time, either."

Manny followed her to her desk. "Are you okay?"

How could she answer? Sweat slicked her hands and white noise still filled her head. At least the room was no longer spinning.

"I ought to give you the day off."

"I need to work, otherwise I'll keep thinking about it. Without something to distract me, I'll be a basket case by sunset."

Manny patted her shoulder awkwardly. "Casey's on break. When you're done with the review, send the copy back to both of us. He'll make the changes and get it posted to the web. I'll be in my office." He hurried across the room's brown industrial carpet and down the narrow hallway.

Claire closed her eyes for a fraction of a second and quickly opened them. She would never forget the look of a dead man's face.

Circulating air tickled her skin. She glanced at the ceiling fan before refocusing on the article. In his clear, concise writing, Casey Stinson quoted the sheriff and the deputies. He'd also talked to another of the Oklahoma mustang and burro preserve owners. A woman who operated a similar but smaller operation east of Ponca City had said, "J.B. Floren will be greatly missed. He had unparalleled passion for these beautiful, wild animals. I can't imagine who would have done this or why."

Claire inked in a few grammatical changes and scribbled her initials at the top of the first page. She laid the piece on Casey's desk as her coworker strolled into the room. The stale odor of cigarette smoke followed him.

"Finished your review, Claire? Good." The lanky writer collapsed into his desk chair. "Called the sheriff to check on any new developments. They've found the murder weapon. One more gory little detail to add." He jiggled his computer mouse. When the screen lit up, he punched a few keys. The article she had reviewed appeared.

"A scythe," Casey said. "Bloody handle, bloody blade."

Claire shuddered at the ghastly image her mind conjured. The bloody face, sliced from ear to mouth on both cheeks, and a tattered blood-soaked shirt, still tucked in, his pants cinched by a leather belt with a silver belt buckle.

"And when they dusted the weapon and the big barn for fingerprints, they found dozens. They're processing them as a rush request, running all the databases. They could have a suspect soon."

"Does the sheriff have any theories?"

"Someone who knew him. Someone with a grudge." Casey looked from the edited draft Claire had provided to the computer screen and made the edits as he talked. "Probably someone local."

Someone local and extremely angry. Claire crossed her arms and hugged herself to stop the trembling. Her own personal crime scene appeared in her mind. The living room. A sofa pillow on the floor. A broken lamp. And a naked man stretched out on the carpet with a bullet hole above his heart, spurting blood for a few more seconds.

"Claire?"

She headed for her desk, and collapsed in the desk chair.

Casey followed. "Can I get you a glass of water? Coffee? Anything?"

Claire rubbed her forehead. "A glass of water. I'm a little dizzy." She folded her arms on her desk and rested her head on them as Casey rushed off. Instantly, her thoughts returned to the Cimarron Valley Rescue ranch, to sitting in the patrol car watching the police officers swarm across the grounds. Ranger barreled out of the barn.

Claire sat up.

Someone local. Someone who'd been able to lock the big black dog in the barn.

Someone who *knew* the dog.

Chapter 5

Hours later, after she had written short articles for the paper on the upcoming arts festival and the annual reunion barbeque for Stillwater High School alums, Claire packed her backpack and left the office. Her muscles quivered as if she'd been on a cross-trainer, and her head ached. The dull ringing in her head began again whenever her thoughts turned to J.B. Floren.

She parked in the grocery store parking lot and forced her mind to compile easy-to-cook comfort food menus. First on the list was Cade's favorite–lasagna– followed by mac & cheese with smoked sausage. She grabbed a grocery cart and wheeled into the store.

Why do I always get the cart with the squeaky wheel?

Claire headed toward the produce section. She wasn't hungry. Experts said that was the best time to shop for groceries. But, with a 15-year-old at home who devoured everything in sight, her own appetite when shopping did not matter. She shook the water from a head of organic romaine lettuce and bagged up apples, bananas and oranges.

Someone rammed her grocery cart as she cruised past the rows of soups, selecting cans of Cade's favorites.

"Hey, beautiful. What's for dinner?" Holt Braden smiled as he leaned against his cart.

"Nothing special. Lasagna with a green salad and French bread."

"Sounds great. Can I invite myself to dinner? We both could use company after that grisly scene this morning." He fell into step beside her. "Wonder if they've got any suspects yet?"

Claire ignored his question and squeaked through the bins of potatoes and onions to the meat section where she selected a package of ground beef and a pound of sausage; she tossed them into her cart. Her stomach twisted at the smell of the raw meat drifting from the butcher's counter along the wall. Holt walked with her, smiling, occasionally dropping an item into his cart.

"How about it?" he said. "I'll help cook. Haven't seen Cade much the last few months since your nephew came to train Blaze. How's that going, anyway?"

Claire's Southern upbringing made it nearly impossible for her to be rude, no matter how annoying someone was. Her mother's voice was always in her ear: 'a lady is always polite and considerate. Bite your tongue, young lady, before you say a cross word.'

Claire shaped her mouth into a semblance of a smile. "The training's going great. Blaze has calmed a lot. She takes a saddle now, and Denver and I have both ridden her a few times. But you've seen us riding her from your place, haven't you? You can easily see the ring and the barn from your back porch."

"I've seen Denver working her." Holt pitched a loaf of bread into his cart. "But, I don't spend all day staring at your place, Claire. I'm on the computer, trading."

He'd told her about his day trading profession many times. Because of his successful investments, he'd moved from Oklahoma City and bought the acreage next door six months ago. And he'd been after her ever since.

Holt followed her squeaky cart when she veered through the pet supply section. She selected a medium-sized bag of Izzy's food, and a large bag of dog chow for Ranger. Holt helped her wrangle it onto the bottom shelf of the cart.

"Has Izzy's appetite grown? That's a lot of kibble."

"I brought Ranger home with me today from the ranch. There's no one there to feed him. And he and Izzy like to play."

"Okay. Hope you're not stuck with him forever, though. That's one big dog."

Stuck with him? She had never regarded any animal that needed help as something she was *stuck* with. She stopped her cart in front of the doggy toys and selected a long, skinny squirrel with no stuffing to be Ranger's first toy.

"You're not serious. You're buying the dog a toy?"

She dropped the stuffing-free squirrel into the cart, and chose another smaller animal for Izzy. "Dogs play, you know. They like toys. Especially squeaky ones."

Claire steered the cart to the front of the store with Holt hot on her heels.

"So, how about it? Can I come for dinner?" he asked when they were finally in line for the cashier.

Holt irritated her, but at least she had not thought about the rancher since he bumped into her grocery cart. Holt's presence would keep her thoughts at bay. His bad jokes would quash any thoughts of today's horrific scene. Not such a bad idea to have him over for the evening. "Don't expect anything fancy. I don't have dessert."

He shrugged. "So? Your sweet presence is enough sugar for me."

Claire rolled her eyes. "Cut the corny, okay? It's not working for me. Drop your groceries at your house and come on over."

Cade wouldn't be happy about this. Truthfully, he hadn't liked any of the men who wanted to date her—another of the many reasons she hadn't done much of it since her divorce and the move to Oklahoma. Her son's approval of her choice for his stepfather mattered. She could wait until he'd graduated from high school to find romance again if need be. Meanwhile, though, occasional companionship was nice. Especially tonight.

She did not want to be alone.

Chapter 6

A sheriff's car was parked in Claire's driveway. She pulled up to the garage and got out, opened the back hatch and cradled a grocery bag in her arms. Deputy Purdue climbed out of the cruiser and approached.

"Ms. Northcutt? Or is it Mrs.?" His breath smelled of licorice.

"Ms. is fine." Claire hadn't expected the sheriff's office to follow up with her so soon. "I answered all your questions earlier. I don't remember anything else."

"Maybe not. But you've had all day to think about it. Maybe you remember something you noticed while you waited at the gate or drove into the ranch? Maybe you heard a noise? Anything different from your previous visits?"

It was a long way for the deputy to drive to ask a simple question. She thought for a few seconds. "No. Nature sounds. Birds, insects, the wind. Nothing else."

"You're sure?" He tilted his head as he looked at her. A smile worked its way onto his face.

"There wasn't anything." She shifted the grocery sack to the crook of her other arm and closed the back hatch.

"You had a shock. Initially such a shock might either erase a memory or intensify it. You've had experience with that, haven't you?"

Her face burned. The deputy must know what had happened when she lived in town.

"Interesting you've now been present at two violent deaths," Purdue said. "Are there more I don't know about?"

She cleared her throat and steadied herself. Anger bubbled inside her. "I found J.B. Floren's dead body. I was not *present* when he died."

The deputy shifted his weight and leaned toward her. "I stand corrected. Still, the coincidence of *you* finding the body is intriguing."

"Do you have any more questions? If not, I need to get inside and fix dinner for my family."

"One more thing. We've learned both your son and your hired hand, er … nephew, volunteered at the ranch. When were they last there?"

"They were weekend volunteers. My agreement with the rancher–I adopted two of his rescued animals–included their volunteer work."

"So, you'd met the man before you started writing this article about him."

"I met him when my son and I went to the ranch to see the mustangs. We adopted two animals. Last fall."

The deputy pulled a notepad out of his pocket, flipped it open, and wrote a quick note "That takes care of everything for now." He loosened his tie. "Long day. I'll be in touch again soon."

He smiled and returned to the cruiser.

Dust hung in a cloud above the gravel drive long after the deputy's vehicle disappeared, and an unpleasant taste filled her mouth.

The queasiness in her stomach worsened as she prepared the evening meal. Why all the questions about Cade and Denver and when she had met the rancher?

Did the sheriff consider one of them a suspect?

Chapter 7

Claire and Holt sat across from one another at the dining room table. Above them the ceiling fan turned, circulating cool air. She picked at her plate of hot, cheesy lasagna. A Caesar salad sat untouched next to the plate, as well as a full glass of her favorite pinot noir. Claire listened for the crunch of tires on the gravel driveway.

"Why doesn't Cade at least call?" she wondered aloud. She tapped her fingertips on the table. Ranger and Izzy rolled their eyes her way from where they lay on the cool wood floor near the doorway.

"He's 15. He's lost track of time. That's all." Holt covered her hand with his. She pulled her hand away.

"At least Denver left me a note. He's having dinner with Jenny in Stillwater." Claire reached for a slice of French bread from the basket on the table, pulled off a piece and chewed absently at the buttery crust.

"I didn't know Denver had a girlfriend." Holt shoveled a forkful of lasagna into his mouth.

"He's been seeing Jenny Prather for several weeks. She owns a hair salon in town."

"Didn't take him long to get a girl. Despite his background."

"What do you mean?" Claire sipped her wine. Irritation built in her head.

"You know. He could be a loose cannon. Dangerous. PTSD may be a clinical diagnosis, but it doesn't mean people are any safer with those people than they would be with a psychopath." His gray eyes hardened.

"Denver is not dangerous. For God's sake, Holt, my nephew just returned from serving in Afghanistan. He's recovering from a leg injury. He needed a place to stay and a job. He has both of those here, and family." She wadded her napkin, dropped it onto the table and folded her arms. She wouldn't listen to an attack on Denver. He was a good man. No telling what Holt would say if he knew she suffered from symptoms of PTSD, too. Would he think she was as dangerous as a psychopath?

"You are generous to offer a place for him to stay and a job." Holt smiled and swallowed. His look softened. He studied her face. "You look great tonight, by the way."

She frowned and started to tell him to lay off the compliments, but a noise at the front door stopped her.

Ranger and Izzy bolted up from the floor, tails wagging in unison. The front door opened and Cade stomped into the house. The knot of worry in Claire's stomach relaxed.

Her son stopped in the dining room doorway. He petted Ranger's head with one hand and Izzy's with the other. "Hey, dogs. How's it goin'? What are you doing here, Ranger?"

"Come have dinner," Claire said. "It's lasagna."

"Not hungry." Cade scrutinized the room. "Where's Denver?"

"Out with Jenny. Did you have soccer practice or a club meeting after school?"

"No. Got tied up. So, why's Ranger here?"

"Come sit," she repeated.

Cade slipped his backpack off his shoulder and dropped it, tramped through the dining room and into the kitchen. A few minutes later he emerged carrying a plate of steaming lasagna, salad and garlic bread. "I'll eat in my room. Tons of homework tonight." He stepped between the panting dogs and snagged one strap of his dropped backpack with his free hand.

"Cade, wait. I need to tell you something." Claire scooted her chair away from the table.

"About J.B. Floren? You brought Ranger home because he's dead, right?"

"You know?"

"It was all over the internet news, Mom. And TV."

Claire frowned. "You don't seem surprised."

"Stuff happens. Floren probably had enemies." Cade disappeared into the hallway, but his voice still reached them. "I'm glad you brought Ranger home." The dog's wagging tail thudded against the wall as the animal followed Cade.

She'd worried for nothing. *Stuff happens?* She glanced at Holt.

"Typical teenage response. You were worried for no reason." He reached for her hand again, but she lifted it to rub her forehead where a headache throbbed.

She picked up her plate. "I'm done in, Holt. Time for you to go home."

She needed a shower to wash the day away, including the bloody images she couldn't seem to shake.

Her hair, long and soft, falls over my chest, the thick strands shimmer in the moonlight like the surface of the ocean. Her mouth, turned up in a half-smile, beckons me to her even in sleep. Her skin, so soft. She rouses at my touch, turns toward me, and I move into her arms. She does not expect what comes next.

Who'd want to get out of bed when you're dreaming that?

But work calls. The charade calls.

I drink the first cup of coffee of the day looking out at the trees. The hot liquid sears my throat. I feel her presence.

Just like the others.

My brain wants to plan it all out, but those plans never work. And this time is different. I've got marching orders, someone else calling the shots. I can work with that. They'll oblige my desires, eventually. So much better to let it play out naturally, not force it. The only unknown is when.

I'm good at delayed gratification. Dad taught me well.

Chapter 8

The dream woke Claire from a deep sleep, and she vaulted from the bed. Her hammering heart thrust adrenalin into her blood stream and her muscles trembled. The curtains flapped as stormy air flowed through the partially open window. She blinked and looked around the moonlit room.

I'm okay. Nothing's wrong.

She didn't want to close her eyes again. The images would come back. The dark apartment. The low voice. Unwanted hands roaming her body. The scent of an unfamiliar man's sweat.

She flicked on a lamp. J.B. Floren's murder had made the memory resurface. *Blood. And death.*

She swiped a hand across her face. Neither memory would ever fade.

No one had known that Max Dyson had followed her newspaper byline and become infatuated with her. She'd paid little attention to the unsigned notes and anonymous flower bouquets, not seeing them as warnings. Then, he'd broken into her apartment, crept into her bedroom and into her bed. His low voice had rumbled into a good dream. She still remembered that dream. She'd been loping her horse across prairie grass, the blue sky above laced with cloud streaks.

"Honey, I'm home," he'd whispered in her ear as his hands caressed her body like a lover's.

A thunder clap jerked her from the memory. Claire shuddered. Her bedside clock read four a.m. Wide awake, she pulled on her robe.

Outside the kitchen window, lightning split the sky and the windows shook. She stepped out onto the porch into ozone-scented air. Light flashes revealed towering thunderheads miles away and roiling nearer.

Back inside, Claire stuffed a pod into the coffee maker, flipped the *on* switch, and sat at the kitchen table listening to the thunder boom. The coffee maker gurgled as her cup filled. She carried it into the living room and flicked on the Weather Channel. Relief flooded her mind when the tv's weather warning was for thunderstorms only, no severe weather that could produce hail or tornados.

The wind and rain raged outside. Something cold touched the back of her knee. *Ranger.* She stroked the dog's head, scratched his muzzle and his ears. He pressed against her hand and grunted softly. "Morning, boy. So, storms don't bother you, huh? Izzy neither. That's lucky for us." She ran her fingernails down his spine. One rear leg lifted and scratched at the air.

When rain no longer pounded the roof, Claire stepped out onto the screened-in back porch with the dog to savor another cup of hazelnut coffee. With Ranger beside her on the cushioned glider, she watched the lightning display fade. The black sky above her softened to gray. Ranger sighed and scooted his head onto her thigh. She ran her fingertips over his skull. His closed eyelids fluttered.

In the early dawn light, Denver strolled across the lawn and into the barn.

Claire finished her coffee and prepared herself mentally for work. Denver led Blaze out of the barn. She watched him begin the training session in the ring. Standing beside the horse, he shifted his weight up and into one stirrup, and stepped out and down to the ground again, all the while talking softly. Denver was intent on the job at hand, absolutely focused on the horse.

Ranger stirred and jumped off the glider. He padded back into the house.

When he and Izzy raced out of the house a few minutes later, she knew Cade was up as well. The dogs streaked past the training ring and headed for the river.

Claire returned to her bedroom to dress in jeans, a soft blouse, and a tailored jacket. She dropped to the floor to tug on a pair of cowboy boots, and clambered back up. Not so easy to get off the floor these days. In her head, she counted the days until her fortieth birthday.

On the driveway, a car honked.

"Bye, Mom." Cade's voice echoed down the hall to the bedroom. A door slammed.

Claire poured kibble into the dog bowls on the back porch. She grabbed her purse and work satchel from the kitchen counter. An ache pounded in her jaw. *Clenching again.* An undercurrent of worry ran beneath the normalcy.

J.B. Floren had been murdered.

An isolated incident? No reason to suspect that it was anything more. Life would go back to normal in another few days.

Claire rubbed her jaw and headed out the back door. She paused. Denver looked up from the training ring, gave a brief nod and clucked to Blaze.

At the end of her driveway, Claire turned her SUV onto the street. A man jogged toward her, his t-shirt draped over one shoulder, his bronzed legs and muscular torso glistening with perspiration. Holt. When he neared her driveway, he grinned and threw her a kiss.

What had life been like before Holt moved in next door? Boring, she acknowledged. As she drove away, Claire watched him in her rearview mirror; he stretched his calves and quads at his mail box.

Claire pulled out of the neighborhood and onto the highway, still thinking about Holt.

"So, what do you know about 'Mr. Perfect'?" Sally Ferguson had asked months ago when the two were having coffee in the break room. Earlier in the conversation, Claire had mentioned her new neighbor.

"His parents are dead, so is his only brother. He's been married, his wife already had kids. He describes himself as a solitary person who prefers to work from home on the computer. I think he's a day trader." Claire recited what little Holt had told her about himself, but didn't add what Holt had said to Claire only a month after moving here, 'When I spend time with another person, I'd like it to be you.'

Most women would be excited when a handsome man like Holt flirted. Not Claire.

Not now, maybe never again. There were too many creeps out there.

Deputy Sheriff Purdue was perched on her desk when she entered the newsroom.

"Good morning, Ms. Northcutt." He removed his hat and laid it on her desk. "I'm following up."

She dropped her work bag on the floor beside her desk. "I thought you did that last night."

"It occurred to me you've known the victim several months and interviewed him at length. You could shed light on his business practices."

Claire shrugged. "I'm not sure I can help, but I'll try."

"When you were at the ranch, did you see Mr. Floren interact with employees or volunteers?"

"Our conversations took place in the living room of the ranch house. The only other person I saw was his housekeeper."

"Opal Hilbert?"

"Yes." Claire had seen the woman dusting lamps one day when she arrived; another time, she was in the kitchen, cooking.

"You saw no other interactions? Heard no other conversations?"

"No."

Purdue picked up his hat. "Thanks for your time. Have a great day." The deputy positioned his hat on his head and grinned at her before he sauntered out of the newsroom.

Claire watched him walk away. *Why hadn't he just picked up the phone and called her to ask about the rancher's interactions? It would have taken a lot less time.*

A bouquet of red roses arrived mid-afternoon. Manny brought them in, a sly grin plastered across his face.

"So, a secret admirer, or do I know the guy?"

Manny set the vase on top of Claire's yellow pad. Claire sniffed the fragrant blooms as she pulled out the card.

Your ardent admirer, Holt. She stuffed the card back into the tiny envelope.

"From the look on your face, you're not thrilled. Poor idiot." Her editor leaned against the corner of her cluttered desk.

"He's not getting the message. I'm not interested."

Manny chuckled. "Are the roses going to make any difference?"

"Nope. And Cade doesn't like him." She pitched the envelope into her desk drawer.

Manny put up his hands and backed across the room. "Don't say anything else."

She grimaced. "He lives next door."

Later, as she completed her final edit on a piece about the mayor's initiative on adult literacy, she heard Holt's voice somewhere in the building. It swelled and grew louder. He ambled around the corner into the newsroom. Manny hurried to keep up with the other man's long strides.

Casey looked over his shoulder at her, shook his head, and mouthed, "He's in love."

"Always wondered what a newspaper office looked like. Thanks for the tour, Manny." Holt patted the editor on the back and headed for her desk. "There's my girl. You got my gift." His eyebrows lifted as he grinned.

"You shouldn't have, Holt."

"But I wanted to cheer you up." His gray eyes glinted.

Claire shoved her desk chair back and studied him. Graying hair over his temples, tanned face, trimmed facial hair rimming his chin and curving into a mustache. She imagined he'd created a stir in the advertising department when he walked through the front doors of the newspaper office. A tiny headache blossomed in her head. *Here we go again.*

"I've been thinking about Cade. Can I take him fishing at Sooner Lake this weekend?" Holt perched on the edge of the desk and leaned towards her.

Her email notification beeped and she glanced at the computer monitor. "I've got to check this message."

"Of course. You're busy." Holt straightened. "Guess I should get out of here. Can I stop by your house for a little nightcap tonight?"

Claire chewed at her bottom lip. Lie to the guy, her brain said. She didn't like to lie, not even to Holt. She looked at her computer screen.

"About 7:30? After supper." His expression darkened. "I need to keep an eye on you. There's a murderer on the loose. Floren's ranch isn't that far from our neighborhood."

"I don't need you or anyone to keep an eye on me. I can take care of myself." Her irritation with Holt pounded in her head. "That murder was personal, an isolated incident. No serial killer is at work around Stillwater, Holt."

"I didn't say there was." He glanced at the bouquet and smiled wryly.

She pushed up from her chair. "Thank you for the beautiful flowers."

He shrugged. "Welcome. See you later tonight."

Casey cleared his throat and Sally coughed as Holt crossed the room and disappeared down the hallway. Claire turned back to her computer where several assignment emails had popped up on her computer screen. She moved her cursor down the list. These assignments would take time to address. She'd have to make phone calls and conduct fact checks before writing the stories.

One of the emails was not from Manny. The email subject of that email read, *Question.*

She clicked it open.

Another dead man. Did you kill this one, too?

Chapter 9

Three hours later, Claire slowed her RAV a half-block from her house. Five sheriff's department cars with lights flashing were parked up ahead.

She drove closer and realized that the vehicles lined her single-lane driveway. Her heart thudded. *Had something happened to Cade?*

Claire drove around the cruisers and parked in front of the garage. She dashed for the house. Ranger and Izzy barked furiously, somewhere.

"Hold up there, Claire," Sheriff Warren Anderson said as he plodded down the porch steps. "We're executing a search warrant for Denver Streeter's living quarters and any areas of your home he has access to." He handed her a folded document.

She opened it and scanned the legalese. Sweat beaded on her forehead. "What ...?"

"State lab rushed the fingerprints we lifted at the scene yesterday, and the fingerprints on the suspected murder weapon. Match came back to Mr. Streeter."

The blood drained from her face. Usually, this time of day, Cade and Denver were working with Blaze in the training ring. "Where's my son?"

"I haven't seen your boy. We found Denver in the barn. One of my deputies drove him into town for questioning. We're searching the barn now. Denver lives in the room off the garage. Right?"

Claire nodded toward the add-on next to the main house, and hurried up the front steps to unlock the door.

"Cade? Son, are you here?" She dashed to Cade's bedroom, sweeping the teenager's messy room with a quick look before racing back to the kitchen. Ranger and Izzy whined and barked from the back porch.

At the back door, a deputy stopped her. She peered around him and across the double garage to Denver's room. The door stood open. They'd stripped the sheets off the mattress and piled them on the floor. Another deputy was rifling through the oak chest of drawers.

"Ms. Northcutt, I have a few questions," Sheriff Anderson said from the front of the garage. "Would you prefer to go to my office?"

"I can't leave until I find Cade. He's supposed to be here." She peered through the open back door of the garage toward the small barn. Something thudded in Denver's room.

"Why is Denver Streeter living out here with you and not in town?" The sheriff came up and stood behind her, arms crossed.

"His mother, Patty, is my sister. She lives in Raleigh." She rubbed her forehead. Perspiration broke out on her neck. "Can we go inside? It would be much cooler."

Claire led the sheriff into the kitchen. She reached for the thermostat and flicked on the a/c.

"Why is Denver here and not in North Carolina?"

The a/c kicked on and air whooshed from the ceiling vent. Claire lifted her face to catch the cool current. She filled a glass with water. "During his second tour in Afghanistan, shrapnel from an explosion broke his leg. The incident left him with a slight limp, PTSD, and an uncertain future." She took a long swallow. "He's always been great with animals. Last fall he completed a horse training course in California and became certified."

The sheriff retrieved a small notebook from his pocket and scribbled in it as she talked.

"Things came together for Denver when I got Blaze for Cade as a Christmas present. Denver needed a horse to train, I needed a trainer. He agreed to do the work and moved here to live with us last January." She drained the last of the water from the glass.

"Any particular reason why Mr. Streeter didn't get a place of his own instead of moving in here?" The sheriff tapped his pencil on the little notepad.

"I wanted to be sure he liked it here. It's so different from North Carolina. And California. He has plans to find an apartment in Stillwater this summer. He's dating a woman who lives there."

"I need her name and contact information."

Claire hated to pull Jenny into this. She'd introduced the pair, believing that a friendship with someone close to his age was critical to Denver's healing. But on the other hand, Jenny might be able to help. She could be a good character witness and vouch for Denver's state of mind. "Jenny Prather. I have her number on my phone." Claire pulled up Jenny's number and read it to the sheriff.

"Did you see Denver Monday night? Where was he about midnight?"

"He had dinner with his girlfriend. Got home around midnight. I didn't hear him leave again." Claire dropped into a kitchen chair and clasped her trembling hands together. "He's a grown man. I don't keep tabs on him. Denver didn't do this."

"But he's a soldier. Like law officers, he's been trained to protect in any way required. Even killing. And with the PTSD ... Who knows what might have set him off."

Holt had said basically the same thing last night. She fingered her empty glass, drawing a line in the condensation that had formed there. "He didn't do this. No way."

Claire lay curled on the sofa in the living room. Izzy had wedged her body between Claire and the back of the sofa. Ranger lay stretched out on the carpet. Cool air poured over her. She hugged a pillow to her chest and breathed in the fabric's flowery detergent smell. Thuds and bangs reverberated from the garage end of the house and Denver's room as the search continued.

Denver had been a soldier, but he didn't have the look of a man who would lose his temper and kill without considering the consequences. But she had to admit his response, when she'd told him about the murder, had been odd.

Someone rapped three times and opened the front door. Ranger lunged for the hallway, a low growl rumbling in his throat. The door opened and Holt stuck his head into the house.

"Claire?" A deputy followed Holt inside. Ranger growled.

"Ranger," Claire warned. The dog's shackles lowered and he sat, focused on the men. "Denver is a suspect in Mr. Floren's murder," she told Holt. "They're searching his room." She sank back into the pillows, pulling her knees to her chest and resting her chin on them.

Something crashed in the garage. Claire winced. *How long would this go on?*

"Hope they don't find any drugs." Holt dropped into the recliner.

Drugs. She had firsthand experience with how drug users looked and acted, thanks to Tom, Cade's dad. Denver was not using.

The noisy search moved to the driveway. Doors slammed. Claire fisted her hands. *They won't find anything.*

A radio crackled and another car door slammed. When a knock sounded at the front door, the deputy pulled it open. Static and blurred voices erupted from the radios on the driveway.

"As a courtesy, I'm informing you we found a large amount of a suspicious substance in Mr. Streeter's vehicle," Sheriff Anderson said from the doorway. Deputy Purdue stood close behind him. "He'll be charged with possession and intent to distribute. We are also questioning him on suspicion of murder."

Claire stepped back and into Holt. His hands cupped her shoulders and pulled her a half-step further back and tightly against him.

"He doesn't do drugs," Claire insisted. *He doesn't do drugs.*

Anderson cleared his throat. "The evidence indicates otherwise." The sheriff tramped across the porch and back to his vehicle.

"I'm sorry, Claire, but I'm not surprised." Holt turned her around and led her to the living room sofa.

But I am.

Tears burned behind her eyelids. Denver didn't do drugs. Her heart constricted.

What if I don't know Denver after all?

The thought startled her, and then an even worse one settled into her brain.

What if he does do drugs?

What if he'd introduced Cade to them?

Chapter 10

The minute hand inched around the clock as she and Holt waited in the living room, the evening news blaring from the television in the entertainment center. From the floor, Ranger watched Holt. Eventually, Claire called the dogs and locked them on the back porch. Her empty stomach rumbled, but she ignored it. How could she eat?

Where was Cade?

She sat through the news broadcast with unseeing eyes. As the credits rolled afterwards, the front door banged open and her son rushed inside.

"Is it true, they arrested Denver?" Cade stalked into the living room. He slumped onto the edge of the sofa near Claire.

"Yes." The sweet-piney scent of soap from the high school gym shower still lingered on his skin. "Where've you been?"

"After practice, Antonio and I hung out at Struck's."

Claire was familiar with the local hangout where the kids often went after school, a convenience store with an old-fashioned soda shop in the back with booths and foosball tables.

"They turned on the news at five," Cade continued. He rubbed his face. "How could they arrest Denver, Mom? That's fu—."

"Language, son," Holt cautioned in a stern voice from where he sat on the nearby recliner. "Apologize to your mom."

"Why are you telling me anything? You're not my dad. You're an asshole who's trying to hook up with my mom." He stomped from the room. Down the hallway, his bedroom door slammed.

Claire winced. Holt had a point, so did her son. "I'm sure you meant well, but you had no right to say anything to Cade about his language." She rose from the sofa and trudged into the kitchen.

After a few seconds, Holt followed.

On the back porch, Ranger and Izzy whined. One of the dogs scratched at the door panel.

She glanced at the clock. The dogs had not been fed, and it was time for them to come in the house. Izzy had a long-established routine of spending the evening inside with her human companions. Ranger enjoyed the routine, too. Left outside all night, the nocturnal ramblings of the area's raccoons, possums and coyotes drove both of the dogs crazy. Their barking would keep her and her neighbors awake all night. Ranger was even more protective than Izzy. He'd become chief of security the minute he arrived.

Reluctantly, she left the door closed and the animals outside on the porch. Neither of the dogs had warmed to Holt. And he didn't make much effort to befriend them, either.

Holt leaned against the granite countertop. "My parents didn't take any lip from me or my brother. You shouldn't take any from your son. Nip it in the bud before it gets any worse."

"You shouldn't have intervened. Cade knows my rules about profanity." Claire kept her voice even although her temper roiled at a slow boil. She opened the dishwasher, pulled out the silverware bin and put the utensils away. "He doesn't need you to remind him." She shoved the cutlery drawer closed. "I need to talk to Cade about Denver."

Claire pushed past him and headed for the bedrooms.

"You need my support, Claire. It's tough raising a kid alone."

"You don't think I already know that? Leave, please," Claire ordered. *And never come back.*

Holt's face darkened even as he smiled, showing beautiful bleached teeth. "Whatever you want. Can I call you later?" He followed her across the living room.

"Not tonight." She opened the front door and Holt stepped out onto the porch.

Claire pushed the door closed and locked it before she rushed toward Cade's room. *Drugs in Denver's truck?* She ached at the thought that Denver might have resorted to drugs. Sometimes he didn't think straight, but he was so much better than he'd been a year ago.

Denver hated J.B. Floren for a reason she had yet to find out. Even so, she still couldn't imagine him murdering the man.

Her mind leapt down a narrow path to another thought. Cade had not been surprised at the news of the rancher's murder. What if Cade, because of Denver's dislike of the man, had been involved in his death?

My world is crashing.

Chapter 11

"**S**on, I need to talk to you." Claire spoke into Cade's closed bedroom door.

The door flew open. Cade glared. "I hate him, Mom." His fingers closed into a fist.

"Holt's right about your language. You know I don't tolerate profanity in our house."

"And I won't tolerate him," Cade blurted.

"That's not your decision, it's mine." Claire's body stiffened and her ears rang.

"I live here, too."

Memories resurfaced. Cade sounded like his father, Tom. *Don't go there.* "You do live here. But I'm the parent. Ultimately, I make the decisions."

Cade stomped across the room to the bed and threw himself on top of the tangled sheets.

"We need to talk about Denver," Claire said.

The room reeked of sweaty t-shirts and dirty socks. Cade had dumped his gym bag out on the floor. Claire perched on the edge of the bed.

His look could have burnt a hole in the carpet.

"The sheriff came this morning with a search warrant because Denver's fingerprints were on a scythe they found at the ranch. They think it's the murder weapon." She fingered the stitches in the quilt her grandmother had pieced together from worn-out clothing sixty years ago.

"Doesn't mean anything," Cade insisted. "They could have found my prints, too. I used one last weekend to cut the grass around the water trough."

She forged on. "The deputies searched Denver's room, the garage and the barn."

"So? They didn't find anything, did they?"

"They found what they called a suspicious substance. And not just a little. They arrested Denver for possession and intent to distribute."

"That's so screwed," Cade fumed. He swung his legs over the side of the bed. He punched his bed pillow, and sprang off the bed to pace the room.

The bloody scene at the base of the flagpole flashed into her mind, soon followed by that other pool of blood and that other body. One hand covered her mouth. The world began to spin. She grabbed the bed's footboard, tried to stand up, and dropped back onto the bed.

"Mom?" Cade rushed to her.

"I'm okay. Dizzy for a second."

"Finding Floren brought it back, didn't it? When you killed Max Dyson?"

Claire took a deep breath. The room steadied. Cade didn't know Dyson had tried to rape her, or how she had gotten away from him. She shivered with the old horror. "I never told you anything about it."

"All the kids at school knew, Mom. I was the kid who had a mom who killed somebody. It was actually cool."

She was stunned, and instantly imagined the scene at school: the kids crowded around him, whispering, eager for details. And she'd stupidly believed he'd been ignorant of the event. "I'm not proud of killing him, Cade." But she couldn't undo what had happened any more than she could purge the memories.

"He would have killed you, right? You had to do it."

"Doesn't mean I wanted to." At the time, she'd been protecting herself. She'd wanted to survive. She'd not known Cade had become a celebrity afterward. She had tried to keep life as normal as possible for them both. She'd bought the acreage and moved them out of Stillwater.

Cade shrugged. "Maybe that's what happened with him. Maybe someone thought they *had* to kill him."

From the back porch, the dogs barked in unison.

"I'll take care of the dogs, Mom. And feed Blaze and Smoky. Denver didn't do drugs. And he didn't kill Floren. They better find the real killer, soon."

He stomped from the room. The backdoor slammed and the dogs quieted.

Claire clung to the edge of the bed. Who could possibly have felt they *had* to kill the rancher? Why? Did Cade know something he wasn't sharing with her?

She stared at the page of the mystery she'd been trying to read. The lines of text blurred. She closed the book. Cade had shown no emotion when they talked about J.B. Floren's death until they discussed Denver's arrest. *Denver. In jail.*

She felt as if she'd been slapped. *In jail? Has he called anyone?* She'd been so worried about Cade that she hadn't even thought about what Denver needed.

Claire ran to the kitchen and dug her phone from her purse. The phone book, though seldom used, still sat on the counter beneath the house phone. She looked up Trina Romero's phone number.

The attorney she'd consulted three years ago after the Max Dyson incident had been knowledgeable, intelligent and compassionate, the exact combination of traits she'd needed at the time. Now, the attorney was needed again. She expected to get Romero's after-hours answering machine when she made the call, but the attorney herself answered.

Claire explained what had happened to Denver, and listened as Trina detailed what might happen next. An attorney would be appointed by the court if he couldn't afford to hire one himself. Once he was charged with a crime, bond might be set by the judge unless he was deemed to be a flight risk. If bond was set–and paid–he could leave the jail. As for the bond, he could pay it in full himself, or pay a bondsman a percentage of the bond as a fee. The bondsman would then pay the full amount so Denver could stay at home in the interim between being charged and being tried in court.

"He needs an attorney. Will you represent Denver?"

"I don't usually represent drug offenders, but it sounds like there are extenuating circumstances. Tentatively, I'll say yes, Claire. I'll stop in to see him first thing in the morning."

"He's been railroaded into this. Denver's not a criminal."

"I'll find out what I can about the evidence that led to Denver's arrest."

"Fingerprints on the scythe hardly seems enough to get a search warrant. It's an implement many of the ranch staff and volunteers used around the property. And as far as the drugs, I've never seen Denver appear to be high."

"I'll keep you posted, Claire. And don't worry about a retainer. Let's see how this plays out."

Claire watched the low evening sun while her mind sifted through recent events. Fingers of pink glowed in the clouds and the red orb silhouetted the forest of river bottom trees a half-mile away. The light in the little barn blazed, signaling Cade's presence with the animals.

She poured herself a glass of pinot noir. Surely the wine would relax her tense muscles and calm down her buzzing brain. Her cell phone rang.

"Claire? I don't understand. Why did they arrest Denver?" Jenny Prather's voice broke. "No way he sells drugs. And they suspect him of murdering Mr. Floren? How could anyone think he could commit murder?" Jenny sniffed.

Claire leaned against the cold edge of the farmhouse-style kitchen sink. In the yard, the mercury vapor light clicked on. A hundred insects swarmed to the glow. "Denver hasn't been formally charged." She ran her fingers through her hair. A bat swooped through the cloud of spotlighted bugs.

Denver's girlfriend sobbed softly.

"His fingerprints may be on the murder weapon, but he and Cade both used the implement in their volunteer work."

"You don't think Denver killed him, do you?" Jenny whispered.

"Absolutely not." Even as she spoke, Claire remembered how carefree Denver had been as a little boy and how antisocial he had become after his tour in Afghanistan. As a child, he'd been the life of every family gathering, sharing jokes he'd heard at school and sometimes putting on a magic show with card tricks. Now, he rarely went anywhere that might be frequented by large crowds. He had few friends. War had made him prefer animals to people, with few exceptions. "Denver told me he didn't like Floren. But that doesn't mean he killed him."

Cade's shadow moved inside the barn. The interior lights flicked off. Cade stalked across the yard with long strides, Izzy yapping at his heels and Ranger trotting behind.

"Can I visit Denver? He needs to know I believe in him." Jenny blew her nose.

"The jail has visiting hours every day."

"Will he be released on bail?"

"Once he's been formally charged, his bail hearing will be held. Trina Romero has tentatively agreed to defend him. She'll talk to him tomorrow. Hopefully, she'll agree and once bail is set, Denver can come home. I'm sure Trina will do all she can for him."

Jenny sniffed again. "How much will bail cost?"

"I'm not sure. The charge is 'intent to distribute.' In Oklahoma, it's a major offense. Bail could be high. Maybe even $100,000."

Jenny gasped. "Denver doesn't have that kind of cash."

And neither do Denver's parents. They were under water with medical bills for Michael Streeter's cancer treatments.

"Where did those drugs come from?" Claire asked.

"I don't know. Denver doesn't take or sell drugs. I'd bet my life on it." Jenny's voice broke. "Is there anything we can do?"

Jenny sounded absolutely sure of his innocence. And suddenly Claire was certain that Denver would not skip out on his bail. He'd stay to face the music, whatever it was. "I'll post bail for him, Jenny. As soon as I can get the money together."

Her mind raced. A bail bondsman charged a percentage for providing the needed money for bail. Instead, she'd cover bail herself by taking out a second mortgage. If that wasn't enough, she could sell some of the stock she held in a small Fidelity account. She'd get the money back once the trial was finished and everything would go back to the way it had been.

"I've got to see him. I believe in him, and ... I love him." Jenny's voice, stronger, cut through her thoughts. "Thanks for being on his side, Claire."

Trina Romero would find out tomorrow how serious the drug charges were. She would probably also find out if the D.A. had collected enough evidence to charge Denver with J.B. Floren's murder.

Claire could imagine Denver must feel defeated and hopeless. Jenny wasn't the only visitor he'd have tomorrow; Claire would find time to visit him, too.

Cade barreled through the garage door and rushed past on his way to the bedrooms, bringing the stench of manure with him and the two dogs. A few minutes later, music blared from his room. Ranger trotted in and sat beside her. He rested his big black head on her knee and sighed.

The wine had not yet worked its magic. Claire sank back into the cushions. The relentless beat of a rap song vibrated the walls of the house. *If you let yourself go, it's like white noise. Sort of.* Tonight, that technique wasn't working.

The 'music' didn't quite pound out the memory playing behind her closed eyelids, a memory of unwanted fingers featherlight on her skin, working their way down her throat to the neck of her nightgown. Her eyes opened to stare at the pulsing walls of the kitchen. The air pressed in around her. She gulped for air, propelled herself off the sofa and across the room to the front door.

Outside, the cool air she breathed in did more to calm her than the wine had. She sat on the porch swing. Ranger eased through the half open door and sat on the porch in front of the swing. She tickled his ears. He groaned and pushed closer.

The rhythmic beat of Cade's rap music faded into the background.

Well, lookee here. She's on the porch. And so's the damned dog. If she keeps that mutt, he'll spoil everything. Even at the ranch, he knew I'd as soon kick him across the barn as look at him.

The dog has to go, one way or another.

She looks hot in her jeans and t-shirt. And she's drinking wine. Alone.

What's she thinking about? Floren's dead body? Denver in jail? Or me, maybe?

What's she got in that wine glass? Looks dark. Pinot noir? Could be a nice anonymous gift before our first night together. Bonus points if I get the wine right.

Wait. Her son is there. Close the door, idiot. Go back inside and turn off that damn rap music. It's spoiling the atmosphere.

You won't be playin' that crap anymore once I'm in charge of things. You can count on that.

Aw, Claire. Wait. Don't go in.

Damn it.

Chapter 12

Claire slid open the window and breathed in sweet, moist morning air. Pink outlined the scrubby blackjack oaks defining the property line between her place and Holt's. Mourning doves cooed. The blooms on the fuchsia azalea bushes had begun to wilt and drop after weeks of brilliant April color.

Two days ago, her mind had buzzed with unasked questions for J.B. Floren. Today, the article was on the back burner, and her only nephew was in jail. A dull headache throbbed in her temples.

Claire headed for the kitchen. She needed coffee. Denver had brewed a full pot each morning for the past four months, a way of saying a daily 'thank you' for opening her home to him. His home-ground coffee beat a single-brew K-cup any day.

No fresh coffee aroma floated in the air.

What would happen to Cade's relationship with Denver now? If she knew Cade at all, she imagined there would be no change. He loved Denver. The two cousins acted more like brothers, despite the ten-plus year gap in their ages. As far as her own relationship with Denver ... The man he'd become made her proud. She loved her nephew. Unconditionally. She would love and support him always.

She plugged in the Keurig and dug through the nearby drawer for a dark roast K-cup that would deliver a hefty caffeine dose. She had to call her sister in Raleigh before another minute passed.

Claire glanced at the clock. Patty would be driving to work. In another five minutes, she'd pull into the parking lot of her skyscraper office building to start the work day.

When the *ready* light came on, Claire punched the *brew* button. Coffee trickled into her favorite cobalt-blue mug. She breathed coffee aroma into her brain, and thought about Patty, about how her sister's life had changed so drastically when she got pregnant at sixteen. To their credit, the couple stayed together and got married after high school graduation. Patty and Michael were still so good together–and happy.

Michael's diagnosis of Stage 1 lung cancer last year had thrown them for a loop. News of Denver's arrest was the last thing they needed.

Claire sipped her coffee and gazed out at the yard. A family of bluebirds flitted, chirping, into the enormous green ash tree which shaded the west side of the house.

She grabbed her cell phone, braced herself for the difficult conversation and pulled up Patty's auto dial number.

Seconds later her sister answered. "Claire. What a great surprise. I'm walking into work. How are you? How's Denver?"

"Do you have a minute to talk?" Claire stepped onto the porch.

"Is everyone all right? Denver's not good about calling regularly; it's been a couple of weeks since we've talked." Patty paused. "What's up?"

Claire plunged in. "Denver and Cade have been volunteering at that Mustang Rescue Ranch where we got our animals."

"Ye-es. He's mentioned the ranch." Her voice took on a cautious tone.

Claire pushed back against the stiff cushions of the loveseat glider. "Someone murdered the ranch owner. And Denver has been arrested for possession of drugs and intent to distribute."

"Wha-at?"

"But not for the murder. At least not yet." Claire gulped. "They searched his room. And his truck. They found some drugs. More than enough for personal use. They've arrested him for 'intent to distribute.' And I think they're trying to find evidence to charge him for the murder, too." She bit her lip. *Why did I gush everything out like that?*

"Oh, my God." Patty's quivering voice dropped an octave.

"I've hired a defense attorney, and as soon as bail is set, I'll post it."

"Oh, Claire," Patty whispered, her voice suddenly hoarse. She cleared her throat. "Michael knows people in Tulsa. I'll have him make a few calls about the bail. And I can fly in tomorrow."

"Sis, there's nothing anyone can do until they set bail. You can call Denver. I'll visit him in jail today. I know you're worried, and so am I. But you have things to take care of there." She was making a mess of this conversation. "What's happening with Michael?"

"He has a chemo session this afternoon. I promised to go with him, but with this news ..."

"Patty, you and Mike have your hands full. I'll take care of all I can here. See how he does with today's treatment. Maybe you can come out next week. I'm hoping it will all have blown over." And she was hoping it would. But it didn't seem likely.

"I pray you are right."

"There's an explanation for those drugs, and I'm sure Denver didn't murder J.B. Floren. The authorities will get to the bottom of it."

"I can't stand the thought of him in jail. Not after Afghanistan and everything he's endured." Patty sucked in a shaking breath. "What about bail? How much it will be?"

"I can raise bail. I know Denver won't skip out and I'll get it all back. Call Denver at the jail. I'll give you the number."

"You've already done so much for Denver. I can't ask you–"

"I love Denver, Patty. He's like my own son. I'm glad to do this for him."

Muffled sobs came through on her cell phone. "We'll get through this, Sis."

"I don't know what I'd do without you." Patty sniffed.

"I'll call you tonight if I have an update. In a little while, give Denver a call at the jail."

Claire read the phone number of the Payne County jail to her sister before she disconnected. She stepped into the house. Her jaw ached. *Clenching.* Down the hall, the bathroom door snapped shut.

She headed to her bedroom to dress for work.

When the bathroom door clicked open again, Claire called to Cade from her room, "Can you feed the animals before Antonio gets here?"

"Sure," Cade's athletic shoes squeaked down the hall toward the kitchen. "Come on, kids," he called to the dogs. Doggy toenails clicked on the kitchen floor. The back door slammed.

As she applied her makeup, she replayed her conversation with Patty. Her sister had sounded devastated, just as she was, and she had not done a good job of easing the blow about what had happened.

But she'd laid it out there, and Patty had needed to know. Her sister would call him, and, if she could keep from crying during the conversation, Denver's spirits would be lifted. As for herself, she'd visit Denver at the jail today and talk with him about bail. He needed to know she was putting her life savings on the line. She didn't think he would skip bail, especially since he was innocent, but the conversation had to happen.

Denver was not guilty of either crime. She was 100 percent positive. Wasn't she?

Chapter 13

"Coffee break time? Mind if I intrude?" Holt startled her when he leaned against her desk mid-morning.

She'd thrown herself into her assignments when she'd arrived, grateful there were no anonymous emails like the day before. She wrote, rewrote and sent a variety of stories on for final edit. She'd been so deep in thought on an article about the successes of the local historic preservation group she had been unaware of anyone moving about the room.

Claire's chair creaked as she pushed back. Holt at her office two days in a row? She had to nip his new habit of dropping in on her. He leaned toward her over the stacks of folders cluttering her desk. She shoved the chair even farther from her computer, and from him.

"Can you take a break?"

"I'm busy, Holt. On a deadline. I have about one minute."

"Okay. That's all I really need. I'm sorry I've disturbed you." The tense muscles of his forehead relaxed. "I've been thinking about Cade. I know he needs his space." Holt picked at his fingernail. "I'm not taking it personally."

"Denver's arrest upset him. Although they haven't exactly pinned the murder on Denver, he seems to be their prime suspect."

"And should be. I can't think of any motive other than bloodlust. Has Denver's trigger temper ever shown itself before?"

"No. And I don't believe he has a temper. He's so gentle with the animals." Heat burned on her face. Trigger temper? Holt knew nothing about Denver.

"But he doesn't like people much. And with the PTSD ... The sheriff and I were talking yesterday about how unpredictable that disorder can be. Anyone who watches the news knows that. Take the killings at Fort Hood, for example."

Holt had discussed the case with the sheriff? Claire rubbed her fingers against the edge of her desk. "Not liking and not trusting people doesn't mean Denver would snap and murder someone."

"Snap he did, from the look of the crime scene." Holt grimaced.

Claire's eyes narrowed. Holt shouldn't have even been at the crime scene. Apparently, he'd gawked at Floren's body enough to have all the details memorized.

The message indicator beeped on her computer. An email from her editor appeared. *Have you finished the piece about Floren's ranch? Publisher wants to run it Sunday with the obit. Can you wrap it up?*

Will do, she typed. That meant reviewing and editing the article and finding another source to fill in the gaps. Several hours of work added to an already busy day. And she had yet to make it over to the jail to visit Denver.

"I've got to get back to work."

"Okay, sweetheart. Later, okay?" Holt bent toward her as if he expected a kiss.

"Knock it off, Holt." She sighed in exasperation. "I'm at work." Her look flashed from his goofy grin to her keyboard while she shook her head.

Holt's footsteps plodded across the room.

Holt Braden was the last thing she needed. She'd allowed him into her life this week because she needed a distraction. Her thoughts constantly hovered on the edge of a precipice, ready to crash into a spiral of fear and anxiety like she had experienced after the Max Dyson episode. She couldn't do that again. If she did, she might very well lose custody of Cade. And maybe lose her job.

On her computer, Claire clicked on and opened a saved document she'd named 'Final questions for Floren.' She'd planned to ask the questions at their meeting Tuesday morning, but that didn't happen. And she'd already tried finding the answers in the digital files and by using internet search engines. The only remaining alternative was another search of old clippings in the newspaper's morgue.

She glanced toward the doorway in the corner of the newsroom. The overhead lights were on. Seventy-five-year-old Maggie Stiner was there, sorting through the previous week's news stories and turning them into PDFs for the digital morgue. Hard to imagine that she'd been cataloguing the news stories for decades, long before the world became computerized. She'd done what hardly seemed possible; she'd spent her entire fifty-year career as this newspaper's librarian.

Claire entered the morgue. All four walls of the room were lined with four-drawer file cabinets. The spry elderly woman was seated at her computer. Maggie pulled off her reading glasses and laid them on the desktop. "Morning, Claire. How can I help you?" Stacks of filing boxes sat behind her on a six-foot table, labeled by months and years. She fluffed her short, full bob of silver hair as she smiled.

"I need to pick your brain about J.B. Floren." The scent of vanilla hung heavy in the air, rising from the wax warmer plugged into an electric socket next to Maggie's computer.

"You're writing his obit?" Maggie's wooden desk chair creaked as she stopped rocking and the chair shifted on its roller legs.

"No, I'm finishing a feature story about the mustang rescue ranches in Oklahoma; the man was a major player. Mr. Eames wants to run the article in Sunday's issue with the full obituary."

"Have they finished the autopsy? Released the body to the funeral home?" Maggie fired questions in her gravelly voice, inquisitive blue eyes sparkling.

"Probably not yet. By Saturday the family should be able to add services pending info to a full obit. The publisher doesn't want to hold it any longer."

"Let me put my thinking cap on." Maggie straightened in her chair and rubbed her temples with crooked fingers. She carefully set her glasses back on her nose and reached for the keyboard.

"I remember when J.B. started that ranch," she said, her fingers flying across the keyboard. "Had a wife. Pretty thing. Didn't seem to be a fit for a big flirty man like him. Of course, I'm not telling you anything new. You know what he's like if you've interviewed him." Maggie peered at the screen.

"No sign of a wife during any of my visits. Just a housekeeper," Claire said. "Mustangs, burros and his dog, Ranger. I brought the dog home with me; he's keeping my dog Izzy company. No one's come looking for him, yet." Claire balanced on the edge of the chair next to Maggie's primary work desk.

"I think Ranger originally belonged to the wife." Maggie frowned at her computer screen. "Give me a minute while I search the files." She tapped a few keys, and then a few more. Not two years after he started the ranch their names appeared in the *Divorces Pending* column, and a few months after, the *Divorces Granted* listings. Here. Take a look."

Claire bent for a better look at the screen. The photographer had snapped Floren and his wife with a dog. The rancher was a younger, thinner version of himself, and the dog was a gangly pup. Claire read the caption aloud. "'Owner/operator of the new Cimarron Valley Mustang and Burro Rescue Ranch J.B. Floren, his wife, Cassandra, and their mixed hound pup, Ranger.' Any follow-up articles?"

"A couple of news items about the divorce, but nothing on the ranch. Don't think anybody expected the venture to take off like it did. Who'd have thought money could be made by rescuing and selling mangy old horses?"

"The couple didn't have kids, I'm guessing," Claire said. "Any idea where the wife went after the divorce? Why didn't she take Ranger with her?"

"Rumors were that the wife didn't want to take anything that reminded her of him. I heard Cassandra moved to Europe. People speculated about other women. J.B. liked to flirt."

"I got that impression."

Maggie's fingers flew over the keys again. "Here it is. I *thought* I remembered something about this."

Claire leaned toward the computer screen and read: "'Rescue Ranch Neighbor Files Complaint. Lucia Valdez has filed a complaint with the SPCA against J. B. Floren, the owner of the Cimarron Valley Rescue Ranch. According to Valdez, she discovered two starving animals after noticing turkey vultures circling low over

Mr. Floren's property." Claire straightened. "Did the group investigate?"

Maggie's fingers typed a flurry of words and another article flashed onto the screen. "Yep. Investigated and found the claim of animal cruelty unsubstantiated." The librarian clicked more keys and waited as the computer searched. *No files found* flashed on the screen. She pulled off her reading glasses. "That's it on the ranch. No more complaints, no more stories."

"Does Ms. Valdez still live near the ranch?"

"We can check the White Pages." She typed in the website's *url*, and Valdez' name. An address listing appeared on the screen. "Lucia Valdez. Rural route. 4700 Western."

"Why does that name sound familiar?"

"She used to be active in state livestock associations. And she was on the board at the bank for a while."

"I probably met her at a bank social, years ago. I'll recognize her when I see her."

Maggie looked over the top of her glasses. "You don't seem the 'social event' type. What were you doing there?"

Claire pursed her lips and shook her head. "I dated a banker briefly. Met him when I applied for pre-approval for a home loan."

"I bet Lucia will remember you. You'll like her, she's a straight shooter."

Chapter 14

Back at her desk, Claire grabbed her cell phone and keyed in the number. The phone rang four times before a woman answered.

"Lucia Valdez."

"Ms. Valdez, this is Claire Northcutt with *The News Press*. Could I have a few minutes of your time? I'm working on an article and would like your input."

"Input? On what? Not that old fart Floren, I hope," the woman snapped.

The neighbor didn't like him. No surprise. If she'd found emaciated horses on her neighbor's property, she wouldn't like the neighbor either. "Would you have a few minutes for a brief interview?"

"Don't know what I could tell you."

"I need your expertise for a story I'm writing about the state's mustang rescue ranches."

"You want both sides of the story, or are you pro-rescue?"

"I can be there in ten minutes."

Lucia waited a beat before she said, "You know how to get here? Drive on up to the house. The gate's open."

Claire punched off her phone, grabbed her purse and headed for the parking lot. A negative side to rescue ranches? None of the three Oklahoma sources she had interviewed for the article had alluded to anything but positive aspects. But there was always another side.

Claire's SUV rumbled down the dirt driveway toward the Valdez house. She parked in front of the connected two-car garage.

Sparrows whistled and a meadowlark trilled. The sweet scent of honeysuckle from a flowering vine on the front porch trellis tickled her nose.

Lucia Valdez threw open the door as Claire bounded up the front porch steps of the ranch-style home.

"Ms. Valdez? I'm Claire Northcutt."

Lucia Valdez nodded. "We've met before, haven't we? I never forget a face." She motioned for her to come inside. "This way. We'll sit on the back porch and enjoy the morning."

Claire remembered Valdez, too. Angular features and ebony eyes, strands of gray hair blending into straight, dark hair that hung halfway down her back. The attractive woman's smile didn't hide her bloodshot eyes.

Claire followed her into the house. In the large living room, area rugs covered a floor of wide walnut planks. Deep sofas with large pillows formed conversation areas and bookshelves filled with volumes of all sizes covered two walls. A large dining table with eight chairs filled the far end of the room.

In the kitchen, a granite-topped island separated a breakfast nook from the kitchen. A compact stereo unit on the counter played an early George Strait ballad.

Lucia indicated the kettle on the stove and an empty mug. "Help yourself. I've got coffee packets and teabags, sugar and milk." She shoved a turquoise pottery sugar bowl and creamer of milk across the counter.

Claire selected a teabag and poured hot water over it in the cup. Herbal-scented steam rose into the air. A picture in a tile frame next to the kitchen's wide sink had caught two dark-haired toddlers squatting near a puppy in a grass yard. Lucia's children?

"This way, Ms. Northcutt." Lucia led Claire through a double garden door and stepped across the flagstone patio to a tile-topped table.

Claire inspected the vista as she settled into a chair. "Beautiful." Her look swept over pastureland and stopped at the towering cottonwoods and bushy willows of the river valley a half-mile or more away. A small herd grazed halfway between the house and the river. She peered at the animals. Too small to be horses. Donkeys? Or a breed of pony?

"Those animals are mixed equids. Do you know the term?"

"Equid? In the horse–or equine–family?"

"Only three equid species exist: horses, zebras and donkeys. The largest animal you see is a mule, a cross between a male donkey and a female horse. The other is a hinney, a male horse and female donkey cross."

Claire squinted toward the field. "Does one of them have stripes or am I just imagining?"

"Yes. The smallest one is a zonkey, a zebra–donkey cross. I also have a zorse, a zebra-horse cross. They all have such different personalities, but each has traits common to their parent equids."

"Are you building a herd?"

Lucia smiled. "Not in the way you might think. All those equids are sterile. The species can breed with one another, but their offspring can't bear young. I'll add more zebra crosses. The kids love to come here on school field trips to see those."

"It's a magical-looking animal." Claire could see the faint stripes on the animal's hide when the sun peeked through the clouds. Here was an idea for a future article. Surely very few people in the area were aware that such a herd existed on the Valdez ranch.

Lucia shifted her look away from the animals. "You're here because of the complaint I made against J.B. years ago, aren't you? Dug it up in an old newspaper, I'm guessing." She sipped her tea, keeping the mug at her mouth and blowing air over the steaming brew between each swallow.

"That's what brought me here. But I'm hoping you can fill in some gaps I have about Mr. Floren's operation. I went to his ranch earlier this week for a final interview about his mustang rescue. I found the body."

Lucia studied her. "I'm sure that was horrible. I'm neither shocked or upset about his death. And I won't apologize."

Maggie was right. Lucia Valdez was a straight shooter. Claire pulled out her spiral notepad and searched for a pen in her purse. "You filed a lawsuit against Mr. Floren?"

"The buzzards were flying. I'd seen them circling before, but that day a dozen or more of those birds were soaring around, preparing to feast. Turns out they were waiting for the horses to die." Lucia's hands cupped her mug as if her hands were cold. "Things changed between J.B. and me. We'd been lovers."

Claire held her pen still. Lovers? She'd heard no trace of affection in Lucia's earlier comments. She remembered the photo Maggie had found of Floren and his wife in the archives. Valdez was the opposite of his petite, blond wife.

"People suspected, including Cassandra." Lucia's eyes had a hard glint. "I wasn't the first or the last of his lovers. You spent time with J.B. You saw how he was about women."

Claire recalled the man's flirtations and the discomfort she had felt around him. "I interviewed him a few times." She let it go at that, Lucia didn't need details.

Lucia nodded. "You read about the lawsuit. It didn't go anywhere. J.B. bluffed his way through it and the carcasses had disappeared." Her eyes narrowed. "You mentioned gaps in your article. I'm not sure I can help, but I'll try."

"Were you supportive of the ranch when Mr. Floren changed his focus to mustang rescue?" Claire held her pen poised, ready to write.

"Most rural people here are ranchers. Cattle or horses, maybe both. And the fact that those mustangs and burros needed homes, well, I was a softie about that, too, until J.B. began to exceed his grazing numbers. Too many horses on his range. And we were in a drought. He couldn't feed that many animals on his pastureland. His choice was either to let them starve or buy hay, and he was a cheapskate."

"So, he wouldn't buy the hay. Why didn't he stop accepting the animals?"

"Folks out west, where the mustangs and burros come from, want them gone. They'll have more free forage and range for their own cattle or sheep. But there are so many animals. Trouble is, when they bring them here, we've got the same problem, only it's not free range. The rescue ranch owners get paid by the government for alleviating overgrazing on BLM land back in Montana or wherever the animals come from. Paid to be nice guys, essentially. It's a decent income."

"So, Mr. Floren depended on that income, but it wasn't enough money for him to buy hay during the drought?"

Lucia shrugged. "How much is enough? We all have our wants, don't we?"

"Did you see the vultures again? Were there more emaciated animals?"

"Not that I saw. And as far as turkey vultures ... it's not unusual to see one or two together. Vultures are part of the food chain like coyotes or bobcats. We have those around here, too."

Claire glanced toward the river. "Is Floren's ranch on the other side of the river?"

"Actually, the river cuts through his property. My boundary is that distant fence line. I'm not riverfront, but I've got water rights and wells. These days, I raise a few foals each year and train." Lucia rubbed her eyelids and sighed heavily.

Claire sipped her tea and looked out at the emerald pastures, the leafy trees and the wide, blue Oklahoma sky. To the right of the house stood a stable with an adjacent paddock and a training ring. "Do you train mustangs?"

"They are feral horses. Their ancestors arrived in North America with the Spanish conquistadors and they've been living on their own for centuries. They do just fine without people. But that's not what you asked. Eventually, with a lot of patience and careful work, wild horses will trust people a little. They can be trained."

"My son and I bought a mustang mare and a burro from Mr. Floren earlier this year. My nephew is training her."

Lucia drank from her mug. The nails of her leathery hands had recently been manicured and painted a pale pink. Her fingers trembled.

Claire's inquisitiveness kicked into high gear. Maybe Lucia wasn't as unaffected by J.B.'s death as she appeared. When Claire leaned toward her, Lucia shifted in her chair.

"Have the police talked to you about the murder?"

"Why would they? Like I said before, he and I weren't on speaking terms."

"I would think they'd interview all of his neighbors, anyone who might have seen something."

"Only saw animals grazing that day. That's all I'll say if they interview me. I'll tell them what I've told you. I didn't like the way J.B. ran his ranch. He was a snake charmer." Valdez drained her mug and set it firmly on the patio table. "I've said all I can."

"I appreciate your time, Ms. Valdez. Is it all right if I quote you in my article as a neighbor?" Claire stuffed her notebook and pen into her purse.

Lucia's forehead creased. "I suppose so. I am–was–his neighbor, and his critic."

"I won't mention your complaint to the SPCA since the case went nowhere."

"No need to rehash it. The man's dead. Let me know if I can help with the mustang you're training."

"I will." Claire plodded through the house and out to her SUV, her mind racing.

Lucia had a motive to kill the rancher. Hatred. Had it been deep enough, fierce enough, to murder him so brutally?

Chapter 15

Claire's truck zipped along Highway 51 back into town. Now was as good a time as any to stop by the jail and see Denver. Afterward she needed to begin the process of gathering the money to post Denver's bail. Could she get a second mortgage? With a high credit score, bills paid on time and low balances on two credit cards, loan approval should be easy, shouldn't it?

She tugged her cell phone from her purse. At the next stop sign, she touched the speed dial number for Reed Morgan.

"Hello, Reed. It's Claire Northcutt," she said when he answered his extension at the bank.

"Claire, it's great to hear your voice. What's going on?"

"Do you have time to meet with me later this afternoon?"

"I always have time for you. I hope everything's okay with you and Cade."

Old memories surfaced at the sound of his voice. She remembered how, when they were dating, Reed had tended to be a control freak. He'd wanted to oversee each aspect of her life; finances, appearance, friends, Cade. She suddenly had second thoughts about asking for his help with a loan for Denver's bail. "We'll talk when I get there. Say, in an hour?"

"I'm headed into a lunch meeting in five. Can you make it an hour and a half?" His voice had become all business.

Claire glanced at her dashboard clock. She had to get back to work, but she still needed to visit the jail. And there was one other stop she could make quickly, on the way. She turned right on Perkins Road and pulled into a strip mall. She parked in front of Clippers, Jenny Prather's hair salon. Stylists were busy with clients at each station and more people waited in a side area. Claire grabbed her iPad. She could use any 'wait' time to add Lucia's comments to the rescue ranch article, check her work emails and schedule time for the afternoon's assignments.

Inside the shop, two of the stylists, Shea and Martina, were snipping hair in their booths; Jenny was chatting with a customer as she dried the woman's hair. A ceiling fan circulated the scents of floral shampoos and pungent hair dye throughout the shop.

"Be right with you, Claire," Jenny shouted over the whooshing hair dryers. The shop's owner had fashionably messy shoulder-length brown hair with highlights and lowlights. Even from the doorway, Claire could see dark circles under her beautiful hazel eyes, indicating a sleepless night.

She settled into one of the padded folding chairs in the waiting area and turned on her iPad. Claire pulled the spiral notebook from her purse, clicked the rescue ranch article on her iPad and added a few paragraphs about the national debate over wild horse rescue.

"Okay, Claire," Jenny called a few minutes later. "I have another customer coming in shortly for a cut. Let's walk next door and get a soda pop." Jenny stuffed a few dollars into her pocket from one of her work station drawers and rubbed lotion into her hands before joining Claire at the front door.

"I'm going to see Denver this afternoon," Jenny said as they walked out the door.

"He'll be glad to see you."

A little light gleamed in Jenny's tired eyes. "Have you seen him?"

"I'm going by after I leave here. Then I'm meeting with a banker. Hopefully, I can post bond Monday and get Denver out of jail."

"Can't it happen any faster?" Jenny asked with a quivering voice.

"It's a lot of money to raise." Claire didn't like the scolding tone of her own voice, so she added, "But I'm happy to do this for Denver."

They headed toward one of the Naugahyde-covered booths in the small café. The thick odor of fry oil hung in the air.

"I can't believe he's been arrested. And they think he might have killed Mr. Floren?" Her shoulders slumped. She wrapped a long strand of highlighted hair around one finger, unwrapped it, and wrapped it again.

"They'll find the person who killed him." Claire wished she felt as sure as she sounded.

"I want to believe that. It seems unreal."

A thirty-something waitress with bright red hair stopped at the end of the table. "What can I get you to drink?"

"To-go cups for both of us," Claire said. "I'll have an iced tea."

"And I'll have a Diet Coke."

"That it?" the waitress looked at each woman.

Claire glanced over at Jenny's pale face. She probably hadn't eaten since hearing the news yesterday about Denver. "We'll also take an order of your homemade potato chips, with salsa."

"You got it. Be right back."

Jenny ran her fingers through her hair, clasped her hands together and rested them on the black plastic surface of the table. "You were out at the ranch to interview the rancher. Any idea why someone would want to kill him?"

"When I interviewed him, we talked about the rescue ranch operation, and a little about horse care. There was no chitchat. He answered my questions, smiled and flirted a little."

Jenny's smile was weak. "J.B. was a flirt, wasn't he? He must have been in his seventies."

"Doesn't stop men from trying for a younger conquest. Did you know the rancher?"

"I cut his hair. Could it have been a woman, another 'conquest' who killed him?" Jenny suggested.

"Mr. Floren was at least six feet tall and probably weighed over two hundred pounds, didn't he? I don't know how a woman would have gotten his body out to the flagpole."

"Maybe she drugged him. Or maybe he'd been drinking."

"At eight in the morning?" Jenny's idea intrigued her. It was an angle the sheriff should consider.

"Denver didn't kill him. And someone planted those drugs. Denver doesn't do drugs. We've been going out for two months, and never–"

The waitress arrived with their drinks and a basket of the cafe's famous homemade potato chips. "Anything else I can get for you, ladies?"

"No, thanks. Leave me the tab, please," Claire said.

"You got it." The waitress tore a page off her order pad and laid it on the table. She looked closely at Jenny. "Say, I've seen you with that horse trainer, haven't I? At the Red Angus? Didn't I hear he's been arrested? Doing drugs, and he maybe even killed that rancher."

Claire pulled in a quick breath. The color drained from Jenny's face.

"It's a terrible mistake," Jenny said in a low voice.

"Couple of deputies came in earlier today, and they sounded pretty certain. I overheard them talking about blood on the floor mats of his truck, the one they found the drugs in."

Tears spilled over Jenny's eyelids and ran down her cheeks. She scooted out of the booth. "Sorry, Claire." Jenny hurried out of the café.

"I didn't mean to spook her. Sounds like that guy's a murderer and a drug dealer to me." The waitress turned to Claire and shrugged.

"You're wrong. Put these chips in a to-go box, would you?" Claire shoved the potato chips across the table to the red-haired waitress.

"Sure thing. Be a shame to let them go to waste." She disappeared with the basket.

The deputies had been discussing the case in public. It wouldn't be long before everyone would have heard about Denver's arrest and the drugs thanks to the waitress/town crier.

The redhead returned with a Styrofoam container and picked up the ten-dollar bill Claire had laid on the table.

Claire touched her arm. "Hey, you need to know, Denver Streeter is a decorated veteran. A good soldier and a good man. He didn't kill J.B. Floren, and he doesn't do drugs. I'd stop spreading malicious rumors if I were you." Claire glared at the other woman.

"Just repeating what I heard. From people who would know," the waitress said with a shrug.

As Claire exited, three women seated at a nearby booth stared at her. The trio huddled together, whispering. Denver wasn't the only one being gossiped about.

Chapter 16

Claire waited at the main desk inside the police station until someone came to escort her into the jail's visitor area. She passed through a metal detector archway, had her purse x-rayed, and followed a policewoman down several gray hallways to an open room full of metal tables. The woman left her at a table and disappeared through a doorway. Minutes later, she returned with Denver beside her, handcuffed.

Head down, he dropped onto the bench across the table from her. The policewoman backed up a few yards and stood, hands folded across her stomach.

"Denver? Are you okay?" Claire leaned toward him and reached for his hand.

He lifted his eyes. His pasty-gray skin and greasy hair told her all she needed to know. "Get me out of here."

His icy hand made her shiver. "I will, Denver. Did the attorney come this morning?"

He nodded.

"She's a good one. And I'm getting the money together to post bail."

His eyes glistened with tears. "I can't thank you enough. And I promise you won't lose that money. No way I'm going to run from this. I'm innocent. The drugs weren't mine, Aunt Claire. Why would someone plant–" His voice broke. He swallowed.

"I know they weren't yours. Jenny knows they weren't yours. Who could have done this?"

He shook his head slowly. "I don't know many people here. Before I met Jenny, I didn't know anyone."

"You two sometimes went to the Red Angus, didn't you? Anyone there ever bother Jenny, or you?"

"We went there. Never stayed long. It was noisy. You know how I am with noise." He studied the handcuffs on his wrists.

She *did* know how he was with noise. It was a major trigger for his PTSD, just as thunderstorms and silent houses triggered her own memories. "Did you know any of the other people who worked or volunteered at Floren's?"

"Cade and I kept to ourselves. We were working."

"Who would want to hurt you?" Claire heard the exasperation in her own voice.

"I don't know why anyone would do this."

"Why didn't you like the rancher? What did he do?"

Denver squinted. "J.B. was a fake. I shouldn't have told Cade about it, but I was angry. I couldn't go back there, and I didn't want Cade to help the man either once I overheard what he was really about."

"What was he doing?"

"The exact opposite of what people thought he was doing. His rescue operation was a farce. And I think I can prove it."

"Not from the inside of a jail cell. Tell me what you know."

"I overheard a phone call. He was joking about the success of his scam. He mentioned you, and that article you were writing. Said something like, 'the heat is off for now. I'm a hero, don't you know?' Then he laughed."

Claire felt as if she'd been slapped. A hero? Would her article turn him into a hero? Was everything he'd told her a lie? A wave of anger washed over her. "I'm headed to meet with the banker right now. You'll hear something from either me or Trina soon."

Her heart wrenched at his woe-be-gone look.

"You'll be back home soon, Denver. I promise."

Chapter 17

"Reed, he's my nephew. I won't leave him in that jail. He's innocent." Claire leaned forward in the comfortable padded armchair and pushed her sweating hands against the edge of the loan officer's polished walnut desk. She resisted the urge to vault from the chair and pace the room.

"You sure emotion isn't clouding your judgment?" The handsome banker studied her face. "I'm speaking as a friend, Claire. I've known you for ... what, five years? Haven't I always been straight with you about finances, whether you were buying your place, or a horse, or setting up a college account for Cade?" Reed Morgan tossed his pen onto the desk. "It's a lot of money. Represents years of scrimping and saving. You need to be absolutely positive Denver Streeter won't skip out on this bail bond. This is your life savings."

"He won't skip. I'd bet my life on it." Reed had her best interests at heart, but she wished he would agree that posting the bond was the right thing to do. "I'll get all the money back when the charges are dropped." She was taking a huge risk by posting bail on her own, without paying a bondsman's 10 percent loan fee. She felt slightly nauseous.

"And he's got good representation? An experienced attorney?" Reed leaned back in his desk chair, picked the silver pen up again and held it in the air between the two pointer fingers of each hand. A few gray strands of hair blended with the dark ones on his temples. His brown eyes snapped with energy and health. If Max Dyson hadn't invaded her life, would she have let a romance develop with Reed? As soon as her head posed the question, her heart reminded her of the reason she'd broken it off with him. Shades of her first husband, control issues and passive aggressive behavior. She hadn't forgotten.

"Trina Romero has an excellent reputation."

"Yes, she does." He scribbled something on a notepad. "You're absolutely sure you want to do this?"

"Positive. Denver is innocent."

He studied her face for a few seconds before he laid the pen down. "I'll get to work on the paperwork. Should be ready for your signature Monday. We'll have Denver out Tuesday, pending no extenuating circumstances." Reed pushed back his chair and moved around his desk. He smiled and touched her elbow as she rose. "It's nice to see you again. I wish it was under different circumstances. Something pleasant. Like dinner and a movie."

She ignored his implied invitation and stepped away. No need to give him any reason to think she wanted to date again. "I appreciate this, Reed. I'll call Monday morning to be sure the paperwork is in order before I stop in."

"Denver is lucky to have you in his corner, Claire. And you can tell him I said so."

Claire forced a smile. "Thanks." After a quick handshake, she left Reed Morgan's office.

She chewed her lip as she hurried through the cool bank lobby and out to her SUV. It had been all she could do not to lose it in front of Reed. Tears threatened and her throat tightened. Her knees quivered as she lifted herself into the driver's seat. She glanced in the rearview mirror at the dark circles under her own eyes.

She had to hold it together for Denver and for Cade. And she must get to work before she got fired. On her agenda when she got there was convincing Manny to delay–or even cancel–the article she'd written about the Cimarron Valley Rescue Ranch and J.B. Floren. Denver has said the rancher was a fraud, and she believed him.

J.B. had been up to something. No way was she going to make him out to be some kind of hero.

Chapter 18

Claire hurried into the newsroom. She encountered no one in the parking lot or in the hallway on her way in. *Thank goodness.* She had nothing to say to anyone.

She clicked open her email account. A string of messages from Manny began at 10 a.m., while she and Lucia had been meeting. Claire glanced at the wall clock, a constant reminder they were on deadline: One p.m.

Manny's first assignment: follow up on last night's police blotter and get the internet edition updated. Tabling the article would have to wait. She called the police station.

"Claire Northcutt? I have a delivery." The voice cut into her concentrated effort to proof the third of Manny's assignments, the updated agenda for tonight's City Council meeting; it should have been posted to the e-news 15 minutes ago. The meeting time: six p.m.

"I'm Claire." She swiveled in the chair. The delivery man crossed the room with a bouquet of Shasta daisies in a turquoise pottery vase.

"These are for you."

She took the vase and placed it on her desk next to the still-beautiful roses Holt had sent yesterday.

"Looks like you've got an admirer," the man said.

Claire checked inside the blooms for a card from the sender, but found none. She opened her desk drawer, pulled two dollars from her vending machine cash envelope and handed it to the man. "Thanks."

"Welcome. Enjoy." The delivery man strolled from the room.

Claire tapped her fingertips on the desk. Did Holt really think flowers were the key to her affection? She had developed an invisible line for over-eager boyfriends. Reed Morgan had crossed it years ago, and now, so had Holt.

She moved both vases of flowers to the top of her file cabinet and positioned the small desk fan between her desk and Casey's to blow any flower scent or pollen toward the wall instead of her chair. The last thing she needed today was an allergy attack or a sinus headache.

Reed's last statement replayed in her brain: "Denver is lucky to have you in his corner, Claire." *Lucky?* She had insisted he come here after he finished his certification. She had introduced him to J.B. Floren, and talked him into volunteering with Cade on the weekends. Look where that had gotten him.

Lucky to have you ... His wistful voice played again. Her need for space, quiet and safety–after her experience with Max Dyson–had not fit into Reed's plans. He had stormed out of the restaurant the night she'd broken it off, leaving her to walk home to her apartment alone. His apology had come early the next day, along with an offer to continue to help her with her search for property outside of town. "I hope we can maintain a friendship and a business relationship," he'd said. So far, they'd been able to, and thanks to him, she'd soon have the money for Denver's bail. She had to get past her memories of his controlling tendencies and work with the man for Denver's sake.

Her desk phone rang. "You're past deadline, Claire. I need the agenda posted. The Mayor called," Manny said.

"I'm on it. Nearly finished." She hung up. But half of Manny's list remained. She pulled out her cell phone and sent Cade a text. "Working late. Eat without me. Love you."

Seconds later, his response came. "K c u."

Claire's fingers shifted back to her keyboard to crank out the remaining assignments.

What was Holt thinking? Flowers two days in a row?

The sun hung low on the horizon, sending long shadows across the empty parking lot when Claire locked the back door of the office and headed for her SUV. Long day. Long week, and still one more day to get through. First thing tomorrow, she'd talk to Manny about pulling the article.

A white envelope flapped under her SUV's right front windshield wiper.

People often placed fliers on cars around town to sell things or advertise an event. Even the university publicized events in the community using windshield fliers. She grabbed the envelope and opened it. The bold handwriting on the paper inside read: "I hope you liked the daisies. They remind me of you."

A sense of déjà vu slammed her. She unlocked the vehicle and hopped inside, started the engine and locked the doors. She'd been certain the daisies were from Holt. But they weren't. Her stomach twisted into a knot and bile rose up her throat.

She hit the accelerator and zoomed from the parking lot.

It can't happen again. Dyson is dead.

He'd written notes, sent flowers and left phone messages before his final act. She stifled the scream that threated to explode from deep inside her. A chill travelled her back. She punched the accelerator and flew through the corner stop sign on Main Street without looking or pausing.

Red lights flashed in her rearview mirror. She guided her SUV to the curb, turned on her emergency flashers and waited for the policeman to approach, shaking uncontrollably. She wrapped her arms around herself.

Another stalker?

Claire unrolled her window. In her side view mirror, she watched the uniformed man step closer. "Officer, I know I ran a stop sign. I was focused on getting home, I didn't see it." She kept her shaking voice soft.

"Ms. Northcutt?"

She glanced up at the Deputy Sheriff.

"Yes, Deputy Purdue. I'm on my way home from work." She rubbed her forehead. "Long day." She swiped at the beads of sweat on her upper lip.

He leaned over to look inside the vehicle. "I'm sure you have a lot on your mind. The murder, Mr. Streeter's arrest. And you drive this route every day. Right?"

"I, uh, yes. I guess."

"Are you all right?"

"I need to get home."

He straightened. "I shouldn't do this, but I'm going to cut you a break. Because of all that's been happening. Let's say you didn't run that stop sign. Forget it. And be careful on your way home. Okay?"

"I will. I definitely will."

Purdue lifted his hand in a salute and strolled back to his cruiser. She hadn't thought much about the deputy before. Nice of him not to give her a ticket. And he wasn't bad looking.

As she pulled back into the street, she wondered, should she have talked to the deputy about the notes and the flowers? Would he have laughed at her concern about a possible stalker? He knew about Max Dyson. Would he take her concern more seriously because she'd been through it once before, or would he shrug it off as the imaginings of a hysterical woman?

Claire drove carefully the rest of the way home, trying to concentrate on the road, and not think about Floren, Lucia Valdez and Denver.

Or the possibility that another stalker had crept into her life.

Chapter 19

The TV blared from the living room as Claire entered the house through the kitchen garage door. Ranger and Izzy raced into the room, tails wagging, and looked up at her.

"Hello, kids. Have you had dinner?" she petted heads and scratched ears until the animals settled down. "Cade, I'm home."

"In here."

At the sound of his voice, the dogs trotted into the living room. Claire followed. Her son sat on the floor, leaning against the front of the sofa, a bowl of popcorn in his lap.

"Have you had dinner?"

"Alonzo brought pizza. He just left." Izzy snuggled down close beside Cade, watching each fluffy kernel of popcorn as it disappeared into the teenager's mouth. Cade flipped Izzy a piece and tossed another to Ranger.

The house phone rang. Claire hurried into the kitchen and picked it up. "Hello?" She waited. Silence, followed by a click as the caller hung up. Wrong number, she guessed.

The sound on the television abruptly stopped. Claire turned back to the living room as the television screen went black.

Cade grabbed the remote control and stabbed a few buttons. "Great. This is great." None of his button pushes made any difference. The screen stayed black.

"Cable must have gone out. Do you have homework?" she asked.

"I've done all my chores and my homework." He pitched the television remote control across the room. "No internet. This is crap."

"Cade, it's no big deal. Find something to do that doesn't rely on the cable service. Maybe read a book."

He tossed her a disgusted look. "Mom, everything relies on the cable and the internet."

She didn't want to argue. A headache pounded behind her eyes. "Nothing either of us can do about it. They'll get it fixed. Don't spend your energy ranting about this, son."

He bolted from the room with the popcorn bowl and stomped to his bedroom, both dogs close on his heels. "Easy for you to say." He tossed the words over his shoulder.

In the kitchen, Claire perused the pantry for an easy dinner. Too late to eat much. And she wasn't that hungry. After deciding on a bowl of oatmeal, she cooked it and sat down at the kitchen table to eat. Ranger dashed through the room and growled at the back door. She stiffened.

"Ranger, is someone out there?"

There was a tapping on the window pane. When she peered through the mullioned window, Holt's smiling face appeared. Ranger stuck his nose close to the door's crack and snuffled. A growl rumbled in his throat.

"Ranger, down. Sit." She pulled the door open and Holt stepped into the kitchen.

"Hi, beautiful. Long day?" Holt warily eyed the growling dog.

When she walked back to the table, Ranger padded behind her and lay at her feet. "Very long." She ate another spoonful of oatmeal.

"Want to talk about it?" Avoiding Ranger, he sat in the chair across the table from her.

Claire considered that question as she swallowed the oatmeal. Did she really want to tell him about talking with Jenny, visiting Denver and about discussing a second mortgage with Reed? About the delivery of the Shasta daisies and an afternoon of Manny assignments, followed by the realization that she had another stalker? Not to mention that her article on Floren made him out to be a nice person, which he wasn't.

"The usual," she finally answered.

"Anything new on the murder investigation? Or Denver's arrest for drugs?"

She forced herself to swallow another spoonful before she responded. "No. Is your cable out? Cade says ours is. TV is off, and so's the internet."

The overhead lights in the kitchen blinked once, twice and went out.

"You've lost your cable and your electricity? Sounds like a wiring problem to me." Holt's chair screeched as he shoved it back. As her eyes adjusted to the sudden dimness, she saw his shadow in front of the doorway leading to the living room. "I see lights at my house. And at the Barton's on your other side."

"Mom? Why did the lights go out?" Cade shouted from his room.

"Don't know, son. I'll get candles." She reached her way to the counter, retrieved the flashlight from the top of the refrigerator and walked over to the cabinet where she stored the emergency candles. At least in the darkness, no one could see that her hands were trembling.

From behind her, Holt slipped his arms around her waist. "I like being in the dark with you. Who needs candles?" He nuzzled her neck below her ear lobe.

She shoved him away and grabbed the candles. "Stop." She slipped around him and headed for the drawer where she kept the matches.

"But if we were ..."

"Mom. Where are the candles?" Cade grumbled from the doorway.

"Hi, Cade," Holt said.

"What are you doing here?" Cade muttered.

"I stopped in to see your mother. And how are you?"

"I need candles, Mom."

Claire struck a match and lit two of the pillar candles. "You can take these to your room. I'll put some in the bathrooms. Hopefully, it's just an outage and the lights will be back on soon."

"Could be there's a storm coming. It's that time of year." Holt grabbed a few of the candles she'd already lit. "I'll take these to the living room."

Claire stood in the dark kitchen, watching the flickering light and Holt's shadow as he crossed the living room to the coffee table. A long time ago, she'd loved it when the lights went out. Three years ago that had changed. Darkness was no longer romantic; it could be a nightmare. She didn't want Holt to be here, but she didn't want to be alone, either. A shiver raced down her back. She'd thought she was doing better, but J.B. Floren's death and the delivery of the daisies had brought it all back.

Holt plodded into the kitchen. "Claire? You're shivering." He rubbed her arms and pulled her close. "Are you cold?"

"No. It's ... I don't want to talk about it."

"I wish you'd quit saying that to me. I want you to talk to me about everything. Life isn't all roses." In the dimly lit room, his eyes gleamed as he looked at her.

Claire fought the urge to step away from him again. His warmth enclosed her. *Comforting. Safe.*

"Let's sit down and talk." He took her hand and led her into the living room. "Is it Floren's murder? Or something else?" He clasped her hand tightly and pulled her down onto the sofa next to him. Their thighs touched. Two candles cast a pool of light on the coffee table.

"I'm listening." He rubbed the side of her hand with his thumb.

Claire took a deep breath. She didn't care what Holt thought about her. If he was horrified at what had happened, at what she'd done ... that was okay. And she needed someone else to know about the possibility that another stalker had intruded on her life.

"Something happened to me three years ago. On a stormy night like this. No electricity."

"Go on."

Claire worried her lip with her teeth. She considered how much of the actual events to tell him.

"Claire, nothing you say could diminish the way I feel about you." The candlelight flickered on his face. He didn't know that she didn't care what he thought. And she truly didn't. What had happened was part of her. What had happened was the reason she didn't care what Holt or anyone thought. And the reason she didn't date.

In her mind, a movie played. The darkness ... the terror ... hands, groping ... the gunshot ... the blood.

Holt touched her arm, she flinched.

"Oh, babe. What is it? What happened to you?"

She pulled in another breath. "Three years ago, I had a stalker, a fan who read my news articles and saw my picture in the newspaper. He sent gifts, notes, flowers."

Holt enfolded her hand between his larger ones.

"One night, when Cade went to spend the weekend with his dad, the stalker broke into our apartment." Claire pulled her hand away and scooted forward to the edge of the sofa. "I got away from him and grabbed my gun. I shot him."

"Killed him?'

She nodded.

His hand stopped rubbing for an instant, and then started again. "Wow. You did what you had to do to protect yourself. I'm sorry it happened. Was it someone you knew?"

"No. But he knew all about me."

Holt rubbed her arm. "I bet you still have nightmares."

This time of year, it was dark, rainy nights that brought nightmares. She sank against the sofa cushions. "Did you send me daisies today?"

Holt pressed back against the cushions, too, and patted her thigh. "Today? I sent roses yesterday, Claire, but no daisies today. Should I have?"

"I got daisies. No card."

"Do I have competition?" He said light-heartedly.

How could there be competition? She wasn't dating Holt. She didn't intend to ever 'date' Holt. And if he had not sent the daisies, she was certain. She had another stalker.

"Do I?" he asked in a more serious tone.

"I told you I don't know who sent the flowers, and you and I are not dating."

"I wish we were." He grinned, but his smile turned into a frown as he stared at her solemn face in the flickering candlelight. "We can find out who sent them. What florist made the delivery?"

"I didn't ask."

Holt perused the dimly lit room. "Where are they?"

"At the office."

A hole opened in her stomach. She didn't think she had another stalker–she *knew* she did. She felt the same as she had then, the tenseness, the trembling throughout her body. Her inability to think about anything else. "I can't stop thinking about shooting that man. It was horrible. And finding Floren was horrible, too."

Holt slid one arm around her and pulled her close against him. "I'm sorry. But you're safe now. Nothing like that will happen again. I'm here with you."

She let him pull her close. He stroked her hair. She laid her head against his chest and heard his heart beating in the quiet house.

She sat up. "I don't hear any rain. If it's not storming, why did the lights go out?"

Holt looked out the front window. "Guess we should call the power company and let them know."

"I'll get my phone. The number is on my speed dial." She charged toward the kitchen.

"Does this happen often?"

"There's a generator near the highway that trips, especially whenever there's a close lightning strike." But she didn't voice her other concern, the one that indicated her continuing PTSD. Max Dyson had cut her electric wiring. Had this stalker done the same?

Claire found her purse and made the call on her phone. She asked about the outage, and was given an automated response. *No outages have been reported at this time. If you want to leave a message, do so after the beep. We'll have a service technician contact you shortly.*

"No outages have been reported," Claire told Holt. "Could it be a fuse?"

"I'll check. Is your fuse box in the garage?"

She led the way, stopping briefly in the kitchen to grab the flashlight. Once there, the two of them checked the fuse box and found every fuse in the correct position. The uneasy feeling in Claire's stomach intensified.

"I'm happy to stay and keep you company until the lights come back on," Holt said as they re-entered the house. "We can listen to music on iTunes. Maybe do a little two-stepping."

"You can two-step?" She forced herself to focus on what he was saying and not her shivering body.

"Shocking, isn't it? But, yes. Learned in college. That's the only kind of dancing this girl I liked wanted to do. I learned." Holt grinned. "Besides, the songs are kind of catchy once you get used to the twang."

She smiled at the image of Holt learning to two-step. As tense as she'd been minutes ago, she felt as if she'd been given an anti-anxiety drug.

"How about you? Can you do the two-step?"

She nodded. "It was the first thing I had to learn when I relocated to Stillwater. The country bars, like the Red Angus, are definitely the most fun."

"That's the place with the bucking bull ride, peanut shells on the floor and steer horns on the wall, right? I bet it gets crazy in there. We'll have to make a date to go two-stepping, but for now, I have my trusty iPhone and my iTunes app." He fiddled with his phone, pushing buttons, and more buttons, until finally a song played. She recognized an old Keith Whitley song, "Don't Close Your Eyes."

Holt stood, reached for her hand and pulled Claire into his arms. They swayed to the music as the song played. When it finished, he stepped back and looked at her.

The lights blinked and stayed on.

"Thank God," Claire said as she dropped his hands and moved away from him.

Cade burst out of his room. "Great. Wonder if the cable's back on." He hopped onto the sofa and grabbed the TV remote. Seconds later, the television blared.

Holt's face registered dismay. But she didn't feel like laughing at the man. They'd had an isolated outage, just like the night Max Dyson had assaulted her.

Tonight didn't go exactly like I had planned. Proves it once again, better not to plan. Dad used to say, 'Spur of the moment is always best. Grab it when you can. Take your chance and go for the gusto.' I think he got that one from an old beer advertisement on television.

Sorry, dad. I didn't go for the gusto tonight. Her son was there. The dog was there.

Excuses, excuses.

But it's early. She's wondering. Good. With her past, worry will turn to terror. She ought to be getting good and freaked out now. The daisies. The note. And the black out.

Good things come in threes.

Good night. Thinking of you. Sweet dreams.

Chapter 20

"*News Press*. Claire Northcutt. How can I help you?" As she answered her office desk phone Friday morning, she glanced at her list of assignments for the weekend edition. Many were nearly complete, others needed major additions or edits. And she still needed to talk to Manny about pulling J.B. Floren's rescue ranch story. It might be Friday, but it was already a hectic day. She would be challenged to get everything done even if she had no interruptions.

"This is Lucia Valdez." In the background, Garth Brooks sang about friends in low places.

Claire pushed away from her computer and grabbed a notepad, not anticipating that this was a social call. "Hi, Lucia."

"I've been thinking a lot about J.B.'s murder. The guy they arrested didn't kill him. The sheriff should talk to the partner." She spoke fast, in a hushed voice.

"Partner?" This was news to her. She'd seen no evidence that anyone else was in charge at the ranch.

"Silent partner. That's how he got the money to keep his quote nonprofit unquote business going. An investor bought in after his wife left."

"Any idea who that investor was?" Claire tapped the eraser end of a pencil on the desk.

"No. I learned about it in Floren's bed, not long after Cassandra moved out. He said they had big plans to expand the ranch into a riding academy for delinquents. I found the dead animals and we were no longer on speaking terms. The expansion never happened."

"Does the sheriff know about this business partner?"

Ice tinkled in a glass. *A cocktail at 9 in the morning?*

Lucia cleared her throat. "You want to write an investigative piece, find out about the partner, Claire." The phone line went dead.

Claire stared into the swirling blue-green waves of her screen saver. A silent partner? She scrolled through the list of contact numbers on her cell phone until she found the Payne County Sheriff's office.

After a short wait, Sheriff Anderson came on the phone.

"This is Claire Northcutt. I've learned J.B. Floren had a silent partner. Have you interviewed that partner?"

The Sheriff cleared his throat. "Ms. Northcutt, the investigation is under way. We are pursuing all possible leads. No need for you to call about the investigation. We'll announce details when we can. No sooner."

The sheriff's stonewalling didn't keep her from wanting to uncover the identity of the silent partner. The partner was a logical suspect. She dropped her phone back into her purse and returned her attention to her computer. Her daily deadlines loomed.

About 10:30, she was interrupted once again when her cell phone rang.

"Claire? Have you got time for a quick lunch? I've got good news to share about your second mortgage," Reed Morgan said.

"That's great." She glanced over the remaining research questions and article edits on her to-do list for the day. "I'm not sure about lunch ..."

"Just a quick one. I don't have much time, either. But I'd prefer to meet face-to-face."

She looked at her assignment list again and calculated times for each task. "How about Millie's Café in an hour? We're early and the food service is fast."

"See you there."

Claire slipped down the hall to Manny's office, holding a printout of the article on the Cimarron Valley Rescue ranch. She peeked around the door frame through the half open door. Manny and Publisher Eames were in deep conversation. She didn't interrupt.

Claire arrived at her favorite diner five minutes before she'd agreed to meet Reed, expecting to find a wide booth and answer a few emails before he arrived. Instead, she found him already seated at a corner table, sipping a cola.

He looked up as she crossed the room.

Years ago, Reed's smile had warmed every time she entered his office, and she'd thought him very handsome as they discussed her mortgage needs. Now, as she walked toward him, a smile spread across his face again. She shivered.

Maybe Reed had sent the daisies? Was he hoping to date again?

"Hi, Claire. Glad it's Friday?"

"It's been a week." Sighing, she slid into the wooden chair.

"I need thirty minutes." He opened his briefcase and pulled out a file folder. "Do you have big weekend plans?"

"The usual. Without Denver's help, my place is looking neglected."

He handed her a few papers and a pen. "If you need an extra hand, I might be able to spare a few hours."

The waitress arrived with two water glasses. "What can I get you?"

"A hamburger, no cheese," Claire said. "No fries. Salad with Italian on the side. And an iced tea. Thanks." She focused on the document. The second mortgage on her acreage and home required another monthly payment of $1,000 if she defaulted on the bail bond. No way could she ever pay that amount. Her monthly obligations required every penny she made at the newspaper. But she couldn't think about that. She signed her name, added the date and handed the papers back to Reed. "So, I'll have the money Monday?"

"I'll do my best." Reed made a note in pencil on the top of the page.

"It has to happen. Denver shouldn't be in jail for something he didn't do."

Reed folded the papers and stuffed them into his briefcase. "I'll tell you what I'll do, and don't tell anyone. It's strictly a personal favor between the two of us. If the paperwork is not approved by Monday afternoon in time for his Tuesday release, I'll advance you the money from my own personal accounts. We'll get Denver out of jail, Claire."

"Wonderful, Reed. But I couldn't expect you–"

"Don't give it another thought. Happy to help. Tell me your plans for the weekend."

She wouldn't tell Reed about the stalker. He knew about Max Dyson, and he might think she was exaggerating, pushing a small incident into a full-blown stalker attack. "I already told you what I'm doing, Reed. And I can't see you mucking out the barn with me, or mowing and edging and raking and turning compost. I'm used to doing those things. I love living out there."

"I see that. I hope you don't think I'm beyond doing a little hard work. I'm the lawn man at my house, you know."

Always impeccably dressed and well-groomed, she couldn't imagine Reed ankle-deep in soiled straw holding a pitchfork. He probably mowed his lawn in khakis and a golf shirt. "I appreciate your offer, but I can handle it."

The waitress slid their plates onto the table. "Enjoy. Let me know if you need anything else." She stuck the ticket for lunch between the table's salt and pepper shakers.

"My treat." Reed grabbed the ticket as Claire added sweetener to her iced tea.

Claire settled into her desk chair and listed the sources to call for her next e-news update. Her phone rang. She didn't want to be interrupted, but she had to take the call. It might be Cade or concern Denver.

"News Press. Claire Northcutt. May I help you?"

"Claire?" The man spoke softly.

"Who's this?"

"I hope you liked your daisies."

Throaty but clear, the voice was all air. In the background, other voices mumbled. She strained to hear something identifiable.

The caller disconnected.

This cannot be happening.

The voice replayed in her mind. *"I hope you liked the daisies."*

Too few words to detect an accent or odd inflection. And he'd spoken so softly.

Claire's mind raced over the men she knew, anyone who might have some hidden interest in her. Men she encountered at work, at Cade's school, at functions she covered for the paper, in her neighborhood, in restaurants she frequented—the list was endless.

Who? And why? Her hands shook uncontrollably.

Chapter 21

Even though two hours had passed, Claire had barely gotten her head back into her work after the earlier call when her phone rang again. She'd just begun an internet search.

This time, she knew the caller's identity after his first word.

"I'm in town to get Cade for the weekend," her ex-husband Tom said. "Can I pick Cade up at school? Does he have his clothes in his backpack? We're going to a ballgame tonight in Oklahoma City and I don't want to be late."

She'd forgotten Cade's weekend schedule with his dad. Usually, she made sure he had clean clothes to take, but last night, preparing his bag hadn't crossed her mind.

"I don't think he packed this morning. You can pick him up at school, but you'll have to run him home to get his things."

"Seriously? That'll take an extra forty-five minutes and we'll already be cutting it close for first pitch."

"That's the reality today. It's been an awful week."

"Well, my week hasn't been a bed of roses either. It's all still about you, though, and like always, I'm the one who pays the price. It would be nice if you could run home and get his clothes, then bring them to the school so I wouldn't have to drive out to your little ranch."

Claire bristled. Five years had passed, yet the same old feelings rose inside her whenever they had a conversation. Her eyes blurred as she looked down at Manny's assignment list. "Not possible. I have too much going on here. It'll be a long day for me without adding that chore to it."

"Our son is a 'chore?' Maybe I need to check into getting joint custody now that I'm living in Oklahoma City."

Joint custody? She didn't think Cade would agree. When Tom had been transferred to the Oklahoma branch of his firm two years ago, he'd asked for every other weekend with Cade, and said he'd wanted to rebuild his relationship with his son. But spending time with him on alternating holidays and for two weeks during the summers had not been ideal. Cade resented the time away from his friends and spent most of his dad's holiday time on the internet or playing electronic games while his dad watched sports on tv.

"Joint custody? That's ridiculous, Tom. We don't even live in the same town. It would totally disrupt his life."

"Not any more than your moving out here after the divorce did."

Claire chewed her lip. She didn't want Tom to be angry when he picked Cade up from school in an hour. The tone for their weekend together would be set with anger. She pinched the bridge of her nose until tears sprang up in her eyes. "Okay. I'll go home and get his clothes. I'll meet you at the high school in an hour."

"Good."

Tom's angry voice resounded in her ears as she grabbed her purse and headed for the back door. She still hadn't talked to Manny about the article, but she didn't want to run into him now. He'd be full of questions, and irritated when she told him what she had to do to keep the peace with Tom. He'd already figured out that Tom had been a difficult husband, and nothing had improved since their divorce.

A trip home was the last thing she needed this afternoon. She'd gotten some quality work in, but the day had been plagued with interruptions, the worst of which had been the call from the stalker. Her body had still not stopped shivering, and every sound in the newspaper office had startled her, causing panic to rise in her throat.

She'd hoped to finish work in time to stop by the jail before she went home, but that wasn't going to happen. She'd be lucky to wrap things up at the newspaper office before the sun went down.

Ten minutes later, Claire stopped on the highway, waiting to turn into her housing addition outside of town. A black car she didn't recognize sat in the center of the neighborhood entrance blocking both the exit and entrance lane. Claire honked her horn and frowned at the other car. Window tinting hid the driver of the sporty sedan. After a good thirty seconds, the driver finally maneuvered the car onto the highway and sped off.

At home, she punched the garage door opener, leapt from her vehicle and raced into the house. In the laundry room, she grabbed a few clothes from the pile on the clothes drier. Cade would want his favorite shirts and his cap, plus two extra pairs of jeans. She gathered his personal items from the bathroom and stuffed everything into his weekend backpack.

Outside, the driver's door of her SUV stood open just as she'd left it. She tossed Cade's backpack over her seat and into the back. A piece of blue paper that had been lying on her console fluttered to the floor. She grabbed it and read, *I asked you earlier, did you like the daisies? If you want more, don't dance with other men.* The words were written in the same slanted script as yesterday's note.

Claire couldn't breathe. She jerked her feet into the car and pressed the door lock. As she tried to still her now-racing heart, she glanced at the surrounding lawns and ranch-style homes. No one was outside.

She reached for the ignition. Her keys were gone.

She didn't remember taking them inside, but she must have. After another quick look around, Claire unlocked the car doors and raced back into the house. She scanned the laundry room and the kitchen. Then Cade's room. No keys. She walked through the house again, purposely looking everywhere for the keys.

Finally, Claire grabbed her spare keys from the kitchen junk drawer. She backed out of the drive and drove to the highway, still scanning her neighbor's yards for strange vehicles or people.

Holt lived in the closest house. He'd had time to leave the note. But, why would he?

Her pulse hammered in her throat as she drove.

Tom and Cade were waiting in Tom's Jeep in the oval drive in front of the high school. As she pulled up, Cade trotted over.

"Thanks for getting my stuff." He opened the backpack and rummaged through the clothing.

"With the blackout and everything that's happened this week ... neither of us thought to pack for the weekend. Sorry." She swallowed, hoping Cade didn't pick up on her distress. "Have a great time at the ballgame."

"Maybe. See you." He leaned in and kissed her cheek.

"Love you, honey," she called. "See you Sunday."

As Cade climbed back into his father's Jeep, Tom stuck his arm out the driver's window and waved.

After they'd driven away, Claire sat in her SUV, watching other students leave the school and saunter toward the huge parking lot. Denver in jail, Cade at his dad's.

She was alone for the weekend with a murderer—and a stalker—on the loose.

Chapter 22

Claire angled into a parking space and rushed toward the employee's entrance, uneasiness trembling inside her. Manny would be angry at her for leaving when she was under deadline, but he would understand once she explained. That wouldn't relieve the source of her uneasiness.

As she reached the building's back door, Lucia Valdez slipped out of a parked pickup truck. The harsh midafternoon light revealed the deep lines on the middle-aged outdoorswoman's face.

"I shouldn't have told you about the silent partner," Lucia said. "Forget it. And be careful." She stuffed her hands into the pockets of her jeans.

"Has something happened?"

"I'm as skittish as one of those mustangs. Sorry I ever mentioned it." Lucia hopped back into the aging Dodge Ram pickup, backed out and zoomed onto the street.

Claire stared after her. What was that all about? Lucia's warning–with no explanation–didn't keep Claire from wanting to know the identity of the silent partner. She was more determined than ever to find out who that person was, especially if the murder investigation continued to stall with Denver as the primary suspect.

When she passed the break room, raucous laughter erupted. Three women huddled around one of the tables. They glanced up, and one of them blushed. Eyes downcast, the other two hid grins behind their hands.

No doubt having a good laugh at my expense. Was the topic Denver or dead bodies?

On the computer at her desk, two emails from Manny waited. The first, *Where are You?* The second, *Are you on track for today's deadlines?*

She didn't need to be reminded. She glanced at the clock. Fifteen minutes to write two more pieces. Claire pushed thoughts of Lucia, the stalker, her son and her ex to the back of her mind. When her desk phone rang, she didn't answer it.

"Claire? I'm talking to you."

Manny's voice penetrated her brain. She'd been deep into her writing, the computer screen filling with words. She kept typing. "Sorry, Manny. I'm trying to get this done."

"Good. I'll be in my office."

Claire finished the last sentence of the short article, read it once, eliminated one comma and one missing hyphen and hit *save,* followed by a quick *send.*

Somehow, she'd finished the two pieces by deadline, and three more scheduled for tomorrow's evening paper were nearly finished. A quick review after she gave these to Manny, and she'd send the articles to the proofreader. She glanced at the clock. Six p.m. She bolted out of her chair.

"You look like a woman on a mission," Casey said.

Claire walked briskly across the newsroom to his desk. "It's Friday, and I am so done with this week. Can't wait to get out of here."

"Me, too. Signing off on this proof, and I'm done. Have a good one." He turned back to his computer as she hurried down the hallway toward Manny's office.

She rapped on the door frame and glanced through the open door. When her editor looked up from his computer, she entered the cluttered office. A pile of papers filled his only visitor's chair. Claire shifted the pile to the floor next to two other stacks of papers and magazines. Manny might have a filing system going on here, but only he knew the placement instructions.

"You look tired," he said. "And you were gone half the afternoon. What's going on?"

"It wasn't half the afternoon, Manny. An hour, at most. I had to run home. Cade's with his dad this weekend, and I forgot to pack his bag. The two of them were in a hurry to get to Oklahoma City for the ballgame."

"So, like the good little wife you weren't, you dashed home to get the clothes so you could make it all easier for him?"

Claire glared at her editor. "I did it for Cade. So his dad wouldn't be in a piss-poor mood and rant at him about me the entire way back to the city."

"Doesn't erase the fact you still let him tell you what to do."

"What do you care how I handle my ex-husband?"

"I care when it affects your work. You nearly pushed us over an already extended deadline. For the second time this week."

"I'm sorry. It's been a hell of a week. I'll do my best to see it doesn't happen again."

"Did you file a revision on the article about J.B. Floren's ranch?"

"I wanted to talk to you about that. It needs a complete rewrite."

The editor took off his glasses. "No time. The publisher wants to run it with the obit on Sunday."

"But ..."

"It looks good to me. We'll pair the two together on facing pages."

"But ..."

"It's already done, Claire." Manny leaned back in his chair, putting his feet on a small coffee table full of empty cups and to-go food cartons. "Now we've gotten that out of the way, how are you doing? The murder, and Denver, and everything else."

The murder and Denver and everything else had taken a back seat to her latest concern. Her front teeth pinched down on her lip. Talking about the stalker to Manny would make it real.

"Claire? What's going on?"

Her face was an open book. She rubbed her chin, reconsidered keeping the stalker to herself and decided that she had to tell him. "It's ... it's happening again."

"What's happening again?"

"I think I have another stalker."

His feet hit the floor as he leaned toward her. "What?"

Claire told him about the daisies, the letter under her car's windshield wiper, and the note that had been left on her SUV's console just a few hours before.

"Someone's watching me, Manny. He saw me last night, dancing in the living room with Holt during the blackout. He was outside, watching."

Manny frowned. "Any idea who it might be?"

"One of my readers, I guess. Like before. No one I know would do this. Especially not anyone who knows my history."

"You should tell the sheriff."

"Tell him what? I've been given flowers, a note, had phone calls and emails. That's not evidence of anything dangerous. I've been through this before, Manny, remember? The police can't do anything until something sinister or harmful actually happens."

He grabbed a pencil and twirled it on its point on his desk blotter. "What can I do?"

"I'm not sure. Other than, don't let me be the last one out of here at night." She ducked her head and picked at a piece of lint on the bottom of her jacket. She couldn't stop her lip from quivering.

"Okay. I'll walk you to your car. Can you finish in thirty minutes?"

Claire nodded.

"Good. We'll both get out of here, and I'll lock up for the night."

As Claire crossed the newsroom to her desk, her cell phone rang in her purse. She hurried to grab it before the call went to voice mail.

"I tried to call you earlier. I need to know if you have arranged for the bail money? Can it happen Monday?" Trina Romero asked.

"Yes. I'm sorry I didn't call you earlier. It's been a whirlwind day and I fully intended to let you know that I signed the mortgage papers today, and Reed Morgan promised the money on Monday."

"Great news. The paperwork is ready to take to the courthouse, so I'm good to go Monday as well. I talked with Denver for over an hour today, and he is ready to get home. I saw on the log that both you and his girlfriend had been to see him. That's good, too."

"Jenny wants him out as badly as I do."

"He appreciates what you're doing, Claire. He's keeping his head on straight, taking his medicine. He's not over-agitated, but he really hates being in jail."

"Who wouldn't hate being locked up?"

"True. Call me Monday as soon as you know the timing for the money." Trina added, "Have a good weekend."

"You, too." Claire dropped the phone back in her purse.

Have a good weekend? *All alone.*

Thank God for the dogs.

"Goodnight, Claire. Hope you can relax this weekend." Casey stopped beside her computer thirty minutes later.

"You, too." She gave him a quick smile but kept typing.

"Any plans?"

"Working around the house. Cade's with his dad."

"He still does the every-other-weekend deal? He's getting a little old to put up with that."

Claire pushed back in her chair and looked at Casey. "He doesn't like it, but that's the way our custody agreement is set up. And I don't think he's ready to openly defy his dad about it."

"Won't be long, I bet." Casey swung the strap of his messenger bag over his shoulder. "Um, a couple of the women in advertising were talking about what happened to you when I got back from lunch today. I googled your name and read about your stalker. Sorry you had to go through that." Casey reached into his pocket and pulled out his keys. "Anyway, take it easy."

"You, too."

Casey sauntered across the newsroom. Her heart was leaping in her chest. It had taken a few days, but the connection had been made to her previous 'dead body' experience. She knew exactly which women had been talking about it; they had probably wanted Casey, the newest newspaper staff member, to hear their comments. Something clicked in her mind. One of the women gossiping at the restaurant had been an advertising staff member, too.

She didn't think it would make any difference in the casual working relationship she and Casey had developed.

Claire filed the loose papers lying on her desk and pushed her desk chair back. The work day was over. She'd gotten it all done, but, like last night, she'd worked several hours overtime. She didn't want to make a habit of this and she didn't think Manny wanted her to do that either. It had been a grueling week, and she didn't want to repeat it, ever again. Her biggest regret was not convincing Manny to pull the article on J.B. Floren's rescue operation.

She turned around, and her pulse leaped. Manny was standing in the hallway, watching her.

"Ready to go?" he asked.

"How long have you been standing there?"

"Only a couple of seconds. I could tell you were wrapping it up."

"You startled me."

"You're on edge. Sorry. Let's get out of here."

Like the previous night, Manny walked with her to the parking lot. After checking under the car and peering into the backseat, he opened the door of her SUV.

"All clear, Claire. Be careful this weekend. I don't like the idea of you having a stalker. I'm sure that neighbor of yours would be happy to come over and spend time with you." Manny frowned and squinted at her. "You don't think he's the stalker, do you?"

"He lives next door and we see each other almost daily. He's on my doorstep constantly as it is. I can't imagine he'd carry it to the level of anonymous notes and flowers when he doesn't need to."

"Good point. If you think of anything I can do, or you'd like Serena to bring the kids and come hang out with you, please call. Okay?"

The thought of Manny's wife and twin girls made her smile. "That's a great suggestion. And I'll take you up on it if I feel the need."

Claire slid into her vehicle and hit the lock button.

What was she going to do all evening? As she drove toward the edge of town, she considered her options. She didn't want to spend it wandering from window to window in her house, scared, anticipating her stalker. And she didn't want to spend it watching the Hallmark cable channel or Lifetime. If they weren't showing a romance, they were showing a suspenseful movie about a woman in danger. The storyline might hit too close to home.

She could clean out her closets–she'd been meaning to do that for weeks. Usually, after the clean out, she'd have bags of clothing she never wore to take to the Goodwill store.

She could piece together that quilt she'd been intending to make.

Or she could read a book. She'd accumulated several on her Kindle. Her choice in reading material was usually a murder mystery. Not a good thing to read while her mind was full of the images of bloody bodies.

Claire pulled into the parking lot of her favorite deli. She didn't have to think twice about picking up some great salad toppings and fresh thin-sliced meats for weekend sandwiches, not to mention a brownie or two. Inside, she got in line behind the other customers, pulled out her phone and checked for messages. Behind her, the bell on the door jangled when another customer entered.

"Claire?" Reed Morgan stepped up behind her. "Twice in one day? We must be traveling on the same wave length."

She doubted it. They hadn't agreed on much when they had dated. She smiled anyway.

"Needing a protein fix before the big yardwork weekend?" he prodded.

Her mind raced through possible answers. She didn't want him to know that her calendar was open and Cade was gone for two nights. She'd already told him her plans to work at her place. He didn't need to know more.

"Guess I'm just hungry for their smoked meats, and all those great vegetables." Claire nodded at the display case.

"And maybe some pie? I remember you really like their lemon meringue."

"Good memory. That was years ago."

"But I bet it's still your favorite. And cookie dough ice cream. And brownies."

Worry sprouted in her head. Why would he remember all those things? "I guess some things never change."

The customer in front of her finished his transaction and Claire stepped up to the counter. She placed her order and ignored Reed's presence close behind her. She didn't want to be rude. He had done her a favor by rushing her mortgage through so she could post Denver's bail.

She checked her phone messages and kept her look averted from Reed. In a minute, the cashier set her 'to go' order on the counter.

Claire grabbed the bag, smiled at Reed and headed for the door. He gave a quick nod from where he stood waiting and looked as if he might come after her.

She walked faster. She locked the doors as soon as she had slid behind the wheel of her RAV.

Could Reed be the stalker?

Ridiculous. He was a well-respected banker, and had probably never even had a speeding ticket. Everything was by-the-book for Reed Morgan. By-the-book and his way or no way.

At home, she carried the bag into the kitchen. When Ranger and Izzy barked from the back door, she stuck the bag in the refrigerator and stepped outside. Both dogs trotted beside her to the barn where she fed Blaze and Smoky.

Back in the house, with the dogs inside, she locked the door behind her. Claire fixed a green salad, topped it with the deli meats, and then carried her salad plate, a glass and a new bottle of wine into the living room. She closed all the curtains, and found a sappy romance on the Turner Classic Movie Channel. Ranger settled at her feet and Izzy snuggled in next to her.

She was going to make sure the night passed in a good way with as little suspense as possible.

Still, the weekend loomed.

After the movie ended, Claire poured another glass of pinot noir and sat down at the kitchen table. When she picked up the glass, bringing it toward her, wine sloshed over the lip. She set it down and clasped her shaking hands together.

What am I doing?

She didn't need wine. She didn't need alcohol of any kind. Had she forgotten everything she'd learned in those weeks of therapy after she'd killed Max Dyson?

She shoved the glass across the table until it was out of reach. Then she cradled her head in her hands and closed her eyes. The movie she'd watched had depressed her. She was alone. She'd been alone for too long. But she didn't want to let anyone in. Not Holt. Not Reed. Not anyone. She felt the familiar quivering inside her body.

The same quivering she'd had since the day she'd shot Max Dyson.

Be present. Be in the moment.

Don't try to dull your thoughts or your pain with drugs or alcohol. Let the feelings and the memories come to the front of your thoughts. Confront them. Feel them. Accept them. Leave them.

The therapist's words whispered in her head. The full experience of killing Dyson was there, too.

She kept her eyes closed and let it replay. Her body chilled and her heart raced.

He spoke in her ear. His hands roamed her body.

Her eyelids jerked open to see a naked stranger next to her in the bed, whispering. He pinned her beneath the sheets, lying on top of her.

She struggled.

He nuzzled her neck, pinned down her wrists. Whispered.

The sheets were between them. He had to let go of one hand to slide beneath them, to get to her.

In her mind, it played in slow motion. He released her hand. She scooted to the far side of the bed, threw the sheets and blanket over him and ran for the living room.

The gun was on top of the tv wall cabinet.

Behind her, he fell to the floor, tangled in the sheets. He cussed, cried out, "Claire."

She stretched to reach the gun, cocked it, held it tightly between both hands as she'd learned on the firing range back in North Carolina.

Dyson lunged across the room. She pulled the trigger.

He fell. Eyes open. Looking toward the ceiling. His arm opened, his fingers jerked. His head dropped to one side.

She held the shaking gun. Her body shivered. Blood poured from the hole in his chest.

In the distance, a siren cleaved the silence.

And there, tied to the flagpole, was J.B. Floren. His cheeks split open. Dark stains splotched his shirt.

A crow flapped overhead, cawing. The chickens clucked and scratched in the barnyard. Far away, a dog barked.

Ranger.

Barking.

Barking now.

She opened her eyes. Ranger stood stiffly at the back door, growling and barking.

"Someone out there, boy?" Her voice quivered.

The dog whined.

What's she doing, sitting at the table?

And where's the boy?

The damn dog knows I'm out here.

She'd got that place locked up tight and the curtains drawn. Except for over the kitchen sink. Not a bad view inside the house from out here.

Chapter 23

The a/c came on and whipped the curtains in the living room, startling Claire awake at six a.m. She rolled off the sofa and pulled the drapes open a foot. In the front yard, two birds battled their way through the air toward a large oak tree. Days like today, when the forecast was humid with a high in the upper 80s, the wind was a blessing.

She pulled on shorts and a t-shirt, turned on the coffee maker, and stepped out onto the back porch. Blaze nickered when the screen door closed behind Claire, and the dogs dashed toward the neighboring meadow. By the time she'd reached the barn, the mare was stomping in her stall.

"Easy, girl. I'm here." Claire grabbed the pitchfork and attacked the bale of hay Cade had brought in from the shed Thursday night. She tossed some into the stalls, and poured oats into the feed troughs. While Blaze and Stormy crunched their food, she opened the back doors to their stalls and the gate to the pasture. They would enjoy this warm, windy day as much as she would.

In the garage, she loaded a new spool of plastic line onto the weed eater and filled it with gas from a five-gallon can. She carried the tool up the driveway to the front fence and turned it on. The buzzing filled her head. Bits of grass flew around her and stuck to her bare legs.

Later, satisfied that the fence line looked neat, she went back to the house. She treated herself to a cup of coffee and a bagel, and ate while standing on the back porch. Blaze and Smoky grazed in the pasture. Whenever her mind turned to thoughts of Denver, or J.B. Floren, or her stalker, she forced herself to think about this moment. She had chores to accomplish.

Back in the garage, Claire hopped onto the lawnmower, threw it into gear, and drove to the front half of her five acres. The buzz of the motor was hypnotic.

She had cut four swaths and was headed back to the front fence when Holt jogged past on the street. He looked her direction and waved; she waved back. The lawnmower chugged along, cutting another ribbon through the thick grass.

Seeing Holt jolted her out of a trance-like state, but instead of thinking about him, her mind replayed each time the stalker had made contact. She gave in to the thoughts and tried to recall details of anything she'd seen in the parking lot at work or on her own driveway. Nothing she remembered provided a clue about the person's identity.

Last night, when Manny had walked her to her car after work, he'd said, "Keep your doors locked at all times. And be alert. Don't space out, Claire." But she'd been   spacing out just now. She wouldn't let it happen again.

She appreciated Manny's concern. She trusted him. A good boss, a good editor, a good man. In many ways, he treated her like a younger sister. And his wife treated her like a sister-in-law might; friendly surface talk when they saw each other. Serena Juarez had invited Claire and Cade to their home for dinner several times after the Dyson shooting.

Claire's thoughts skipped back three years. How could Dyson have watched her closely for so long without her noticing? Had she been that oblivious to her surroundings?

After the event, she had read books about 'being present.' She had learned to focus, to see her surroundings–whether walking, shopping or driving. She tried to be present in all conversations, to be an active listener, and to respond when people asked questions or said something deserving a response.

As a reporter, critical listening and observation skills were necessary. Both abilities provided ways to detect an interviewee's discomfort with a question, or possible lies. Easy liars could be sociopaths like Max Dyson. Could anyone else in her life be a sociopath? Impossible to know. Those types of people could also hide their lack of emotions. They were good actors.

How could it be happening again?

She navigated the mower in a tight circle and headed back toward the street. Holt stood by the front fence directly in front of her, his t-shirt slung over one shoulder, his sweaty chest heaving from his recent run. The mower crawled across the yard toward him. Holt waited. Her neighbor had great muscle tone for a man his age, mid 40s, she thought, a few years older than she was.

Claire reached the fence line and shut the motor off. "Morning, Holt."

"You got an early start with the yard work today. Where's your helper?"

"He's with his dad, and I've got lots to do."

"Need any help?"

"No, thanks. After I finish the front yard, I'm heading out."

Holt's face registered his disappointment. "Any chance we could spend a little time together later?"

"I'll be gone most of the day."

"I had hoped . . ."

"Another time, maybe?" She started the mower and chugged away.

She'd told Holt the truth. As soon as the yard work was done, she had a date with her SUV. She didn't know her destination. Anywhere but here. Anywhere her stalker couldn't find her. Anywhere she could relax.

After watching a movie and drinking a half bottle of wine last night, the restless dogs had spooked her. Claire had grabbed a pillow and a blanket and slept on the living room sofa. Izzy had slept on the cushions at her feet; Ranger had snoozed on the floor beside her. If the dogs hadn't been there, she would have driven to a motel or crashed at a friend's house.

Dogs were the best alarm system available. When Dyson attacked, she'd been without a companion animal. He'd caught her totally off guard. It wouldn't happen again.

Claire finished mowing the front yard and chugged to the storage shed to store the mower.

"Ranger. Izzy," she called. Seconds later, a streak of white followed by a much larger streak of black dashed across the grassy meadow. She called again, and the dogs bounded into the yard. Stick-tights and burrs clung to Izzy's long coat, but Ranger's short, dense fur had repelled the prickly seed hitchhikers.

"Izzy. Look at you. There's a bath and a haircut in your future. And you'll have to stay here the rest of the day. Ranger, you're coming with me."

On the back porch, she filled the water bowl on the screened-in porch and locked Izzy in.

Claire grabbed the picnic basket from the top shelf in the pantry and filled it with deli meats, cheese and a bottle of tea. As she packed her lunch, she contemplated a drive to the west, where the rolling land gave way to flat fields of wheat and maize. She considered going north into the Osage and the tallgrass prairie.

But her thoughts settled on a different destination.

Chapter 24

Ranger pushed his nose out above the lowered passenger window, sniffing as the RAV-4 shot down the highway. Twenty miles to their destination–the property that had once belonged to her grandparents.

Before leaving home, she'd found a phone number for Corbin Brook, who'd bought the property three years ago. *This number is no longer in service,* a recording had said after she punched in the number.

So, Brook had truly gone 'off the grid' as he'd promised. It had not been enough for the new owner to unhook the electricity and gas, opting instead for a propane tank buried in the side yard. No cable, no TV antennae or satellite dish, and no land line.

Brook had told her he intended to live a simpler life.

At the property closing, Brook had offered her access any time she wanted it. If she called him first, he would leave the front gate unlocked and she could visit freely. Part of her felt reluctant to burst in on the man today, but there was no way to contact him.

Claire acknowledged many reasons a person might want to disconnect from society. Family issues. Legal issues. Political issues.

Or it could be something entirely different. Maybe he was a nudist. What if she drove in and found him enjoying his property *au natural?*

Maybe he'd started a commune of people living off the land. Maybe there were dozens of them living together in the old house, sleeping on the floors.

It didn't matter, it was his property. During the few visits she'd made to the acreage since the sale, she, Cade and Izzy had hiked, picnicked and fished in the farm pond. Brook had approved each visit when she phoned, but not once had she seen the man–or any other people–during their afternoon visits.

Claire drove up to the gate two miles off the county line highway. She hopped out of her SUV, pushed the gate open, drove through, and closed it behind her. A sense of dread fell over her. This scenario reminded her of that morning at J.B. Floren's ranch.

She shook the feeling off. No tire tracks marred the dirt road leading across the pasture toward the house where her grandparents had lived. Other than a scissortail flycatcher hovering overhead, and crickets chirping in the tall grass, nothing seemed to be living on the old farm. The breeze that had made the day so pleasant earlier, was non-existent. The hot sunrays scorched her arm through the open car window.

She drove another hundred yards through knee-high prairie grass to the house. In the small front yard, Bermuda grass had gone to seed.

Claire parked, hopped out and opened the tail gate for Ranger. He jumped down and sniffed the ground before he meandered across the yard, nose in the dirt, tail wagging.

The scents of earth and grass filled her head, and memories rushed back. Summer weeks spent here with her grandparents, the little room upstairs where she slept, night breezes flowing through the house.

Mornings in the garden with Gramma, digging potatoes. Hot afternoons on the shaded north side in the cool dirt, watching earthworms wiggling in the soil.

When she looked at the house, she expected it to look as it had back then, lovingly cared for, siding painted sky blue, porch railings shining white in the morning sun. Instead, paint was peeling from both the railing and the trim around the windows. Dirt crusted on the boards of the front porch floor and the steps leading up to it.

Claire bounded up the steps and knocked at the door. "Hello?" When no one answered, she knocked again and peeked through the grime-streaked front window. The room was empty.

She knocked at the door once more before traipsing down the steps and into the overgrown front yard. No signs of anyone. Corbin Brook was no longer here. Truth be known, there wasn't really any evidence he had ever lived here.

Ranger followed Claire to the small barn behind the house. The doors were padlocked shut. She circled the structure.

Weeds had overgrown the former vegetable garden between the house and the barn. Broken corn stalks tilted over the rotted remains of other unidentifiable vegetables, and scarecrow rags fluttered from a pole in the center of the plot.

A rabbit's tail flashed white a few yards away as the animal darted out from beneath a bush.

"Woof." Ranger took off.

Brook had cleared out, and his animals were gone, too. Had he sold the property? Would the new owner care if she and Ranger wandered around?

Claire headed for the old dirt road which meandered through the blackjack oak grove to the pond. Corbin Brook had kept the tree branches trimmed for a while, but spring growth had been unchecked. The branches would make the road impassable before the end of summer. A few small oaks had already established themselves in the center of the red dirt track.

Claire had caught her first sunfish at the pond. The grassy area on the wide earthen dam would be a perfect spot for her picnic.

She returned to the SUV, grabbed the picnic basket and quilt, and set out on the road. The scents of green growing things perfumed the air. Insects buzzed around her and pollen particles floated past as she walked.

Not far away, Ranger barked his 'play with me' bark. She imagined that a rabbit had run into its hole or taken shelter beneath a downed tree limb. Last winter's ice storm had broken many branches. They lay helter-skelter on the ground throughout the dense oak forest.

Claire studied the red earth for animal tracks. The curving hoof prints of deer were easily identifiable. In many places, she saw evidence of wild pigs—ruts in the ground where they'd dug for mushrooms, bulbs or acorns. If Corbin had been gone for months, the pigs had probably readjusted to life in the wild without people. She'd stay on the lookout.

"Ranger? Here boy," Claire called. Seconds later, the dog loped through the grass to her, stopped and leaned against her leg. "Having fun?" she asked.

The panting dog wagged his tail. On a nearby flat spot, she dropped the unfolded quilt over the grass and poured a drink for the dog. Ranger lay on the cool red earth. Claire sat on the quilt.

A swarm of gnats selected her head as an arena for some insect sport. She swatted them away.

Claire forced herself to lay back and look at the sky. Fluffy clouds meandered from west to east. A grasshopper sparrow twittered and a hawk soared overhead. She closed her eyes and breathed slowly. Ranger bolted up and raced away. Another rabbit?

In only a few minutes, the skin on her arms and face began to tingle with the heat of the noontime sun.

In the distance, Ranger barked an alarm bark.

Claire got up from the quilt and picked her way through the thicket toward Ranger's barks. She stepped over fallen limbs, avoided prickly green briar and poison ivy. When the barking stopped, so did she. Insects and birds chirped.

"Ranger?"

The dog crashed through the undergrowth to her. Whining, Ranger looked back the way he had come, tilted his head and looked at her.

"Okay, show me."

The dog picked his way through the trees and she followed. Suddenly, an unpleasant and recognizable odor permeated the air. She covered her nose and scanned the undergrowth for an animal carcass.

One more step through the buckbrush and sumac and, unexpectedly, the earth dropped off into a ragged gully. Sunlight from an opening in the tree canopy lit up the ravine and everything around it. At the bottom, a pile of bones glistened, jumbled with bits of animal hide and hair.

Ranger whined. Claire covered her nose and mouth, and tried to hold her breath. She counted five large animal skulls, easily identifiable as herbivores. A horse, a cow or goats? She grabbed a quick breath and gagged with the strong odor.

"Let's go, boy." Claire whirled and hurried back through the trees. Had Corbin Brook killed his animals and left their bodies to be ravaged by coyotes, pigs and vultures?

At the old farmhouse, Claire pitched her picnic things into the back of the SUV. So much for a quiet picnic at the old farm pond. The skin of her arms itched relentlessly. She must have plunged through a chigger nest in the tall grass as she'd raced back to the car. She bit her lip and forced herself not to scratch at the bites.

A low growl rumbled in Ranger's throat as she opened the SUV's back door for the dog. Claire glanced at the tree line and caught a glimpse of something moving behind the green bushes and brown-black trunks of the trees.

"Hello? Who's there?" She strained to see into the shadows as she slid into the SUV and locked the doors.

When her grandparents had lived here, nearby residents often sneaked onto their farm to hunt, hunting season or not. Deer, turkey, quail or even wild pigs–each animal was equally desirable to a hunter any time of year. She shared her grandfather's opinion that hunters were always welcome, in season or not, if the hunted game fed a hungry family. But when hunting for sport, a person's property lines should be respected. Were there hunters on the property now?

Claire had lost her desire to linger and enjoy the seclusion of the wooded acreage.

A cloud drifted over the sun. Claire glanced at the thick forest. Something had happened here. The air felt different. This farm held gentle memories of another time, but after today, she wouldn't come here again.

She started the SUV, turned it around, and headed for the county road. She didn't look back at the house.

Chapter 26

When Claire reached Highway 177, she accelerated to the speed limit. Gradually, her thumping heart slowed. What had happened to Corbin Brook? The man had left the property. He owned it, it was his to do with as he chose. But she felt blindsided. He knew how attached she was to the 'family farm' and that she would want to visit again. Couldn't he have at least called to let her know he'd moved on?

None of your business, her mind said. But her heart didn't agree. She hated to see the old farm house empty. Without an inhabitant, the ninety-year-old structure would decay further and eventually fall apart. A sad end for a property that had nourished a family for many decades.

Claire's cell phone rang as she neared Perkins. She glanced at the Caller ID, but didn't recognize the number. Her new stalker? She didn't want to think about that. Her mind was intent on the bleached bones in the gully. Why had animal carcasses been dumped there? She couldn't think of a good reason.

Her phone beeped with a new message. She glared at the phone. The rest of the weekend loomed ahead with just her and the dogs at the house; she didn't need a new message from the stalker to worry about. But would a stalker leave a voice mail?

The SUV sped past green fields and leafy trees.

As she drove into Perkins, her stomach rumbled. She pulled into the Sonic Drive-in. Forget the lunch she'd packed; she wanted a Cheese Coney.

Claire punched the order button on the menu panel beside her parking slot and placed her order. On her phone, she retrieved the voice message someone had left earlier.

"Hello? Claire? It's Lucia Valdez. Please come to my ranch as soon as possible. I'll be here." Lucia's voice was shaking. "Hurry."

Lucia probably wanted to insist again that she forget J.B. Floren's mysterious silent partner. She didn't want to hear it. Come Monday, she'd begin her own search to locate the partner, even if the police weren't interested. As far as she knew, their investigation into the murder had stalled with a focus on Denver.

What if Lucia's call had nothing to do with the silent partner? She'd sounded upset.

Claire punched *call back* on the phone message screen.

"Thank God," Lucia said when she heard Claire's voice.

"Sorry I missed your call. I can be there in ten minutes if you'd still like me to stop by."

"Yes. You must. You'll understand when you get here."

Her curiosity aroused, Claire said, "I'll be there soon."

Claire ate another tater tot. Ranger whined in the back seat.

"Okay, boy. You can have the last one. But don't expect anything else to eat until we get home. One more stop to make."

Claire pitched the last tater tot toward the back seat. The dog's jaw snapped as he caught it in mid-air.

Claire slowed to a stop in front of Lucia's tile-roofed home. Lucia stepped off the front patio and waited on the sidewalk, her arms crossed.

Ranger yipped and jumped into the front seat. When Claire opened the SUV's door, Ranger crawled across her, leapt out and raced to Lucia. Claire watched, a little puzzled.

"Good to see you, boy." Lucia knelt to pet the dog. His tail wagged furiously. "How are you? Is Claire treating you right?" She looked at Claire, her face gray and her eyes blood shot. "Calm down, boy. Thank you for coming, Claire."

Ranger sat beside Lucia, his tail sweeping the ground as it wagged. He nudged her with his head, seeking attention.

"Lucia, what's wrong?"

The other woman gestured toward the house and stood. Claire and Ranger followed her through the living room and out to the patio, then along a flagstone path to a storage shed surrounded by blooming azalea bushes. Lucia stopped at the shed's doorway. She wrapped her arms around herself and seemed to shrink, then shoved the door open.

Claire peered into the gloom of the small building. The coppery smell of blood hung in the air. Her eyes adjusted. Horrified, she drew back, not sure she was accurately seeing what was lying on the floor of the shed.

Between the two women, Ranger growled.

Surely it wasn't ... The blood rushed from Claire's face. She grabbed the doorway to steady herself.

Chapter 27

But it was ... the severed head of a small horse? Faint dark lines striped the animal's neck.

"My God. What ...?"

"I found it just before I called you." Lucia's voice quivered. "Petreus."

Claire looked closer at the head on the floor. It wasn't real, but the head of a stick horse with dark lines painted on the neck. "Why would someone pull such an awful prank?"

The older woman shook her head. "It's a personal message. And I think this message is meant for you as well as me."

"A sick message. I thought for a minute it was real. How could it be a message for me?"

Lucia's voice caught in her throat. "It could have been Petreus. Instead, it's one of Miguel's old stick horses, covered in what's probably pig blood." She glanced at the head again, before turning away. "Come into the house."

Ranger padded along next to Lucia. Her fingertips touched the dog's head, and he seemed to lift on his toes to meet them.

In the living room, Lucia sank onto the edge of a chair cushion. Ranger remained near her, his head resting on an arm of the chair.

"I don't understand why someone would do this," Claire whispered. The familiar ringing in her ears grew louder.

"Only a barbarian would do such a thing." Anger trembled in Lucia's voice. "And I thought Floren was the only barbarian in this part of the country." She stroked Ranger's head.

Claire remembered Denver's reaction to the news of Floren's death. And his admission that he hadn't liked the man.

Lucia's hands clenched into fists. She sat, silent and seething.

Someone had brutally murdered Floren, and days later, someone had left another brutal message for his former neighbor and lover. What did Lucia know that the murderer wanted kept secret? A chill raced down her back. This was someone threatening to kill Petreus. She thought of Blaze and Smoky. Would the murderer threaten to kill one of them if she continued to investigate?

"What do you cherish, Claire? I cherish those animals," Lucia whispered.

Claire shook her head. "But I cherish my nephew. If the sheriff doesn't pursue other suspects, what choice do I have but to continue to dig into J.B.'s life and his silent partner?"

"You mustn't, Claire. Will you sacrifice one thing you love for another? It's a horrible choice."

Claire heard something new in Lucia's voice. Resignation. Had she made such a choice before? With Floren?

"I've not been able to eat all day. But my son Miguel must eat. Would you join us for a late lunch? We'll share paella and a bottle of wine.

A son? Claire had seen no evidence of anyone else living here with Lucia, but she had seen a picture of a boy in Lucia's kitchen.

She'd hurriedly eaten a Coney and tater tots just a few minutes before. She wasn't hungry, especially after seeing the stuffed stick horse head in the shed.

Spending the evening with Lucia had an appeal. She needed companionship and conversation to occupy her mind. Otherwise she'd be staring at the walls of her empty house and wondering about Denver in jail, the stalker or the head in Lucia's shed.

She'd shared a paella dinner with Reed Morgan once in a Tulsa restaurant. Those first few dates, Reed's knowledge of cosmopolitan cuisine and wine had impressed her. Before long, she realized Reed believed he possessed extensive knowledge about everything. Annoying. "I haven't had paella in years," she finally said. "Sounds delicious."

"I'm glad to have your company." Lucia sat back in her chair and took a deep breath. Color rose in her face, and her eyes lost their terror. "Miguel? Come and meet my new friend."

Footsteps sounded across a hardwood floor. When a handsome pre-teen boy stopped in the doorway, Ranger trotted over to him, tail wagging. The dog dropped his head and pushed in close to the boy.

"Claire, this is my son, Miguel. Miguel, this is Claire Northcutt. She's the reporter I spoke of who wrote the story on your father. She found him that day."

J.B. Floren's son? Lucia surprised her again.

"Nice to meet you, Ms. Northcutt." The boy's straight white teeth gleamed. He stooped and threw one arm across Ranger's back.

"It's nice to meet you, Miguel." He had his father's hair, but his mother's dark brown eyes and olive skin.

"Claire will stay for dinner. Would you set another place at the table and stir the paella? And pour a glass of wine for both of us, will you?"

"Sure." The young man stood up. "Come, Ranger." He left the room and Ranger followed.

"I told you Floren and I were lovers," Lucia said. "Miguel came along. Not long after that, Cassandra left."

"You didn't mention a son."

"Our love affair and our child were unnecessary sidebars to your news story."

Miguel carried in two half-full wine glasses; Ranger trailed him into the room, and laid down. When the boy had gone back to the kitchen once more, Lucia continued. "J.B. and Miguel had a good relationship. Miguel moved freely between us, and his life has been better for it." She lifted her glass in Claire's direction. *"Salud."*

The conversation shifted to other things. Miguel carried a platter of cheeses, smoked meats and crackers to the table. Claire picked at the appetizers to be polite, but when a delicious aroma floated in from the kitchen, her appetite roared back.

Outside, the blue sky deepened into evening.

Now that she'd met Miguel, she recognized his face staring out from photographs placed on tabletops and shelves. One photo showed Lucia with Miguel; another showed a different woman with a girl. The family resemblance was obvious. Lucia's niece? The two young people were probably the toddlers in the kitchen photograph she'd seen on her previous visit.

Miguel appeared in the doorway again. "Mother, Mrs. Northcutt, supper is on the table."

Lucia led the way into the dining room. "Sit here, Claire, between Miguel and me."

Ranger padded in and collapsed under the table.

"Son, I think Claire would like to know about your relationship with your father."

Miguel looked at his mother and a roulette wheel of emotions spun across his face, ranging from sadness to anger. When he finally spoke, the bouncing ball had landed on sadness. "I'm sorry he's dead." He picked at the seam of his jeans near one knee.

"Your mother said you spent a lot of time with him."

His face darkened. He reached down to scratch the top of Ranger's head.

"What did you like to do together?"

"We rode horses. Fished. Tossed a football sometimes. And he taught me to drive." The boy grinned.

"Psst," Lucia frowned. "At his age, J.B. let him drive in the fields."

"Already driving?" Claire smiled at the boy. "My son can't wait to get his learner's permit. Have you met Cade? He volunteered at your father's ranch on Saturdays."

"Cade's your son? He's always with Denver." Miguel's face lit up.

"Denver is my horse trainer. And my nephew."

Miguel moved the rice around on his plate. "I remember them." He shrugged. "Saw them on the weekends." He laid his fork on the table and looked up. "You found my father."

"Yes."

"What was it like?"

"Miguel. What a question to ask. Don't answer, Claire." Lucia glared at the boy. "There was blood everywhere, son. Someone used a scythe on him. Do you really want more details?"

Miguel abruptly stood. "May I be excused, Mother?" He hurried to the kitchen without waiting for an answer.

The vivid image of J.B. Floren's body flashed in Claire's mind. "That was harsh."

"What did he expect? He wanted you to tell him. He wanted to know how much someone hated his father. Now he knows." Lucia lifted her wine glass and looked at Claire over the rim. "How old is your son, Cade?"

"Almost sixteen."

"Miguel is in private school. He's home for the summer but he'll go out of state next fall. The one good thing J.B. did for his son was to provide an educational trust account."

"That's wonderful. What I wouldn't give —"

"The money was payment to me to keep my mouth shut about Miguel's paternity and mind my own business." Lucia put down her fork and leaned over the table toward Claire. "You saw what might have happened to my Petreus. Someone wants to be sure I don't tell what little I know. Whoever killed J.B. is warning me."

Chapter 28

"What *do* you know?" Claire asked Lucia.

"J.B. and his partner were up to something. I don't know what. I will say nothing. I won't risk Miguel's future. You need to keep silent, too. We must let it be."

Let it be? Denver was in jail and might be charged with a crime he didn't commit.

"Lucia, what if Denver is being set up? He's innocent. What if he's convicted and sent to jail? Oklahoma has capital punishment. What if he's sentenced to die? We can't just 'let it be.'"

"I must protect Miguel. I have no choice."

"Maybe I can find the silent partner and talk to them. Surely you have some idea who that is."

"You have a son, too. You have possessions, things you love, things you want to protect. Sometimes there must be sacrifices."

"But that's blackmail. If we go to the police, they can offer some protection."

"You're naïve," Lucia insisted. "The police can't protect anyone from people who care nothing for the law, greedy people who'll remove any obstacle blocking their quest for more money."

"Lucia, you make it sound hopeless, like we can't save Denver." Blood pounded against Claire's temples. "The evidence against Denver may all be circumstantial, but people have been convicted with less. I can't let that happen."

"If you choose this battle be prepared for bad things to happen to your family. I've made my decision. The stuffed horse head was a message. Next time, a real animal–or person–might die. Claire, I can't help you with anything related to Floren. I've been warned." Lucia laid her napkin over her plate. "As have you."

Claire pushed away from the table. "If you won't help Denver, we can't be friends. He's my family."

Lucia lifted her hands. "That is how it must be."

Claire stood. "Ranger, come" She grabbed her purse and stormed out of the house leaving the front door standing open behind her.

Claire's head was still pounding when she got out of her SUV in the garage a short time later. At the back door, she paused to watch the garage door rumble down. Ranger whined at her feet.

Lucia would do nothing to help Denver. And Claire might be putting Cade and herself at risk to try to save him. What kind of a choice was that? She'd thought she and Lucia could work together to solve the murder, but she'd been wrong.

Claire sat at her kitchen table. Izzy and Ranger lay on the floor nearby, snoozing. Twilight cloaked the yard in gloom. The mercury vapor light on the barn blinked on.

In the living room, the television blared a game show. She wasn't interested. She couldn't think of anything but Denver, sitting in jail. He'd be out on bail soon, but without evidence of another person's guilt, he could be convicted during the coming trial. And then charged and tried for J.B. Floren's murder.

Claire crossed the kitchen to the living room and peeked between the drapes. Outside, the world was still.

Lights shone from Holt's upstairs windows. He was home and he hadn't called. She didn't regret being brusque with him this morning, even though it would have been nice to have had company tonight. Just not Holt.

Her mind rolled on to thoughts of Denver, J.B. and Petreus. She couldn't go on like this. Her mind was like a train rolling down a hill on straight tracks with no station in sight. She needed sleep.

He paced in his living room. He hadn't seen her today, but he could guess what she must be feeling. The horse head trick had been gruesome, but the women needed a shock.

Claire had to stop investigating.

Denver would be out of jail on bond Tuesday. He had to get rid of him.

And not just Denver.

Why couldn't it be simple, like he wanted it to be? Why did the women always interfere?

He had to stay focused.

Dad always said, stay focused, boy! The good thing will come. Delayed gratification is worth the time.

But Dad wasn't here. He didn't know Claire. She was perfect for him.

How much longer must he wait?

He closed his eyes and paced. He knew the width of the room. He knew how many steps it took to get from one side to another. Hadn't he paced it for hours last night, unable to sleep, thinking of her with her head in her hands, sitting at her kitchen table with no idea that he was in the yard, wanting her.

Waiting.

Chapter 29

By mid-morning Sunday, Claire had finished washing, drying and folding the laundry. She'd cleaned the bathrooms and the kitchen and vacuumed the carpet floors, work she'd begun at five a.m., an hour before daylight crept over the horizon and into the sky.

All night long, her dreams had been fragmented bits featuring blood and horses and dark unidentifiable images. Even in the bright light of day, remembering the gruesome sight of the bloody stuffed animal head on the floor of the shed sent shivers racing up her back.

The image of Denver languishing in his jail cell left her desolate. Enough was enough. If she was busy, she wouldn't have time to dwell on it.

Blaze and Smoky grazed in the paddock, soaking in the morning sun. Earlier, she'd delivered their breakfast oats and let them out of their stalls to munch grass in the back lot.

Wind whipped her hair as she walked to the barn. Ranger and Izzy dashed up and followed for the first few yards until Izzy took off after one of the barn cats and Ranger loped after her. Claire unlocked the barn and slid the door fully open along its track. Immediately, the scent of dust, hay and manure filled her head, tickling her nose. Pollen from the trees lay thick on the lawn, even coating the edges of the water trough with yellow dust. She rolled the wheelbarrow over to the stalls and grabbed the pitchfork, sneezing.

As she finished spreading fresh hay in the stalls, Blaze clomped her way to the open outer door to her stall.

"Ready for a little exercise?" Claire returned the pitchfork to its usual place and grabbed the curry comb from the tack alcove. The mare's hide quivered as Claire stroked her back and withers. Blaze nickered. Claire slowly saddled the horse and as she led her outside, Smoky trotted into the barnyard, braying.

"Want to try a ride through the back field to the creek? New territory. Let's give it a go." Walking the perimeter of her five-acre property day after day wasn't much exercise for the horse. She had permission to ride across her neighbor's pasture and down to the creek, permission she'd gotten not long after she bought the mustang. The only provision was that she not wander the property or make the ride a daily event. In the six months since he'd given approval, she'd not yet taken advantage of his offer. But now, Blaze was ready.

Claire walked the horse to the back-property line and the seldom-used gate that gave access to the pastureland behind her acreage. Blaze tossed her head and pricked her ears forward, even stomping a front hoof as Claire lifted the latch and pushed the gate open.

"This will be fun, girl." She mounted the horse, settling into the saddle as Blaze shifted her weight and side-stepped. The mare's teeth chewed at the metal bit, and finally let it settle in her mouth. She tossed her head again. When Claire clucked her tongue and touched the horse's flank with the sides of the stirrups, Blaze started forward. "Easy does it."

Ranger and Izzy dashed past in pursuit of something. Claire and Blaze ambled through the greening grass toward the distant stream. The horse shied, dipped and leapt to one side when a meadowlark flitted across their path, but quieted and continued to plod along.

Claire kept the reins loose on the horse's neck and let the horse choose the path, keeping in the correct general direction. Minutes later, they reached the line of willows and cottonwoods clinging to the bank of the small tributary. At a wide opening between the trees, Claire slipped off the horse and led her to the reddish-brown water. Blaze stepped into the stream and lowered her head to drink.

A few yards across the creek, a great blue heron flapped up from the shore. Downstream, a white egret picked his way along the bank, watching for minnows.

Claire led Blaze through the shallow water. Mud sucked at the horse's feet.

When Blaze shied at a jumping frog, she pulled at the reins, encouraging the horse to come out of the water. "We'll walk a bit farther and then head home."

Claire lifted herself into the saddle and urged the horse on. They skirted willow trees with slender trunks leaning toward the water and branches reaching toward the land. They avoided eroded places, where heavy rains had opened cracks and left gullies behind when the red soil washed into the stream.

Ahead, a large flat rock hung partially over the rushing water, baking in the sun. When they reached it, Claire stopped the horse and swung out of the saddle.

"How about another drink?" She held on to one rein as the horse stepped into the water. Claire hopped onto the rock and scooted across it. She stretched out, letting Blaze slurp nearby. Above them, smears of white floated on a bluebird-blue sky.

She stared into the hypnotic rushing water. Birds chirped in the trees and a gentle breeze tickled her face. Abruptly, nightmare images flashed into her head. J.B.

Floren, slashed and lying by the flagpole; the stick horse's blood-smeared head on the floor of the storage shed; and Max Dyson, sprawled on her living room floor, bleeding from a gunshot wound.

Claire had been able to keep the images at bay, letting the minute-by-minute agenda of the day fill her head. But when she tried to relax, the horrible visions flooded her brain.

She scooted off the rock, coaxed Blaze back to the riverbank and stroked the horse's neck before she placed her left foot in the stirrup, ready to swing into the saddle.

Pshew!

Something whizzed past her head. *A gunshot?* Blaze shied and bucked; she fell hard onto the red earth. The horse galloped away.

Ow. Claire massaged her hip; she'd landed on a stone the size of her hand.

Cautiously, she pulled herself to her knees. *A gunshot? Really?* She scanned her surroundings. Maybe a branch had crashed to the ground in the surrounding forest. Maybe a wasp had zoomed past her head.

Birds flitted in the trees, undisturbed.

It couldn't have been a gunshot.

Claire peered upstream, looking for the mare. Blaze could easily injure herself as she ran along the creek. If she fell into a hole and broke her leg, it would be a sad end to the horse's life. She couldn't imagine sharing such news with Cade and Denver.

She limped down the creek bank toward the opening in the trees, expecting to find the horse drinking or grazing on tender grass shoots.

Her hip ached but it could have been much worse. If the horse had fallen on her, she might have broken her leg. Hardly worth complaining about a bruise.

A horse whinnied around the next bend in the creek. Claire picked up her pace and limped around the trees. "Blaze!"

Holt was leading the horse by the reins toward her. Deep furrows creased his brow. "What happened?"

Blaze snorted and tossed her head.

"Where did you find her?" Claire grabbed the bridle and stroked the animal's sweaty neck.

"I saw you leave for your ride and came to find you. When the mare galloped up alone, I was worried you'd been hurt."

"I fell off and bruised my hip. Is Blaze okay?"

"Overheated and sweaty. Otherwise, she seems to be all right."

"Thank goodness." Claire checked the animal's forelegs, and lifted each of her front feet in turn, checking the frog of her foot for stones before setting it down. "She's not limping?"

"No, but you are. You fell off? That's not like you."

"A noise startled Blaze and she bucked. I wasn't prepared." Claire stroked the horse's neck.

"What kind of a noise?"

"I'm not sure. Might have been a gunshot."

Holt stared down the creek. "Did you see anyone?"

"No. Probably someone target practicing, shooting at bullfrogs or something."

"Could be. But they could have killed you or Blaze." Red splotches colored his cheeks and his eyes glinted.

"But they didn't. I'm fine. Really. It's over. Let's go back to the house." She stroked the horse's neck, took the reins from Holt and led the animal in a tight circle, turning back toward the opening in the trees.

"I'll go back in a minute and walk upstream. See if anyone's around." He looked over his shoulder at the creek and then stepped up beside her.

Claire spotted the break in the cottonwoods marking the opening to the pasture and headed toward it. Holt walked silently with her.

"When will Cade be back?"

"Any time."

He ran his fingers through his hair. "Claire, I care about you, but you're not interested in me. Would you mind telling me why not?"

"I've had bad luck with men. I need time to myself."

"What you need is a good experience. I won't hurt you." He stopped walking. "Let me help you, Claire."

"Let's be friends, okay?"

"I want more."

Claire stroked the horse's neck. "I've got to get back to the house. Cade will be home any time." She led Blaze away.

Holt didn't follow.

When she stopped to open the gate, she glanced back. At the creek, a figure stepped through the gap in the trees and disappeared into the shadows.

Chapter 30

Claire turned up the living room stereo as she stripped the sheets off the beds and piled them on the floor. The music pounded through the house; she sang along with familiar songs from the nineties, ones she'd danced to as a teenager. She danced as she worked, lifting her arms to the rhythm. For a while, the music kept the frightening images at bay, but one country song burrowed into a portion of her mind she'd closed off.

She'd gone to the Red Angus with Reed three years ago, when the song had been popular. A week or two later, Max Dyson had attacked her. Could Dyson have seen her for the first time at the Angus?

She stopped dancing, suddenly shivering as if an ice bucket had been dumped on her head.

Another stalker.

When would he contact her again? Would it be a note, flowers, or a phone call with no one on the other end of the line? He could watch her for weeks or even months before making his move.

A car door slammed on the driveway. Cade? She stuffed the sheets into the washing machine, dropped in a detergent pod and closed the lid. As she passed through the kitchen, voices echoed from the front hallway.

"You don't have to walk me in like I'm a little kid, Dad," Cade complained.

"Sure, I do. I want to say hello to your mother."

The three of them entered the living room at the same time from opposite ends of the room.

"Hi, son." Claire extended her arms for a hug.

"Hi, Mom." He brushed past her and slunk toward the bedroom hallway.

"Cade?" she asked his retreating back. Seconds later, the door to his room slammed shut. She turned to Tom. "What's going on?"

"The usual teenage nastiness." Her ex raked his hands through his hair and dropped into the recliner.

"Did you guys have fun?"

"Off and on. He's sullen and argumentative."

"Wonder who he gets that from?"

He glared. "He has no respect. You haven't taught him anything."

"Excuse me? You have no idea what goes on here or what I'm teaching him. You've hardly been present to help with any of it."

"Why is it every time he spends time with me all we do is fight? You've made him hate me."

"That's not true. I never say anything bad about you. If he acts that way, it's for reasons only he knows. Things have been stressful here this past week. The man who owned the ranch where Cade volunteered with Denver was murdered. Maybe he's upset about that."

"And that's another thing. Denver. He's a bad influence. He's teaching him all kinds of things he's too young to know. Why would you let someone like him have so much influence over Cade?"

"Denver is smart. He's been a good mentor. And he's family."

"But he's in jail, isn't he? For drugs? I read it online. Some mentor you picked."

"But he's innocent. They'll find the person who really did this."

"Claire, you're as naïve as ever. No wonder the kid has such idiotic ideas about the way life should be."

Claire clenched her hands. "Enough, Tom. You can't come in here and talk to me this way. You should leave."

"My God, Claire. Can't we even have a simple conversation? You blow everything out of proportion like he does."

"Leave." Claire charged to the door and pulled it open. When Tom didn't move from the chair, she waited at the door, hands on her hips. "Now."

Tom vaulted out of the chair, scowling as he stomped to the door. "You better talk to him. When I pick him up in two weeks, he better show more respect or I'll teach him the lesson myself. He's not too old to have a little respect beaten into him."

Claire slammed the door behind her ex and leaned against it. The man was as impossible as ever. How could she have ever hoped that he and Cade could have a real relationship?

"Mom?" Cade stood in the center of the living room.

"I guess the weekend didn't go well."

"Nope."

"But you wanted to go. The ballgame and everything."

Cade shrugged. "I tried, Mom. But he's sarcastic and makes fun of whatever I say. I don't want to spend another weekend with him. Ever."

Claire studied her son's face. Clearly, this wasn't a tantrum. Whatever Tom had said or done had upset Cade more than usual.

"We can go back to the court and get the visitation changed. You're old enough the judge might let you make your own decisions. But your dad will press the issue."

"I wish Denver was here."

"Did you ever talk to him about your dad?"

"He understands me. He never made me feel like an idiot. But Dad ..." Cade's hands clenched.

"Denver will be home Tuesday. I'll pay his bail tomorrow. The police will figure out who killed J.B. Floren. And they'll find out who planted those drugs in Denver's truck."

"Maybe." Cade plopped down on the sofa.

"I think I'll call in a pizza, and we'll run into town to Hideaway and eat. Sound good?" Claire loved the specialty pizzas at that restaurant as much as her son did.

"I want to see the dogs and Blaze, first. I'll feed them, and we can go." Cade bolted off the sofa and started for the kitchen, then stopped and hugged her.

Chapter 31

As they entered the Hideaway Pizza restaurant a block from the Oklahoma State University campus, Cade stopped to talk with friends at a front table. Claire moved on with the hostess and was seated at a booth in the center of the large eating area.

It was good to see Cade laughing. Relaxed and happy, he was the opposite of the sullen, angry person he'd been an hour ago. Teenagers were no different than adults, they were often different people depending on who they were with. And they were the strangest of all when they were with their parents.

Claire studied the crowd. Most of the customers wore jeans, tees and hoodies–probably university students. Other casually dressed adults were probably alumni with their families; the children wore OSU tees and sweatshirts. When the front door opened again, a man entered, and a bolt of recognition shot through her. He wasn't wearing his uniform. The man edged past the table where Cade stood talking with his friends and headed her direction.

"Ms. Northcutt. How are you?" Deputy Purdue's grin turned his face almost handsome. He flicked the hair off his forehead with one hand. Out of uniform, his usually stiff shoulders relaxed and so did his face. He looked friendly–a far cry from the officious prig he'd been at her home when they'd arrested Denver last week, or when he'd let her off without a ticket after she'd sped through the stop sign Friday night. "I'm okay, Deputy."

"Good weekend?"

"So-so."

Cade bypassed Purdue and slid into the opposite bench seat of the booth. "Hey."

"Hi. I'm Kent Purdue." The deputy extended his hand to Cade.

"Cade Northcutt." He shook the deputy's hand and frowned.

"Nice to meet you. You two enjoy your dinner." He nodded and sauntered off.

"Who is that?" Cade asked when the man was barely out of hearing range.

"The deputy who arrested Denver."

"That dude? Doesn't look much like a deputy." Cade twisted around for a second look.

Purdue joined two other men in a booth across the room; Claire didn't recognize either of them. "I've never seen him out of uniform before,"

"He was flirting with you."

"I didn't flirt back. I'm not interested in dating."

"You're not? Have you told Holt?"

"I may have gotten through to him this weekend. But he's still our neighbor, and I'll be nice to him. You never know–someday we might be glad he lives next door."

"I doubt it. But I guess it's good for you to have someone to call in an emergency. In case I'm not home."

After eating, Claire and Cade stepped out into the humid night. As they walked to their SUV, a low, black car rumbled past. The street lights reflected off the dark windows.

"So, Denver's getting out tomorrow, right? You're posting his bail?" Cade opened the SUV's passenger door and slid into the front seat.

"The paperwork will go in tomorrow and he should be released Tuesday. You'll be glad to have help with the chores again, won't you?"

"I don't mind the chores, Mom. But it's better to share them with Denver than to do them by myself." Cade plugged his earphones into his cellphone.

She put the car in gear and pulled away from the restaurant. A half-block down the street, they passed a black car parked at the curb. The vehicle pulled into the street behind them. Claire watched the sedan keep pace with her SUV in the rearview mirror.

The black car followed when they turned onto Highway 51, headed east out of town. Claire slowed and flicked on her blinker at a cul-de-sac a half-mile before her neighborhood. She turned in; the black car zoomed past on the highway.

She pulled back onto the highway and punched the accelerator. If she could catch up with the car, she could get the tag number.

"What're you doing, Mom?" Cade pulled one earbud out of his ear.

"Nothing." She focused on the car in front of them. Cade stuck the device back in his ear.

The black car's tail lights grew smaller and smaller. She slowed down and released the breath she'd been holding.

Cade let the dogs in and headed off to his room. On the back porch, the humid night air pressed in around her. She'd brought out her cell phone, intending to call Patty to give a promised update, but it rang before she could punch in her sister's number. She recognized the calling number. After several rings, she answered with a cautious, "Hello."

"Claire?" Lucia Valdez asked.

Claire could think of nothing for the two of them to talk about. Lucia didn't want to help Denver.

"I followed your advice and filed a report," Lucia continued. "But they won't find out anything. I put the stuffed horse's head in the trash." Lucia sighed.

Claire heard defeat in the other woman's voice. "At least there's a record of the incident. If something similar happens, the police can connect the dots." She hated the implications of what had happened. She couldn't comprehend a person making threats to cover their bad behavior. She'd been brought up to do the right thing, always. She did, most of the time.

"Maybe." Lucia didn't sound convinced. "Has anything odd happened to you?"

Claire considered telling her about the black car and the possible gunshot on the creek bank earlier today. But she didn't believe either of those things had anything to do with J.B. Floren or his ranch.

Lucia jumped into Claire's pause. "What's happened?"

"There *could* be a car following me. And at the creek this morning, something scared Blaze. Maybe fireworks, maybe a gunshot. I'm not sure." Claire tapped her finger tips against the arm of the glider. She didn't want to confide in this woman. She was not an ally. But she wasn't exactly the enemy either.

"I hope you followed your own advice and called the sheriff about the car and the gunshot," Lucia said.

"There's nothing to report. I didn't get a tag number. And, as far as the gunshot, I didn't see anyone down at the creek, and nothing appeared to be damaged by a bullet. For all I know, it was fireworks, or even an insect, a bee or wasp that whizzed past."

"Claire, this is serious. Especially considering that awful stuffed horse's head. It could have actually been Petreus."

"Lucia, let's not blow this out of proportion. I wasn't hurt. Truly, there's nothing to report to the sheriff." But, her stomach flopped. Someone *was* stalking her. What if Floren's killer was trying to stop her investigation? Could there be any connection between the two?

The mercury vapor light came on beside the little barn. Immediately, insects swarmed into the glow. "I'm glad you called the sheriff. That was a horrible prank."

"That prank was a warning for me to keep quiet, not to tell what I know. Don't play 'connect the dots,' Claire. Seeing that stuffed animal head should convince you to keep out of all this."

"Did you tell the sheriff what you know?"

"I said nothing about J.B., his activities, or the silent partner. And it will stay that way. If the sheriff finds the perpetrator, it won't be because I told him."

Claire's hands curled into fists and a new headache throbbed. Lucia knew something that might lead to a killer. "An innocent person is sitting in jail. As far as I know, they don't even have any other suspects. We *have* to do something."

"I told the sheriff Denver had nothing to do with J. B.'s murder. I told him to look deeper, to do a real investigation, but to leave me out of it. That's the most I can do. Good-night, Claire." Lucia disconnected.

Claire dropped the phone onto her lap. She didn't want to understand Lucia's position, but she did. She'd seen the stuffed animal head, dripping red paint. But Lucia could have the clue that would lead to Floren's murderer. Surely there was a way to uncover it without bringing catastrophe to either Lucia or herself.

Claire scurried through the house in the gloom, pulling the curtains shut and making sure all the doors and windows were locked. Someone, somewhere, wanted Denver to take the rap for the murder. And another person had keyed in on her, wanted her to notice them, even love them.

Claire poured a glass of wine and sat, feet tucked beneath her on the sofa in the darkened living room. She didn't want to sleep; nightmares came with sleep. With Cade in his room nearby and Ranger at her feet, calm normalcy seemed possible for the first time in days.

She leaned down to touch the dog's head and scratch his ears. His tail thumped the floor. He grunted softly and sat up.

"I'm glad you're here, boy." The dog leaned into her fingers, letting her scratch deep into his ears. He groaned, and shook his head. "If you could talk, you'd clear Denver, wouldn't you? You could tell us who killed J.B."

When she pulled her hand away, the dog stood. In one smooth movement, he leaped onto the couch beside her and rested his big head in her lap.

Claire reached for the soft throw on the back of the sofa, enfolded herself in it, pushed back into the pillows and closed her eyes.

He couldn't sit still. What a day!

He'd not expected the opportunity to scare her at the creek. When she and that horse trotted across the pasture, he cut around the other way, anticipating where they would go.

She was beautiful. Older than most of the women he wanted, but that was part of the thrill. She was experienced, she could offer something new. He had no doubt he could bring out the wildcat in her.

She'd laid there on that rock and he had fought with himself. He'd wanted to splash across the creek and grab her. Enough of this waiting like the others wanted. She'd been to the farm yesterday and nothing had happened. Her investigation was dead in the water, especially after what he'd done to the stuffed horse head.

She would drop the investigation. Eventually, she'd welcome him with open arms.

That's how it would go.

He wouldn't let his father's voice inside his head convince him otherwise.

Chapter 32

The neighbor's rooster crowed at first light Monday morning. Claire was still on the sofa. Ranger snuggled close on the cushions next to her legs. He lifted his head and sneezed, closed his eyes and sighed; his head dropped back onto the cushion.

Claire rolled off the sofa to open the draperies, then scurried back, lifted her legs and slid them between the dog and the deep sofa cushions. The sky lightened from black to gray as each of the stars blinked out.

Her mind was muddled with sleep. She yawned and the day's calendar crowded into her head. She let herself relax into the cushions a few more seconds before she vaulted off the sofa. *Might as well get an early start.*

By 7:15, Claire had settled in at her desk and powered on her computer, glad to have a good hour to start on the assignments Manny had sent her at seven a.m. Plenty of time before the usual 9 a.m. staff meeting.

She called the police department and requested a copy of the weekend police blotter. Most weekend incidents involved college students. There were the usual half-dozen domestic violence calls and a convenience store hold-up plus the occasional stolen vehicle or carjacking. The sergeant who was her contact at Stillwater PD answered his extension.

"Hey, Claire. Busy weekend for us," Sergeant Ed Morton said. The sound of papers rustling almost drowned out his voice on the speaker phone.

"Anything unusual I should know about before you send me the report?" She expected to clean up the summary of the incident reports as usual, making only a few additions or changes. Sometimes, an event was worthy of an article all its own, and she would create a brief story for the e-news and several short pieces for the evening print version.

"Here's one you'll definitely want to follow up on. A rape, off-campus, southeast part of town."

"Can you give me details or should I come down to the station for an interview?"

"The story is on the radio. Here's what they've got. The perp surprised the woman in front of her house when she arrived home. She described him as medium build, wearing jeans, a dark t-shirt and a ball cap. He forced her inside where he raped her at knifepoint in the kitchen. Afterward, he threatened her and told her not to call the police or he'd kill her." Sergeant Morton cleared his throat. "The victim saw a newer model black sedan speed down the street just after the attack. She didn't get the license number."

Claire scribbled on her yellow pad. Her heart thumped. A rapist, possibly driving a black car. Her stalker might drive a black car. "What are you doing to catch the guy, sergeant?"

"We're canvassing the area for vehicles fitting the description. Do you have any idea how many men in their twenties and thirties drive black cars? They're as common around here as pickup trucks."

"Should I use that detail in the news story?"

"We'll contact those vehicle owners over the course of the day. No need to tip them off."

"But what about warning potential victims?"

"Once we're sure we've got a serial rapist, we'll publicize what we know. We're working with the victim to narrow down the list of possible suspects. Usually, it's someone the woman knows. In only a few cases, it's not."

"Thanks for the info. If Manny wants more, I'll come to the station."

"You don't need an excuse to come down here. It's always good to see you."

A high-priority email popped up on Claire's computer screen. "Gotta go, Ed."

She hung up and clicked on the email from Manny. *My office. Now.* The wall clock showed another fifteen minutes until staff meeting. She grabbed her yellow pad and tucked her purse into a file cabinet. As she passed Casey Stenson's desk, he looked up and lifted his hand, continuing a conversation on his desk phone.

Manny's office door stood partially open. Inside the room, a blond woman in a knee-length beige skirt and a gold-trimmed white cardigan sat stiffly in his visitor's chair, knees together, feet next to a pile of magazines and newspapers.

"Come in, Claire. This is Cassandra Winchell, J.B. Floren's ex-wife. This is Claire Northcutt. She wrote the story on J.B., and was the one who found him."

The slender blonde shifted her body to face Claire. "I see."

The skin on her face was plump and shiny. The woman had probably had both a face lift and Botox injections to mask her age. She had to be in her sixties or seventies.

Manny cleared his throat. "Mrs. Winchell is in town on business."

Claire looked from Manny to Cassandra Winchell. "How can I help you?"

"You wrote the article. Made him out to be a hero. Whatever he was, he wasn't a hero. What a shoddy piece of journalism. If it had truly been an 'investigative' piece, you'd have exposed him for what he was, cruel and opportunistic."

Claire involuntarily stepped back. She had asked Manny to hold the article, which he didn't, and the reaction had already begun. She looked at her editor. He cleared his throat.

"I investigated the controversy around saving the mustangs, not Mr. Floren," Claire said. "My piece fairly presented both sides of the issue. And Mr. Floren is known as an expert. He ran the largest mustang rescue ranch in Oklahoma."

"Rescue," Cassandra scoffed. "If you want to call it that."

Claire studied the other woman. Lucia was dark-haired with flashing eyes, she'd done nothing to alter her appearance and disguise her age. This woman was pale, a blue-eyed blonde with styled hair, stiff with hairspray, and penciled-in eyebrows. The two women couldn't have been more different.

"You should know that people who knew him are laughing about your article." Cassandra studied her French manicure.

"Mrs. Winchell, Claire and I are both sorry you feel that way," Manny said. "Exactly what do you expect us to do now that you've called this to our attention?"

"It's too late. You printed it. Unless you print a retraction to save your reputation, there's nothing to be done." She smoothed the back of her skirt as she stood. "I'm on my way to the sheriff's office. At least they've caught the man who killed J.B. I know people, including myself, who would like to send the young man a thank you note, but he'll have to be convicted first."

Cassandra Winchell nodded at Manny and stepped past Claire to exit the office. She left the door open; her high heels thudded on the thin, industrial carpet as she headed for the front door.

"What a B," Claire muttered.

"Nice start to the work week." Manny's brows lifted.

"You ran the article even though I asked you to hold it."

"Not my doing. The publisher read it, thought it was a great companion piece with the obituary. I tried to explain there might be reason to hold it, but he didn't agree."

Claire chewed at her lip. "J.B. may have had secrets, but I stand by my article as an adequate discussion of the pros and cons of saving wild horses and burros through rescue ranches and adoptions. J.B. Floren had enemies. They can think what they like about the article."

"I agree. It's not the first time this paper has created a controversy, and it won't be the last." Manny scratched the back of his head.

"So, did she say anything else? Why is she here? Surely her sole purpose wasn't to come here and blast my article."

"Mrs. Winchell didn't share that information with me. She's on her way to the sheriff's office. Your guess is as good as mine as to what she'll have to say to the sheriff or why she's in town. Executor of Floren's will, maybe?"

"She could be in charge of his burial or cremation," Claire said, but she doubted she was any of those things. More likely, Lucia–not Cassandra–had been left as executor and in charge of arrangements upon his death. She had tolerated a relationship with Floren because of Miguel. Another possibility was that the 'silent partner' would step up.

"Wish I had a source at the sheriff's office. I'd like to know exactly what Mrs. Winchell says to the sheriff." Manny glanced at the wall clock. "Time for staff meeting."

Chapter 33

Claire couldn't concentrate in the weekly meeting. The stale air hinted at tobacco residue from Casey and the print shop workers who still took smoke breaks outside. The a/c had been turned off for the weekend, and hadn't yet cooled the building after coming on at 7 a.m. Claire stepped over to the counter and turned on a desk fan, pointing it toward the floor to send the hot air up.

The publisher and managing editor reviewed assignments and business concerns. Her mind was elsewhere. When she'd entered the room, the advertising staff had twittered behind their hands. They either heard what had happened in Manny's office, or were discussing Claire's history with dead men. She shrugged it off.

Her mind replayed Cassandra Winchell's words berating Claire for the rescue ranch article. Cassandra had called J.B. an opportunist and cruel. Tough words. J.B. had been up to something besides an affair. Had there been another reason for their divorce? Lucia had ended that relationship after finding the starving animals. What else had Floren done to alienate these women?

"Want to grab lunch, Claire? It's been a few weeks," Casey Stinson broke into her thoughts as the staff members filed out of the room after the meeting.

Claire pulled herself back to the present. She had a busy day ahead, and the assignments waiting on her desk were only a small part of it. "I've got phone calls to make first," she said. "Let me see where I'm at time-wise after that."

She was anxious to check in with Reed Morgan about the approval of her second mortgage and needed to pick up the check for Denver's bail. She also wanted to contact Trina Romero about the timing of his release. "Can you give me an hour? Maybe it'll be less."

Casey shrugged. "Sure." He grinned, and his long, thin face changed when his eyes brightened. "I've always got another obit to write. The publisher may not make much money with subscriptions these days but he can always count on customers paying for obits."

"Don't forget funerals, graduations, anniversaries and weddings," another voice chimed in. Maggie caught up with them, walked a few steps beside Claire and turned into the newspaper's library/morgue, flipping on the lights as she entered.

Claire stopped in the doorway. "Maggie, you and I checked the clip files for articles on J.B. Floren last week. What about separate files on Cassandra? Specifically, about their divorce?"

"Was that Cassandra I saw in Manny's office earlier? She hasn't changed a bit. Kind of a snot." Maggie dropped into her desk chair.

"Yeah, she complained about my article. Said it made J.B. out to be a hero. And he wasn't."

"Of course, she wouldn't think so. He had an affair and they got a divorce. No hero to her." In a flurry, she typed Cassandra's name into her search bar. After a list appeared, she touched each file name, saying, "We've looked at this, and that one, too. Here's the picture with the dog." Her finger tapped on the screen at the final file entry. "But here's one about the divorce. Don't think we opened this one."

She clicked on the file and a short item appeared on the screen. Divorce proceedings. The article gave the date of the couple's hearing, and the attorney who represented each. Maggie swiveled in her chair. "I'm afraid that's it, unless you go to the courthouse and search out the actual records for the divorce."

Claire shook her head. "I'm just curious. Looking for juicy details, something that might be related to his murder."

Maggie peered at her. "You're divorced. Got juicy details you want to spill to the world?"

"Not on your life." Claire smiled.

Juicy details? Nothing 'juicy' about verbal abuse. Day after day, week after week of being beaten verbally, told you were not a good wife, not a good mother, and pretty much a low-level human being. She didn't want to be reminded of what she had endured for too many years. Yesterday's row with Tom reminded her all too well. Being in the same room with him for more than a minute had brought everything about her suffocating marriage roaring back.

"So, are you conducting your own investigation? Sheriff's not doing a good enough job?" Maggie asked.

"My nephew is at the top of the suspect list. I guess I trust their investigation, but it's not moving fast enough for me."

Maggie took off her glasses and set them on the desk. "Here are my thoughts about that. You are a fine reporter, but you're liable to be poking a snake's den with this one. Lots of things happen behind the scenes, and I personally am just fine with not knowing about most of them."

"But Denver's life may be at stake. If he goes to trial, and they find him guilty–"

"Cart before the horse, my dear. You're anxious and impatient. I get it. But slow down and watch your step. Somebody hated that rancher, and my guess is that they are none too eager to have someone figure out why."

Chapter 34

At her desk, Claire retrieved her cell phone and her purse from the file cabinet before she sat at her desk chair. The phone's screen showed she'd missed a call from Reed. She called him.

"Reed, I hope you have good news for me."

"Your rush paperwork went through. Good thing you've been on time with your payments and haven't asked for any extensions. Your second mortgage has been approved. Celebrate with me at lunch and I'll give you the check."

Claire glanced over her shoulder at Casey on the phone at his desk. "I can't do lunch today, Reed, but I can stop by immediately before or after. And can you make it a money order?"

When he asked, "Can you be here in fifteen minutes?" the tone of his voice had changed.

Immediately after disconnecting, Claire punched in Trina Romero's number. She was with a client, so Claire left a message about the bail money, adding that she would drop off a personal money order within the hour. She swiveled in her chair and found Casey watching her.

"Ready?" he asked.

She slipped the strap of her purse over her shoulder. "Let's go."

At the bank, Casey waited in the car while Claire went in to collect the money order from Reed. She found him in his office at his desk computer.

He looked up, reached into his desk drawer and pulled out an envelope. "Here you go, Claire. If Denver skips out on bail, you'll have a heck of a time repaying this second mortgage. You'll be in debt until you're seventy, provided there are no more catastrophes in your life to throw you even further off track." He frowned at her.

"Denver can't sit in jail another day. He's innocent. Someone framed him." She took the envelope and tucked it into her purse. "Thank you."

"I hope the sheriff finds evidence to clear Denver."

"The sheriff will find the real killer if he'll turn his focus elsewhere."

"Like where?"

Claire considered what Denver had told her before his arrest, and what Lucia and Cassandra Winchell had said. "Floren wasn't a saint, and the truth will come out." She turned toward the door. "Thanks again for your help."

"I'll walk you out. You sure you won't have lunch with me?"

"I'd already made plans to have lunch with a colleague. Another time?"

Reed stood at the door of the bank as she walked the few yards to Casey's waiting car. She glanced back. Reed was squinting after her, still frowning.

"You had a tough week, didn't you? Having nightmares?" Casey asked before biting into his hamburger.

She chewed on a French fry. "Some. I'm not scared of dead bodies. What's scary is the realization that, in Floren's case, somebody killed him." Casey knew Floren wasn't her first dead body, no secret there.

"Did you wonder if the killer was still at the ranch after you found the body? What went through your mind?" Casey bent toward her across the table.

"You're kind of a ghoul, aren't you? I never realized that." She forced a laugh at the younger man.

Casey sat back in his chair. "I confess to reading true crime and murder mysteries, and watching an occasional slasher flick."

She fingered the rim of her iced tea glass. "Truthfully, when I discovered the body, shock set in. I didn't think about my own safety, or whether the killer was still at the ranch. Such violence, and so much blood everywhere. Until you've seen it for yourself, it's unimaginable."

He took another bite of his hamburger, and ketchup oozed over the side of the bun and dropped onto his plate.

Claire shuddered. She gulped some tea and changed the subject.

Chapter 35

Casey dropped her off near Trina Romero's office, a few blocks from the newspaper building. The money order weighed down her purse. She feared losing it or that Reed Morgan might change his mind about giving her the loan and ask her to return it to him.

Trina was standing at the reception desk, talking to the employee, when Claire walked in. "Hey, Claire. Judy's ordered some lunch for me. Have you eaten?"

"Just finished."

"Okay. Come on back."

Trina led the way to her office. "Denver will be so relieved to be out of that jail." She closed the door behind them.

"Has the sheriff told you anything about the drugs they found? Do you think the sheriff has other suspects in Floren's murder?"

"The sheriff hasn't said a word. Truth be told, I'm not sure he's even investigating." The look on Trina's face turned grim.

Claire's heart plummeted into her stomach. "There has to be some evidence somewhere that shines a light on the real murderer." Claire's mind spun through what Lucia had said and what Cassandra Winchell had shared this morning. "Many people didn't like J.B. And he had a silent partner. Other people had reason to want him dead."

Trina shrugged. "The murderer could be a stranger. Isolated ranch. Minimal occupants. Could have been a robbery gone wrong. Did anyone take inventory? Anything missing?"

"Who could answer that? He lived alone."

"The silent partner. Possibly his ex-wife."

"She's in town. She came by the newspaper office to let my editor know I'd done a poor job on the article I wrote about the rescue ranches. She wasn't happy I painted Floren in a positive light."

"That's her privilege. No matter what you write, someone will have a problem with it." Trina tapped her fingernails on her desk. "Interesting she's in town. They've been divorced for a while. Why would she come? Surely, he had other heirs, or other people assigned to take care of his final arrangements."

Claire thought of Miguel. Did J.B.'s acquaintances know he had a son with Lucia Valdez? Did that fact have anything to do with the man's murder?

"J.B. had a son with Lucia Valdez."

Trina raised her eyebrows. "Really? Who knew? The ranchers are out of my social sphere. Other than the occasional article or picture on the social page of their events, I'm clueless about who they are or what they're doing. A son with Lucia. Interesting."

"I met him Saturday. He didn't seem sad about J.B.'s death. He was morbidly interested in what his body looked like when I found him. I guess in today's world of zombies and vampires, young people are used to blood and gore." Claire perched on the edge of a chair. "Floren paid child support and spent time with his boy. Miguel lived with Lucia, but their ranches have common borders. Made it easy for him to see his dad."

Trina tilted her head. "So either one of them could get from one place to the other without being seen. Could either Lucia or Miguel have murdered J.B.?"

An uneasy feeling dropped over Claire. She imagined Lucia's face, and Miguel's. The stuffed animal head in Lucia's storage shed proved Lucia's innocence. Hard to imagine Miguel pulling such a stunt. "No. Lucia has been warned to stay out of the investigation, and she's warned me, too."

"Has anything happened to make you feel threatened?".

Mentally, Claire dismissed the possible gunshot. It might not even have been a bullet, and nothing had happened since. Reality included the daisy delivery and the notes on her car. "I might have another stalker. An unidentified person sent me flowers. Two anonymous notes were left on or in my car. And someone in a black car might be following me."

"Those things probably have nothing to do with the murder, but I hope you've told the police."

"Not yet. I'm hoping it will end."

"Claire, stalkers don't go away unless you make them. I hope you're being careful. Are you carrying a gun?"

Claire's gun stayed on top of the tall cabinet in her living room. "No. But I have one at home. I'm being careful."

"I hope so." Trina laid her hands on the desk and looked at Claire. "Okay. I have several things to accomplish at the courthouse, including this. Do you want to go to the court clerk with me?"

Claire pulled the envelope from her purse, opened it, and stared at the dollar amount on the check.

"It's a lot of money, Claire. Are you sure you want to do this?"

"There's not a doubt in my mind." Claire signed the money order on the back. "Here. I could go, but if you saw the pile of work on my desk ..."

Trina gestured at a stack of folders five inches high on her own desk. "Tell me about it."

"I trust you to get it there and handle whatever paperwork is needed as my emissary."

"Let's have Judy type up a note to that effect. She's a notary, too. That way there will be no question."

The lawyer stood. "I'll let you know when Denver will be released for sure, but I'm expecting it will be tomorrow morning."

"Keep me posted. I'll be there."

Claire stepped outside the office. Sirens blared a few blocks away, moving in the opposite direction. It could be an ambulance siren, or possibly a fire truck. She'd get the details soon enough. The newspaper office was always among the first to know when something happened.

Chapter 36

Two empty police cars sat in the customer parking lot when Claire walked up to the front doors of the newspaper office. Inside, employees huddled behind the counter. Down the hall, two uniformed policemen stood in the doorway of the publisher's office.

"What's going on?" Claire asked the receptionist.

"Someone said you went to lunch with Casey, but you weren't with him when it happened. Did you see it? Where have you been?" The woman dabbed at her nose with a tissue.

"Did I see what? What happened?" Claire scanned the room for clues.

"Claire?" Manny hurried out of Mr. Eames' office. "Step in here, please."

"Sure." She rushed after him. In the office, Carson Eames sat behind his desk. He stood, and asked, "You went to lunch with Casey?"

Claire looked from the publisher to Manny and back again. "Yes. And he dropped me off a few blocks from here. I had an errand to take care of. What's happened?"

"Somebody t-boned Casey's car in an intersection a block from here," Manny explained. "He's been taken to the hospital."

"Is he all right?"

"These officers have no report on his condition yet. One witness saw an SUV leave the scene," Eames said. "They got the license tag number. According to the DMV, it's your vehicle."

"What?" Claire dashed out of the office and down the hall to the back door. In the employee's parking lot, she scanned the numerous cars and trucks parked there. Her SUV wasn't among them.

"Miss Northcutt, do you have any idea where your SUV is?" One of the policemen asked as he caught up to her.

"It's not here."

"Does anyone else have access to your vehicle? Is there another set of keys?"

Claire dug in her purse and pulled out her car keys. "My keys are right here. My other set went missing." She thought about the black car she'd seen in the neighborhood, and the note left on her dashboard. Had the stalker taken her keys?

"Missing? Did you leave them in your vehicle?"

"I'll search the house when I get home." Icy fear filled her head.

"Tell me where you were for the past hour." One of the policeman pulled a small spiral notebook from his back pocket.

"Casey drove us to lunch. Afterwards, he dropped me off at Trina Romero's office. You can call her, she'll vouch that I was in her office for at least the last twenty minutes."

"I have no doubt you were there. But we're talking about only a few blocks."

She didn't like the way the policemen were looking at her. "Casey and I had lunch. We're friends. I had no reason to hurt Casey."

A message buzzed on one of the policemen's cell phones. He stepped away, made a quick phone call and turned back to the group, which now included Manny and Carson Eames. "They found your vehicle abandoned at Couch Park. Extensive damage to the right front fender."

"Couch Park? That's at least two miles from here. If I crashed into Casey, how did I get back here so quickly? I'm not wearing track shoes." She glanced down at her flats. "I'll vouch for her, officers," Manny said. "Carry out your investigation. I'm sure you'll find that her vehicle was stolen and Ms. Northcutt had absolutely nothing to do with this hit-and-run."

Claire smiled weakly at her boss. This was unbelievable. Why would someone steal her SUV and run into Casey with it?

"We'll retrieve the car. Come down to the station later this afternoon for an update. The vehicle will be taken to impound after the examination and can probably be released to you when forensics have been completed."

Taken to impound? How badly damaged was the RAV? But more important, how seriously hurt was Casey?

"Call Hertz, Claire," Manny said. "I'll take you to rent a car. We'll worry about picking yours up later."

Chapter 37

About 5 p.m., Manny took Claire to Hertz to pick up a rental vehicle.

"I called the police department," she told him. "The forensic team hasn't cleared my RAV."

"What do you think they'll find?"

"Fingerprints and DNA from me and Cade. Hair from the dogs. Any other DNA proves someone else was in my vehicle and used it to ram Casey."

"But why would someone ram Casey?"

"Don't ask me. I barely knew the guy. We'd been getting together for lunch occasionally. He's married. Has a son."

"So, I ask again, why would anyone ram Casey? And with your SUV."

Claire felt the chill as it ran down her back. Had Casey been targeted because of her? Because they'd had lunch together?

Once she had her rental, a Jeep Explorer, she called the hospital to check Casey's condition. Rather than provide the information to her, the nurse put her on hold. A few minutes later, Casey's wife came on the line.

"Thanks for calling, Claire. Casey's out of surgery and stable. He has a broken arm, and internal injuries that the surgeons have repaired. He's in serious condition, but they say he'll be out of ICU tomorrow and make a full recovery. I'm waiting for him to wake up."

"Can I bring you something to eat? Do you need anything?"

"No, my neighbor came with me, and another neighbor is watching our little boy. Thanks for offering."

"I'm sending thoughts and prayers his way. I'll get by there to visit tomorrow, when he's awake." Claire dropped her phone back into her purse.

Claire called Manny with the information.

"That's good news. He'll recover. The way those policemen sounded when they showed up at the office had me worried. You'd have thought he died at the scene."

"They'll find whoever did this. The team going through my SUV will find something."

"And what if they don't? Are you sure your alibi is solid?"

"Alibi? Manny, I was at Trina's office. With Trina. And her secretary saw me. We met in her office. There is no way I could have come back here, gotten my vehicle, run into Casey, driven out to Couch Park and gotten back here in such a short time."

"Didn't mean to ruffle your feathers." Manny chuckled. "Better be prepared for any question they may throw at you. Hit and run is a serious offense."

Claire pulled into the shopping center and parked in front of Jenny Prather's hair salon. Seconds later, she pushed through the doorway. Jenny left the client sitting at her station, and hurried to the waiting area. She grabbed Claire's arm and pulled her into the back room. "I hope you have good news for me. Did you get the bond money? Is Denver getting out?"

"Yes. Trina Romero posted the bond. I'll pick Denver up first thing tomorrow morning."

Jenny threw her arms around Claire. "You're amazing. Denver and I will be indebted to you forever."

"I'm glad I could do it. I love Denver, too, Jenny."

"I know you do. And he's told me how much he loves you and Cade, and how thankful he is for everything you've done." Jenny swiped away the tears on her cheeks.

"I'm taking tomorrow off so he and I can spend time together. Shea spent the afternoon rescheduling my appointments. I feel like celebrating. Do you have time to get a beer with a couple of us? In about an hour?"

"You should celebrate, and I wish I could. Truth is, without Denver, Cade and I have fallen behind on our chores at home. One of us has to feed and care for the animals, and the horse Denver's been training really needs to be ridden."

Jenny frowned. "Maybe we can do it this weekend."

"Plan on it. Meanwhile, drink a beer for me, and I'm guessing I'll see you at my house tomorrow morning?"

Jenny beamed. "Yes. But it's a surprise. Don't tell him I'll be there, okay?"

Claire glanced in the rearview mirror several times as she drove through the streets of Stillwater to reach Highway 51 and head east. No black car behind her; no cars at all.

Two days had passed since her 'stalker' had last made contact. Maybe she'd been wrong, and it was only an innocent secret admirer. But if so, why had he taken her keys? She worried at her lower lip. There'd been a house key on that ring with the car keys.

As she drove through the entrance to her neighborhood, Claire checked the rearview mirror and glanced from side to side, perusing the yards as she drove past. No black car, no suspicious vehicles. She drove the loop through the neighborhood, checking driveways at each house. Nothing to be alarmed about.

She pulled into the garage, watched the garage door rumble down and unlocked the back door.

"Cade?"

On the back porch, Izzy and Ranger barked. She opened the door and braced herself for the onslaught of wriggling dog bodies. Both animals greeted her with wagging tails and licking tongues. Each of them in turn pushed close to her, hoping to be petting and scratched. She stooped and hugged them. When she stood again, sticky dog saliva clung to her cheeks.

Claire checked the pantry for dinner supplies, and set her selections on the counter. She did the same in the refrigerator, pulling out frozen chicken breasts, asparagus, and romaine lettuce. Like Jenny, she felt like celebrating for Denver tonight. The ordeal was far from over, but at least he would be free again. They'd deal with the rest of it later. She uncorked a bottle of red table wine and poured herself a glass. Ranger leaned into her leg.

The house phone rang. She let the answering machine pick up. Most likely it was a solicitation, none of her friends called that phone. She didn't plan to make any donations at the moment. Hadn't Reed told her that she had signed her life away?

Her answering machine message requested the caller leave a message. The tone beeped and the dial tone resumed. The answering machine clicked off.

Claire pulled out the bakeware she needed, set the oven temperature, and carried her wine glass into the living room. She flicked on the evening news.

"Meanwhile, in Stillwater, police are searching for a serial rapist ..."

She shifted to the edge of the sofa cushion. This morning, Ed had told her about one rape. *Serial rapist?* Had there been another assault?

Seconds later, the front door startled her when it banged open. Cade called, "Mom? What's for dinner?"

Ranger and Izzy dashed for the door, yipping. She clicked off the news. Hearing about a serial rapist had destroyed her desire to celebrate. The ominous black car she'd been seeing could belong to the rapist.

"Hey, Cade. I haven't started dinner. Thought you had practice. Are you home for the night?" She hugged him when he stopped in the middle of the living room.

"Yeah. I've got to work on my term paper. Mrs. Isaacs wants the list of references Thursday, and I haven't been compiling them."

"Would you take care of Blaze and Smoky first while I get dinner together?" She headed for the kitchen. "Don't forget to lock the doors when you come in."

"Don't I usually?" He followed her into the kitchen and leaned against the doorframe. Izzy yipped and jumped at him, wanting to play. "I heard the news about the rapist, Mom. I doubt he'll come way out here." He headed for the back door; both dogs wagged along after him.

Claire hurried to the front door and locked the dead bolt and the knob. She peeked out the small window, checking her front yard and the street beyond. All quiet.

In the kitchen, she mixed up the ingredients for a sauce, and placed the chicken breasts in the oven. Through the windows over the sink, she saw Cade moving in and out of the barn as he cared for the animals. Her hand shook as she took another sip of wine.

The phone rang, and once again she let the machine answer. The caller disconnected when the message signal beeped. She paused in her preparations. If the caller was a friend, they would call her cell phone. It lay on the counter, next to the sink. But her cell didn't ring, and no message was left on the machine. She pulled out a knife and chopped carrots and onions to go in the dish for dinner.

Outside, Ranger barked his playful bark, and when she glanced through the window toward the barn, the two dogs and Cade were playing chase in the yard. Her son was still a boy, regardless of how grown-up he tried to be. Their lives might have been different–if his father had been a better husband, if the two of them had stayed together. Chances were, they'd be living in North Carolina. Chances were, they would have had another child. She would have liked to have had a daughter.

When the phone rang again, she closed her eyes and counted to ten. The machine answered, the caller hung up, the machine disconnected. She reached across the counter and unplugged the phone at the wall. The land line had become obsolete except for solicitations. Whoever was calling would continue to call, interrupting the quiet house and her thoughts.

The oven beeped; she opened the door and stirred the dish, folded in the chopped vegetables, and closed the door. Thirty minutes longer. She pulled lettuce and other vegetables out of the refrigerator and made the salad.

Outside, the dogs were quiet.

Denver would be released tomorrow, and maybe, after what Lucia had told the sheriff, they would begin to look for another suspect. Maybe, too, her stalker had decided to focus on someone else.

Perhaps she could sleep tonight, if she didn't dwell on what had happened to Casey. Who in the world would t-bone a car and then drive away without checking for injuries? It had to be a random person, no one who had anything to do with the mess Denver was in or Floren's murder. Just a random person with no conscience whatsoever.

The lights are off. She's already gone to bed. So much for thinking she might feel some guilt about her 'friend' Casey in the hospital.

Hah, the look on his face just before her car slammed into him!

He hadn't seen that coming.

The guy's a loser. Too cocky. Too tall. Why would she even want to be friends with him? If friends was what they were.

I've delayed long enough. She going to ruin things, bailing Denver out of jail. Nearly time to take the upper hand, start calling the shots.

As Dad used to say, this'll hurt me more than it hurts you.

Ha ha.

Chapter 38

Thunder growled in a cloud-filled sky on Tuesday morning.

Claire waited in the hallway of the jail for Denver to appear. She folded her arms and squirmed on the wooden bench. A week ago, she'd never have imagined herself here, in the jail, waiting to pick up a family member charged with a crime. Life had a way of throwing unexpected curves.

Down the hall, a door swung open and Denver appeared with a uniformed man. She stood and waited for them. When Denver stopped in front of her, she touched his arm. "Hi. Let's go home."

Claire and Denver walked side-by-side out the door of the Payne County Jail. Denver kept his head low, his look on the ground, and followed her to the truck without making eye contact with her or any of the people on the street. With his pale skin and shaggy hair, he looked ill. Claire's heart ached. *He'd spent six days in jail. Long enough to make anyone ill.*

They had driven to the eastern city limits of Stillwater before he spoke.

"Does Mom know I'm out on bond today?" His voice was low and gravelly.

"Yes. But you should call her. She'll want to hear from you."

"She will. But any conversation about what has happened ends the same way. Why? Who?" His fingernails scratched against the denim of his jeans. "I'd never sell drugs. Somebody planted them."

Claire glanced at him. He peered out of the car's passenger side window and then at the road ahead. "I don't have a clue either, Denver. And I doubt the sheriff would tell me if he knew more."

She wouldn't say anything more about the investigation into J.B. Floren's murder. As far as she knew, Denver was still the focus of their investigation. Both Lucia and the man's ex-wife had implied that plenty of other people might want to harm the rancher. Hopefully, both women had told the sheriff about those people and his dealings.

But Denver asked the question she'd been hoping to avoid. "How's the murder investigation going? Do you think they still believe I had something to do with it?"

"The sheriff has said nothing to me, and I don't expect him to."

"At least they're not after Cade." Denver swiped his hand over his face. "His fingerprints and mine are all over the barn and the equipment. We were both there on weekends. Last weekend, I told him J.B. was a bastard."

Claire felt cold, despite the warm morning sun. "Cade couldn't murder anyone," she said. But Cade's behavior had changed since the murder. He spent his non-school hours outside in the barn or in the training ring with Blaze and Smoky, Ranger and Izzy. She'd seen him working with the horse in the paddock, imitating Denver's moves.

"Cade couldn't murder anyone," Denver repeated. "Not any more than you could, right? Now me, that's a different story." He spoke sharply, without looking at her.

She reined in her hurt at Denver's thoughtless comment and dismissed his insensitivity. He was all too familiar with what had happened three years ago. He had a right to be angry and discouraged about the recent events.

"What do you remember about the last few times you were at the ranch? Did anything out of the ordinary happen? Were there any people there you weren't used to seeing? Did you overhear any arguments?"

Denver shrugged and shook his head. "Didn't see much of the guy while we were there. People came and went. We worked."

She turned the rental SUV into her driveway. An older model blue Honda Accord had parked close to the house. Jenny Prather sat in the glider on the front porch, swinging.

"We'll talk later," Denver said as the SUV rolled to a stop next to the other vehicle and he caught sight of Jenny on the porch. He leapt out and ran for the house.

Jenny rose from her seat in the wicker glider. Denver vaulted up the steps two at a time and embraced her, lifting her off the ground and swinging her in a circle. Their whirl slowed, and they locked in a kiss.

Claire looked away from the pair and peered at the sky; dark clouds had thickened. Lightning fingered through them, and thunder rumbled miles away. Footsteps clattered down the porch steps to where she waited.

Jenny wrapped Claire in a tight hug.

"I'm going to steal him away for the rest of the day." The couple linked arms.

Denver's eyes sparked.

"You two go have fun." Claire waved them away. She leaned against her vehicle and watched Jenny and

Denver hop into Jenny's car. Jenny revved the engine, and made a U-turn.

The Honda raced off.

Chapter 39

Claire's spirit lifted. Denver still had a hard road to travel, but at least he was out of jail. Halfway to Stillwater, raindrops splattered the windshield. Denver and Jenny wouldn't even realize it was raining, they were too glad to be together again. And as much as she loved rainy days, she was glad to be headed to work. Rainy days brought back thoughts of rainy nights, and she'd just as soon not experience any of those by herself, especially when the possibility of a stalker lingered in her life.

Denver hadn't noticed that she wasn't driving her RAV. Or, if he had, he didn't mention it. She wasn't sure what she would have said. How could she have explained everything that had happened since his arrest last week? He knew nothing about the things she'd learned about J.B. Floren, and he knew nothing about the stalker. He had no inkling someone had stolen her extra set of keys and slammed her car into Casey.

Hopefully, Casey would be conscious when she visited him in the hospital. He'd have questions, just like she did. Why had he been targeted? Had they thought she might still be in the car with him? Was *she* the real target of the hit and run?

Questions filled her mind. She had answers for none of them. Reed Morgan's scowling face, as she'd left to have lunch with Casey, superimposed itself over other thoughts. Had Reed been upset with her about posting bail, or about having lunch with Casey instead of him? She knew all about Reed's jealous nature. But to ram a car into someone seemed far beyond what Reed might do.

A police car sat in the customer's parking lot at work. Claire drove on around the building to the back, and parked the Explorer.

She hurried to the newsroom. Once there, she glanced down the long hall to advertising and the executive offices. If there was a policeman in the building, she couldn't see him.

"You're the topic of the day," Sally Ferguson said from behind her.

"What do you mean?" Claire edged past the other reporter and made her way to her desk. Casey's empty work space loomed.

"Policeman was already here when I got back from lunch. He's been making the rounds."

"Have you talked to him?"

Sally nodded. "He wanted to know about your relationship with Casey. How often did you go to lunch together? Did you get along? Was there competition between you? And then the kicker. Were you two having an affair?"

Incredulous, Claire peered at Sally. "You've got to be kidding? So, I'm still the main suspect, and they think I rammed into him because I was either mad or jealous?" She shook her head. "Our police department has been watching too many cop shows on TV." Claire shoved her purse into the file cabinet drawer and sat down at her desk. She switched on her computer.

Sally slid into her own desk chair and smiled over at Claire. "Don't you even want to know what I told them?"

"Of course, I do."

"I told them you were friends. That you tried your best to get along. And that you're not really *into* men right now. But you're not into women either. I didn't imply that."

"Thank you, Sally." Claire sighed. She put her elbows on her desk and rested her head on her hands. Denver was out of jail, and now she was being investigated for a crime she didn't commit. Could things get any crazier? "When the DNA evidence comes back from my SUV, and they find some strange fingerprints or DNA, this will all blow over."

"Don't you mean *if* they find some strange DNA evidence?" Manny's voice carried across the room from the doorway.

Claire lifted her head. "I guess they talked to you, too."

"Oh, yeah. But there is good news. Casey is in stable condition. He's in a private room."

"I'll go see him over morning break, if there isn't anything else you need me to cover this morning."

"Press conference about the new park on the west side of town. Casey's usual beat. I thought you might like to get out of the office."

Claire glanced out the narrow window between her desk and Sally's and then looked at her editor.

"Yep, it's raining," Manny agreed. "But they'll have the conference set up in the picnic shelter. Eleven a.m. You can go there straight from the hospital." Manny checked the sheaf of papers in his hands and looked over at her.

She nodded. "I'll do it." She didn't mind getting out of the office, and light rain was a perfect match for her mood.

Chapter 40

Casey had just been given a dose of pain meds when Claire arrived at his hospital room. They spoke briefly before his eyes clamped shut and his breathing deepened. His wife, Marjorie, remained seated in the chair beside the bed.

"Nice of you to stop by," she said as Claire moved toward the doorway. Casey snored softly from the bed.

"I'm glad he's doing so well. I'm stunned that whoever ran into him had just stolen my SUV."

"Guess that'll teach you not to leave your keys in your car." Marjorie frowned at her.

"I didn't. They were stolen a few days ago. Frankly, I thought I'd just misplaced them, but I was wrong."

"You've told the police?"

"Yes. But I'm sure they're not taking my word for it. I hope they find the thief and nail him for the hit-and-run."

"Me, too." Marjorie settled back into the chair and picked up her paperback book. "Thanks again for coming by."

The gentle rain had turned into a deluge and was coming down in sheets when Claire emerged from her car at the new park's shelter house. Claire flipped the hood up on her rain slicker and ran for cover, assessing the group of people huddled inside the large shelter as she moved. She recognized the mayor, the parks director, and several city counselors. They weren't the people she was used to dealing with and for a minute, she wished she'd handed off the assignment to Sally. She never seemed to know what to say to the mayor and his staff. Politics wasn't her thing.

Someone jostled against her.

"Didn't expect to see you. Not your usual assignment," Reed Morgan said.

Claire shook her head and raindrops flew around her. "No, it isn't. But the regular government reporter isn't available today. Why are you here?"

"Guess who loaned the city the money for construction costs? Temporarily, of course. The project is covered by an appropriation of sales tax."

She stepped deeper into the shelter. "You've got your finger in lots of pies, don't you?" As soon as the words were out of her mouth she wished she could pull them back in. She sounded like a sarcastic b. Not good timing.

Reed blinked and shrugged. "That's the business I'm in, Claire. Loaning money for various projects."

"I didn't mean that like it sounded. I'm glad you're in that business. And I appreciate your help with my own 'project'."

"You're welcome. Now, excuse me. I must speak to the mayor before this ceremony gets started." Reed pushed through the small crowd, heading toward the spot where the mayor's staffer was setting up the microphone.

Claire glanced around at the crowd, keyed in on the park director, and headed her way. She liked the lively woman and respected the way she stood up to questioning from the mayor and the City Council. The director would answer her questions quickly and concisely, and probably provide a great quote to use for a headline.

Rain still dripped from the sky hours later as Claire drove home after work. She pulled the rented SUV into the garage. As she climbed out, tires crunched on the gravel drive. She glanced over her shoulder; Holt parked his truck and hurried toward her, sidestepping a few puddles on the driveway in his leather loafers.

"Have a good day?" He leaned in for a kiss as if their 'friends only' conversation on Sunday had never happened.

Claire ducked her head to avoid the kiss, unlocked the back door, and stepped inside. "You must have been watching for me to get home."

"No, I just drove up myself, and saw you pull in." He followed her into the kitchen.

She considered what to tell him about being a suspect in Casey's accident, about the short hospital visit to Casey, about the run-in with Reed at the news conference. But in her mind, none of them was the most important part of her busy day.

"Denver's out of jail. I picked him up this morning and brought him home. He and Jenny are together."

"So, you sprung for his bail, and then you brought him here?" Holt sat down at the table. Izzy and Ranger barked and whined on the back porch.

"Of course. Where else would he go?" Claire grabbed a glass and filled it with cold water from the tap on the refrigerator door.

"You're going to let him spend the night in your house, after what he is suspected of doing?" Holt boomed. His icy blue eyes flashed. "I should camp out on your sofa tonight. You may need protection."

"You're being ridiculous. Denver didn't kill J.B. Floren. There's no reason to make him find another place to stay."

He shoved the chair back and moved to her, his hands outstretched. "Please reconsider. For safety's sake. I care about you."

Claire's resolve didn't waver. Denver was wrongfully suspected of murder. He should return to her home. It had been his home too, since January. "I believe in Denver's innocence. What kind of message would that send to the sheriff, or to the world, if I refused to let him stay here?"

Holt's eyes narrowed. "You're more worried about public opinion than your own safety?"

"Holt. Stop."

"Okay." He lifted his hands. "I hear you loud and clear. You won't listen to reason. At least, not from me."

He stomped across the room and out the back door, leaving it ajar. Rain tapped on the roof.

Claire trod through the kitchen to the porch door. She let Izzy and Ranger in, patted their heads and gave each a rawhide chew stick. Outside, rain poured from the gutter's down spout and ran into the yard to pool on the sodden grass. She trekked back into the living room and collapsed on the sofa, leaning back into the soft cushions.

Ranger nudged her hand with his big head, and she scratched the sides of his skull. When she stopped, he nudged her hand again. He laid his head on the cushion and sat close. She scratched a little more.

She'd made Holt mad. It didn't make her feel good, but she wanted to have an honest relationship with him. She wanted that kind of relationship with any person in her life. If you couldn't tell the truth and agree to disagree, if need be, what kind of relationship was it, really?

Maybe Holt would leave her alone for a while.

And it seemed that the stalker was inactive as well. She hadn't heard from him in days.

Casey was recovering and Denver was out of jail. Things might be calming down. With any luck, she would get a good night's sleep.

Chapter 41

The front storm door latch opened. Ranger jerked his head out from under her hand and dashed for the door with Izzy. Claire glanced at the mantle clock. Six p.m. The evening news had just come on.

"Son? In here," she called.

Cade barreled into the living room, the dogs pranced beside him. "Did you bail Denver out?"

"Jenny was here when I brought him home this morning. Denver's been with her all day, and I don't expect to see him tonight."

Cade's shoulders slumped. "Oh. I guess that's good. Ought to cheer him up quick." He sat on the ottoman and petted the two dogs. Izzy stood on her hind legs and tried to lick his face.

"Denver needs cheering up. He looked so pale and downhearted on the way home. He lit up like a lightning bug when he saw Jenny waiting for him on the porch."

Cade gave Ranger one last scratch. "Good. I'll go take care of Blaze and Smoky. What's for dinner?"

Claire hadn't considered dinner, but she had an easy fix. "How about pork tenderloin, asparagus and mashed potatoes." The idea of those aromas floating through the house made her mouth water.

Cade grinned. "Sounds great." His smile faded. "Is Holt coming over?"

"No. He's angry I've let Denver come back to live with us."

"Figures. He wants to control you, Mom. Can't you see?"

"Yeah, I see. I'm not interested in Holt Braden."

Relief flooded Cade's face.

Cade strolled off to the kitchen, where he dished up kibble and filled the dogs' water bowls.

Decision made.

The tightness in the muscles across her upper back eased. Denver was out of jail, Holt had finally gotten the message, and the stalker was not engaging with her anymore. The knot in her stomach was gone. It was time to devote her full attention to finding J.B. Floren's murderer, and the silent partner.

She'd put out some feelers among her contacts, including Reed, but if those actions didn't provide a lead soon, she would go to the county clerk's office and check land ownership records for The Cimarron Valley Rescue Ranch. If ownership was listed as an incorporated entity, she should be able to find the owners listed through the Oklahoma Department of State database.

She turned up the sound on the news broadcast so she could hear it better from the kitchen, and headed to fix dinner.

When her favorite TV detective show ended hours later, Claire clicked off the television and downed the last drop of wine from her glass. The wine had done the trick. She was tired and her thoughts had slowed to a crawl, instead of racing around inside her head like they had for the past week.

Her cell phone rang from the sofa table a few feet away. She let the call go to voice mail. Then she carried her glass to the kitchen sink. On the way to the bedroom, she picked up her phone and listened to the message. Lucia Valdez said, "Call me, Claire. Please."

Claire returned the phone call immediately. "Lucia, is everything all right?'

"Is your nephew out of jail?" Lucia sounded worried.

"He's not home. He's with his girlfriend."

"Can you call him, warn him?"

"About what?"

"I have a bad feeling. He's being set up for more than the drugs. They're going to make sure Denver goes to jail for J.B.'s murder. Something's going to happen, I know it. You've got to get him home, and keep him there."

"He's a grown man, Lucia. I have no control over him. He'll do what he likes."

"You don't understand. Remember what they could have done to Petreus? And still might do? Call him, Claire." Lucia disconnected.

Claire punched off her phone and laid it on the sofa beside her. She grabbed it again and clicked through her contact list. The only number she had for Jenny was the salon's number. She scrolled back through recent calls and found Jenny's call last week. The same number as the salon.

Denver didn't have a phone. He hadn't wanted one when he first came here. He said he didn't know anyone who would call him, and if he wanted to reach his mother, he could borrow Claire's phone, couldn't he?

She considered the message from Lucia. Was it worth a drive into town to try to find him? She didn't know Jenny's address. Besides, they were two adults, alone together on a rainy night. Chances were that whatever they were doing, they wouldn't want to be disturbed.

Her cell phone rang again. She punched the phone on without looking at the ID screen. Lucia again?

"Claire? Enjoying a TV night? Have you disconnected your house phone?" a breathy male voice asked.

Claire dropped the phone. She dashed to the living room light switch and flicked it off, dousing the light from the lamps. She darted from window to window, adjusting the drapes to close any gaps. White noise roared in her ears.

She hammered on Cade's bedroom door and threw it open without waiting for an invitation.

"Mom? What's wrong?" Cade looked up from the floor where he sat braced against the bed, his head phones on and his iPad on his knees.

"Someone's outside. Watching." She covered her face with shaking hands and gulped back a sob. "It's happening again." She sucked air as the room spun.

"Want me to go outside and see?" Cade bolted out of bed and started for the hallway.

She grabbed his arm. "No. Don't do that." She held onto him and tried to breath slower. The room came into focus. Her heart slowed. "It's probably nothing. A wrong number." *But he'd said her name.*

"Are you sure, Mom? Really, I can go check."

"I'm tired, and the wine's gone to my head. I'll go to bed."

"I think we should call the police."

"Forget it, please. Your mom's having a wacky attack. Sorry." She backed from the room and closed the door. Her hammering heart had slowed, but was still beating fast. She closed her eyes and counted to twenty, opened them and listened before she scurried back to the darkened living room. She paused in the doorway.

A low, dark shape moved across the carpet from the kitchen. Her heart stopped.

Ranger whined and nudged her clenched fist with his nose.

"Oh, my God." She dropped to the carpet. "I'm going crazy. I truly am."

Claire held the warm dog, her head on his shoulder, feeling his gentle, even breathing on her neck. Gradually, her pounding heartbeat slowed. She thought about the gun and the box of bullets on top of the cabinet.

After she'd crossed the room to retrieve them, she held the gun gingerly. Images flooded her mind, lightning flashed and she imagined Max Dyson, illuminated briefly, stroking her body. Then, the race to the apartment's living room. And finally, the gun blast.

She closed her eyes.

Ranger whined again. Claire's mind jerked into the present.

"Come on, boy. You're sleeping with me tonight." The dog followed her and curled on the floor beside the bed when she closed the door. She carefully loaded bullets into the gun clip, then stowed it and the remainder of the box of bullets in the drawer of her nightstand.

Tomorrow, she'd tell Cade where the gun was. He was old enough to know to leave it alone; he knew it wasn't a toy. It would be a good idea for the two of them to take gun safety lessons and learn how to shoot.

Rain splattered against the bathroom window while she washed her face, brushed her teeth, and slathered on lotion. When she finally climbed into bed, her mind still raced.

She had expected to feel more in control after Denver's release from jail. But the drug charges still hung over him. Lucia's certainty that whoever had framed him for the drugs would persist in framing him for more crimes worried her. How could she prevent it?

Her only choice was to take the offensive and get answers to all her questions. The ruined stuffed horse's head was a warning to her and to Lucia. But would the sicko perpetrator make good on their promise to do something much worse and very personal?

Claire peered up into the darkness, but no answer appeared on the ceiling above her.

His breath came in gasps as he slogged through the rain. Adrenaline raced with the blood in his veins.

His hands hurt. The gloves had not provided much padding during the attack.

He'd not been prepared for what he felt.

Anger seethed, steaming him up so he couldn't think.

HE...WAS...SO...MAD.

Not just at that woman. At Denver. At Claire.

The whole situation had gotten out of his control.

They don't listen to me.

Rain poured onto his face, his waterproof hoody didn't keep it off.

He'd show them all soon enough.

Tonight was just the beginning.

Chapter 42

The radio alarm blared. Claire opened her eyes. The rising sun peeked through a gap in the curtains. She closed her eyes again, rolled over, stretched, and wished she could go back to sleep.

She'd slept fitfully. Wine and the unnerving phone call had resulted in short periods of light sleep and crazy dreams. She'd been awake when Denver came home.

Her head pounded.

Claire showered, dressed and put on her makeup. When she stopped to wake Cade on her way to the kitchen to make breakfast, she found both his bed and the bathroom empty.

In the kitchen, the aroma of coffee floated in the air. A dirty mug on the counter indicated Denver had begun his usual morning work routine.

The kitchen door to the garage stood open, and on the opposite wall of the garage, Denver's door stood wide open, too.

"Hi, Mom." Cade lumbered into the kitchen from the back yard, grabbed a day-old bagel and a small bottle of orange juice from the fridge, and hurried to the front door. "Bye, Mom."

"Cade?" She grabbed at his arm but missed. She needed to talk to him about last night, and to tell him about the gun. This morning, last night's freak-out because of the phone call seemed absurd. It had been raining, no one had been outside looking in. The call had been intended to frighten her. And it had succeeded. In the morning light, the remembered fear made her angry.

Out on the driveway, a car door slammed and an engine revved as Antonio backed his car down the drive.

Her cell phone vibrated on the kitchen countertop, then rang; the caller ID read *Sheriff.*

Too early for the sheriff to be calling. *Something was wrong.* "Hello?"

"Claire, is Denver Streeter there?" The sheriff's voice blasted.

"He's out in the barn, working."

"Don't let him leave. I'm on the way."

Claire's thoughts raced as she disconnected. Lucia had warned her last night. Was Lucia's premonition already coming true? She looked out the window at the barn just as Denver led Blaze into the adjacent training ring. The horse trotted in a circle while Denver held a slack rope and snapped a short whip close to his own body. Ranger lounged in the grass a few yards away. Izzy dug frantically at a mole mound close to the barn.

Blaze cantered around, around, around. Denver's mouth moved with words only the horse could hear. In a few minutes, he slackened the rope. When he eventually dropped it, the horse stopped and tossed her head, whipping her mane from side to side and blowing air from wide nostrils.

Claire's coffee cup trembled and liquid sloshed over the cup's edge and onto the countertop. She dumped the coffee into the sink, nauseated by the smell of the liquid she usually craved in the mornings.

An engine roared up the driveway. Seconds later, boots stomped on the porch and someone pounded at the front door.

When Claire pulled the door open, Sheriff Anderson, Deputy Purdue and two other uniformed men stood with their hands held ready above their holstered weapons.

"Ms. Northcutt, is Denver Streeter here?"

"He's out back in the training ring. What's this about?"

The sheriff's brow furrowed. He nodded at his companions, and the two of them stalked off the porch and ran in opposite directions to circle the house. "We found Jenny Prather beaten in her apartment. A neighbor identified Denver as having been there last night."

Claire stepped back from the door, feeling as if someone had punched her in the stomach. Lucia's prediction resounded in her head. Denver was in trouble again.

Shouting erupted behind the house, accompanied by angry dog barks. The sheriff leapt down the steps and hurried away. Claire rushed to the kitchen window in time to see one of the uniformed men haul a handcuffed Denver up from the ground and shove him across the yard. Ranger stood stiffly a few yards away, snarling and barking. Blaze trotted to the far end of the training ring, snorting and pawing at the ground.

"I didn't do anything," Denver shouted at the deputies as they pushed him toward the cruisers in the driveway.

"Stop." Claire ran up and reached for Deputy Purdue's arm, but he shrugged her away.

"Let me do my job, Ms. Northcutt." Purdue turned back to Denver.

"You have the right to remain silent ..." one of the deputies recited to Denver while the other pushed him toward the vehicles and prodded him into a cruiser.

Sheriff Anderson sauntered up to Claire.

"Guess you know where he'll be. Any questions, call me." Anderson scurried off to his vehicle while the other sheriff's department vehicle zoomed down the drive. Claire stared after them.

Jenny beaten? Denver arrested? Could things get much more messed up? And just last night she'd had the stupid thought that it was all smoothing out.

Holt's dually king cab pulled up the driveway. Claire's stomach clenched. She turned away and climbed the porch steps. The wooden slats tilted beneath her feet and the walls of the porch undulated. She grabbed the porch rail.

"Claire, what's happened?" Holt asked from behind her.

She pulled herself onto the porch.

"Are they taking Denver back to jail?" Holt pounded up the porch steps.

"It has to be a misunderstanding." She pushed the front door open and hurried across the living room. "I've got to call Trina Romero."

"The sheriff must have had good reason to arrest him again." He followed her.

Claire snatched the television remote, clicked on a news channel and dashed to the kitchen to her cell phone. Claire punched into the directory listings and made the call. With her back to Holt, she told Trina the news.

"Mind if I make a cup of coffee?" he asked.

She shrugged.

Holt pulled a K-cup from the storage drawer. He placed it in the coffee maker, and leaned against the counter as the coffee maker gurgled and filled an empty mug with steaming coffee.

She ended the call and placed the phone on the counter.

"Will you listen to me now? Hope you're not planning on posting bail a second time."

"Denver wouldn't hurt Jenny Prather." Claire gritted her teeth as tears welled in her eyes. "You should see them together. They are in love."

"So you say."

"He wouldn't hurt her." Claire rubbed her forehead. She didn't believe for one minute that Denver had hurt Jenny, but someone had.

Holt poured milk into his coffee, dug a spoon from the silverware drawer and stirred the beverage. "You're going to have to face reality one of these days. The man is wounded mentally." Holt chugged half the mug of steaming coffee.

Claire's head filled with noise. She rushed to her bedroom and threw herself on the bed like a teenager. Tears rolled down her cheeks.

In the kitchen, she could hear Holt making himself another cup of coffee. The deck door slid open and closed. Ranger and Izzy barked in the back yard.

This is too much. She pulled in a deep breath and exhaled before she walked back to the kitchen. "Ranger, Izzy, stop it," she shouted from the door. She swiped the back of her hand across her wet cheeks.

Holt had grabbed Blaze's rope and was leading Blaze toward the barn. He disappeared inside with the mare. When he appeared again, the dogs kept their distance. Ranger growled low in his throat.

Holt crossed the yard to the house. At the sliding door, he wiped his feet on the doormat and slid the door open.

"You've lost your hired man," Holt called to her, "and you need help."

He washed his hands at the kitchen sink.

"I have a light day. Let me work at your place, muck out the stalls, exercise the animals. Then Cade won't have so much to do when he gets home from school. Maybe he and I can hang out a little while."

She willed her mind to tell him *no*, but the words caught in her throat. Claire grabbed her purse. "I have lots to do today. Thanks for the offer to help. We are a little behind. I'll take you up on it." Her voice shook.

"I'll go home and put on work clothes, come back and clean the barn. My work can wait. Don't worry about anything."

"I appreciate it." The week without Denver's help to care for the animals had worn her out even though Cade had taken on most of the chores.

He smiled. "I'll even fix dinner tonight. It'll be waiting when you get home. You can have a glass of wine and relax."

She wished it was possible to relax.

In her rental car, on the way into Stillwater on the wet highway, she thought about Jenny and Denver. She'd seen the way the two of them looked at one another yesterday. *He couldn't have hurt her.*

Claire checked the vehicle's dashboard. She hadn't bothered to sinc it with her phone, otherwise, she could have used the steering wheel buttons to place a call through the Explorer's audio system. She pulled out her cell phone and punched the sheriff's autodial. "I want to talk to you about Jenny Prather," she said when Anderson finally came on the line. "You've arrested the wrong man. Wasn't Jenny able to tell you who hurt her?"

"Ms. Northcutt, Jenny Prather is in a coma in critical condition. As far as Denver Streeter, witnesses saw him with her, and he's already the primary suspect in a murder," the sheriff countered. "Soon we'll have DNA from the scene, and I'm confident it will match Mr. Streeter's."

"He readily admits to being there, doesn't he? Doesn't mean he beat her up."

"I'm sure there'll be DNA to back it up."

Claire waited for more, but the sheriff waited, too. After several quiet seconds, he said, "You can make an appointment to talk with me about this but a better use of your time might be to visit Ms. Prather in the intensive care unit at the hospital."

Jenny's face flashed into her mind, and then Denver's.

What had happened last night? And how had Lucia known?

Chapter 43

Claire detoured to the strip mall and the hair salon on Perkins Road. The sign in the window read *CLOSED*, but fluorescent lights blazed inside. As she cruised by, someone walked through the shop. Claire angled into a parking place.

She rapped on the window and Shea crossed the interior to unlock the door. "Did you hear about Jenny?" Her cheeks were wet with tears.

"Yes. Are you okay?"

"I will be when she's out of ICU." The hair stylist's voice shook. "Someone nearly killed her." Shea locked the door after Claire had stepped into the shop.

Claire's mind was full of questions. Had Denver said or done something to make Jenny end their relationship? Had they argued?

It didn't matter. She was certain Denver would never have laid a hand on Jenny. But as long as his girlfriend remained in a coma, no one had the answers; Denver would stay in jail.

"Did Jenny talk about Denver?"

"*Did* she?" The young woman's face broke into a sad smile. "She's madly in love with him. And you can see he loves her, not just lusts after her like some of her clients."

Had another man been jealous enough to beat Jenny because she loved Denver? "Like who?"

"Lots of guys." Shea's eyes misted over. "She was pretty and nice to everyone. Guys came in for haircuts and manicures. They'd start stopping in without an appointment, saying they needed a quick trim when they only wanted to see her. She'd shift them to one of us. Guys recognize a brush-off."

"Anyone in particular who was not happy?" Claire's question echoed in the empty shop.

Shea swiped at her tears. She rushed to the desk and thumbed through the pages of the appointment book. "Yeah. A regular of Jenny's. An older guy, way older, and Jenny didn't want a sugar daddy."

Claire looked over Shea's shoulder at the appointment listings when the stylist pointed at a name in the book. *J.B. Floren.*

"He was still good looking. But Jenny wasn't interested. He sent daisies a couple of times, from 'Your secret admirer' but we all knew who sent them."

Why had Jenny not told her about J.B.'s flirtation? He'd sent daisies, like her own anonymous admirer/stalker.

Claire scanned the open pages of the appointment book. Reed Morgan, Holt, Manny, Casey and even Kent Purdue. All regular customers at Clippers Hair Salon.

"Has the sheriff talked to you or anyone here at the shop?"

"No. Alexis, the assistant manager, called me this morning about Jenny. Today was my turn to open the shop, so I came in to cancel and reschedule appointments. Then I'll go to sit with Jenny at the hospital." She pulled a tissue from a box on the desk and blotted her eyes. "Do you think one of her clients did this?" Shea glanced out the front window at the strip mall parking lot. Beyond it, a steady stream of cars zoomed past on Perkins Road.

"All I know for sure is that Denver couldn't have done this. He loves her. And they've arrested him."

"Oh, no," Shea moaned. "It wasn't Denver. Guys hit on Jenny everywhere. Here. At the Red Angus. We meet there after work sometimes, like Monday night when we celebrated Denver getting out on bail."

"Did anybody bother her that night?"

"Sure. Lots of guys talked to her. Some may be clients, but I don't know their names."

"Tell the sheriff about the Red Angus. It could be a good lead."

"You think her attacker was at the Angus Monday night?" Shea glanced outside again, then scanned the shop's interior. "I don't want to be here alone."

"Don't stay here."

Shea followed Claire out of the shop and ran across the parking lot to her car while Claire climbed into her rented Explorer. She took the fastest route to the newspaper office, down McElroy to Duck, past The Red Angus.

Not long after moving to town, she'd been to the Red Angus with Reed. Most weekends, the bar featured a singer or local band on stage. The paper often assigned a reporter to review the entertainment. That assignment had recently fallen to the newest staff member, Casey.

Shea could be right–an admirer had homed in on Jenny and followed her home Monday night. Maybe that admirer returned to her place Tuesday night, saw Denver, and paid Jenny an angry visit afterward.

"Manny? Got a minute?" Claire knocked on the door frame of the editor's office.

"Claire. About time you got here." Manny set down his coffee cup and crossed the room scratching his head. "Guess you've heard about Jenny Prather."

"Deputies came to my house and arrested Denver this morning. It makes no sense to me. She was the most important thing in the world to him."

Manny shrugged. "Maybe they argued. Maybe she had another fellow. Maybe he was jealous. Is that why you're late? You've been at the hospital?"

"It hasn't been a good morning." Claire had earned Manny's criticism. She hadn't exactly been a reliable employee lately.

"The phone is ringing off the wall. Need you to do a background on Jenny for the news article about her assault. You know the drill." His brown eyes softened. "I'm sorry about Denver. Guess they'll finger him for it until she wakes and tells them different."

"He loves her, Manny. No way he did this."

"The truth will come out. As long as Jenny Prather survives." Manny stepped over to his printer, grabbed a sheet of paper and carried it back to his desk.

Claire stumbled as she headed for the newsroom.

As long as Jenny Prather survives.

Chapter 44

As Claire worked, she kept typing the wrong words, making grammatical errors and writing incoherent sentences. After fifteen minutes of unsuccessfully editing a one-page news article, she pushed out of her chair and hurried across the newsroom past Casey's empty desk.

She'd forgotten to ask Manny about Casey's condition. When she went to the hospital later to check on Jenny, she'd stop in and see Casey, too.

Light poured through the open door of the newspaper morgue. Maggie hunched over her desk, arthritic hands dancing on the keyboard. As always, the room smelled of vanilla from the melted wax in the electric pot.

"Maggie, got a minute?"

The librarian tilted back in her creaky wooden desk chair and looked over her reading glasses at Claire.

"It's your lucky day. Filing, as usual. What can I help you with?"

"Floren's obituary ran Sunday, didn't it?"

"Yes, and so did your article about the mustang rescue ranches."

Claire grimaced. She'd seen her article with the Associated Press tagline, the one Cassandra Winchell had complained about, the same one she'd asked Manny to hold just in case the rancher wasn't the shining star of mustang rescue she'd made him out to be. She'd not bothered to glance at the short obituary Casey had written.

"Do you remember what services are planned?"

"I've got it here." Maggie's fingers whipped across the keyboard and in a few seconds the obit flashed on the computer screen. She scrolled to the last paragraph and read aloud, "Funeral services have not yet been announced."

Claire scanned the screen over Maggie's shoulder. "No survivors are listed, either."

"Nope." Maggie moved the cursor back to the top of the article and scrolled once again to the end.

"Any clues who paid for funeral services and embalming?"

Maggie shrugged. "His estate, I guess. And whoever's in charge of managing things after his death. He was currently unmarried. The executor of his will is probably some attorney."

"How can I find out who that is? According to a source of mine, J.B. Floren had a silent partner."

"Check with the funeral home. Says in the obit that O'Shaunessey's will announce graveside or memorial services later."

"You know anyone there?"

"Brian O'Shaunessey went to school with me umpteen years back. I think his son Joe runs the place now. Give him a call."

Claire headed for the break room, her thoughts swirling. A tray of chocolate cupcakes sat on the bar by the sink; the delicious smell permeated the small room. Claire passed by the sweets and moved on to the soda pop machine. She needed to think clearly, not zone out on a fast sugar high. She selected a diet soda and slid a dollar into the machine.

What could she say to the mortician to get him to reveal who paid for J.B. Floren's embalming and burial? 'I've been out of town and just heard the news. I'm devastated. Can you tell me how to get in touch with his partner?' Or, 'He was like a father to me, and I want to talk to his partner about having a memento from the estate." Maybe, 'Floren owed me money. I need to talk with the representative of his estate.'

She didn't like any of those options. But then, she thought of one that might work. 'I owe Floren money. I have not yet paid in full for the burro I bought from him earlier this year. Do you have a contact number for his partner?' That might work. Claire didn't owe him money, but she'd promised the service of her son and Denver for as long as J.B. needed them. In return, he'd cut her a deal on the burro. The request was believable.

Claire moved into the break room and found it empty. She sat at a table in the back of the room and made the call from her cell phone.

"Funeral home," a woman said in a solemn voice.

"Could I speak to Mr. O'Shaunessey, please?"

"Who is calling, and what does this concern?"

Claire pulled in a quick breath and forged on. "It's a business matter—I owed Mr. Floren money—perhaps what I owed could be applied toward his final expenses."

"Hold on for one minute please, and I'll get Joe."

After a brief pause filled with an orchestral version of a classic Beatles hit, the funeral director came onto the phone.

Claire repeated her request.

"Ah, that's nice of you. I'm happy to take your name and number and have his lawyer's office contact you about your offer and your debt."

He wasn't going to give her the name.

"I wonder how long it will take for them to call me back?"

"I have no way of knowing."

"On second thought, maybe I should wait until they contact me to settle the debt. They probably don't want to deal with this right now. Thanks for your time." She hung up, fully aware her number had displayed on the funeral home's caller ID screen. Claire might get a call from the lawyer or the partner. She would wait.

Next, she called Trina Romero.

"I'm leaving for the jail," Romero said. "These new charges are circumstantial at best. He'll be released within 48 hours unless they have substantial proof."

Trina sounded so confident. Claire hoped she was right.

Claire called the jail to speak with Denver. According to whoever answered the phone, Denver was unavailable for phone calls. What did that mean? Was he in solitary confinement?

She wandered back to her desk and glanced at her assignment list. Plenty of pieces to write, enough to fill every minute of the day without breaks. Just as well. She had to get her mind off Denver in jail and Jenny in the hospital, like Casey.

Would Jenny wake up today and tell the police who had attacked her?

The alternative–that she would never wake up again–was unthinkable.

At the hospital, Claire asked for Jenny's room number; her friend was still in the ICU unit. She followed the signs to the ICU, where she spoke to the head ICU nurse.

"Only family is allowed inside. Who did you say you were?" he asked.

"I'm a close friend, practically family. She has no family in the area. I want her to know someone cares."

"Okay. I guess it won't hurt to let you see her for a moment, since she hasn't had any other visitors. She's still unconscious. This way."

The nurse punched the access button. Air laden with the smells of disinfectant and cleanser rushed out as the doors opened and they entered. Once inside the unit, he led Claire past the nurses' station to a cubicle and parted the curtains. Claire gasped. Jenny lay in the bed, her face swollen purple, blue and red. *Unrecognizable.* Bandages covered one ear, the side of her head and both arms.

"Jenny?" Claire whispered.

Her friend lay still. The monitor on an adjacent machine registered a regular heartbeat; another displayed her oxygen level.

Claire stepped up to the bed. Lightly, she touched Jenny's hand. "I'm so sorry. Please wake up and tell us who did this to you."

Claire sniffed and blew her nose. Her throat clogged.

Jenny in the hospital; Denver in jail. Could things get any worse?

Chapter 45

Once again, Claire sat in the entry hall of the Payne County jail. The place smelled like high school, the same floor polish and vague cleanser smell, mixed with human sweat.

A policeman called her name and she joined him for the same walk down the same hallway she'd travelled before.

"Wait here."

Claire studied the institutional green walls. Light green was calming, wasn't it? Why did it make her feel trapped?

Denver was escorted in, hands cuffed. His eyes were wide, his hair disheveled. "What's happened to Jenny, Claire? No one will tell me anything. They keep asking me the same questions. What happened?"

"I heard you come in at one a.m. But what happened before that? Did you and Jenny argue?"

"You sound just like the f-ing police. No, we didn't argue. She brought me home, and she was fine when she dropped me off."

"She brought you home?"

"How else would I get there? She was at the house when you brought me home yesterday morning. I didn't have my truck, remember?"

"And you've told the police this?"

"At least a half-dozen times. What happened to Jenny?" His eyes pleaded.

- 223 -

"Someone beat her up last night. She's in a coma."

Denver's mouth dropped open. "Who?" he stammered.

"No one knows. Jenny can't tell anyone anything right now. Did she mention anyone bothering her or trying to get a date? Had she noticed anyone following her?"

"She never said anything like that. She wasn't seeing anyone else." He cradled his head in his hands.

"Maybe she didn't *have* another boyfriend, but that doesn't mean someone didn't want to date her. Maybe they want you out of the picture so they can."

"You think someone framed me for the drugs so they could date Jenny? And then they beat her up?"

Claire shrugged. "It's possible."

He stared at his cuffed hands. "I know other guys were interested in her. I saw how they'd look at her at the Angus or when we went out to dinner."

"Anyone in particular?" Denver shook his head. "Who flirted with her when you were out together?"

"A few people said hello."

"What about people you knew from the ranch? Did you ever see any of them when you were with Jenny?"

He rubbed his thumbs together. "I don't know. I was always so focused on Jenny. I just don't know."

The question opened doors in her own mind. *Could* there be a connection between Jenny, the planted drugs and the murder?

Chapter 46

Ranger raced down the driveway to greet her as she pulled into the drive. The happy dog, long tail wagging, revealed Cade was home from school and Holt was not here.

She squatted and hugged the animal. "Hello, you. I've been to the hospital to see Jenny. She looks awful. Who did this to her?"

The dog panted and listened, leaning into her, seeming to encourage her to speak. She scratched his ears, sat on the ground and squeezed back tears. The dog pushed closer and whined.

"I'm coming apart. It's all so unfair to Denver." She wiped her cheeks with the backs of her hands.

"Mom? What are you doing? You going to fix dinner?" Cade called from the porch.

"In a minute, son."

Claire sat quietly on the thick green grass, accepting the comfort Ranger gave.

The dog fit in so well at her home it was easy to forget Ranger didn't live here. "Do you miss Floren?" She asked speaking into the animal's ruff. Izzy barked from inside the house; Ranger flinched.

"Woof." He looked at her, every muscle in his body tensed.

"It's okay. Go. Find Izzy. I'm fine." She stood and trudged to the house as the dog raced ahead of her. It seemed odd that no one had asked about Ranger since J.B. Floren's death. The dog had been here an entire week.

Why had no one asked about Floren's dog, not even Cassandra?

Cade and Claire sat down to a dinner of steaming macaroni and cheese with smoked sausage and buttered peas. Holt had not called, and there was no sign that he had worked around the house as he'd promised. She clanged the silverware against the plates as she sat the table.

"You don't think Denver had anything to do with Jenny getting beaten up, do you Mom?" Cade slid into his chair and grabbed a biscuit to slather with apple butter.

"No. Someone else did it. A client, maybe. Or a person she met at the Red Angus."

"The Angus? Is that where she hangs out?"

"Not usually. But she and some other women from the shop went there after work on Monday."

"Denver had nothing to do with Jenny getting beaten up, the drugs or Floren's murder. You should call and talk to the sheriff, Mom. Be a character witness or something."

"I have talked to him. He doesn't seem to put much stock in anything I say."

"But this is different. Someone's got it in for Denver. We've got to figure out who it is."

"There isn't much I can do."

"You can prove someone else did it. Investigate on your own."

"That's a tall order, Cade."

"But you've got sources. You know people. Surely one of your connections can help figure out who's doing these things to Denver."

Cade peered at her across the table, his eyes bright and full of conviction. She wished she could be as enthusiastic as he was. Instead, she felt a weight on her shoulders and a sense of hopelessness that was immobilizing.

"I'll give it some thought. After dinner." She dished macaroni and cheese onto her plate. "Can we talk about something else?"

"I've got tons of math homework tonight. And all the chores." He stuffed another spoonful of macaroni into his mouth.

"I'll help you with the outside chores after dinner so you'll finish faster. But before that, I want to ask you about J.B. Floren."

He chewed a mouthful of food, then swallowed. "Yeah? What?"

"Did he ever say anything about a partner?"

"Nope."

"So, you think he ran the place all by himself? Nobody else ever gave orders? No one else was hanging around there all the time?"

"People came and went, Mom. He sold horses and burros, remember?" Cade took a long swallow of water and continued to shovel food into his mouth.

"How about someone else who made decisions? A business partner."

Cade chewed and swallowed again. "Nope. No one went into the office except J.B. He kept it locked. Even warned me to stay away. 'If the place catches fire, don't go in to save anything, hear me? Let it burn.' No lie. Exact words. I never went near the office." He scraped his plate clean and laid his fork and knife across it. "Why are you asking all this stuff, Mom?"

"I don't think the sheriff is looking at anyone but Denver. And if he doesn't have any other suspects, he'll continue to push Denver as the guilty party." Unlike Cade who devoured the food on his plate, Claire had only picked at her food, stabbing noodles with her fork and then pushing them off.

She wasn't hungry. The image of Jenny in the hospital bed–her bruised face bandaged, her eyes swollen shut–was superimposed over the image of Floren at the base of the flagpole where she had found him last week.

Her brain raced. Were the two crimes connected? Jenny knew Floren; she cut his hair. The only other person who was directly involved with both people–that she knew of–was Denver.

Chapter 47

Claire rinsed the dishes after dinner and joined Cade in the barn. She mucked out the stalls and two days' worth of feces and urine-soaked straw. The burro had been rolling in the straw; bits of hay and manure clung to his back. She brushed the animal; his hide quivered as she worked. Blaze rolled her eyes at the two humans and laid her ears back, seemingly scolding them for her lack of exercise.

What had happened to Holt's promised day of work and supper? She glanced at his house. The shades were drawn.

As soon as they'd finished the work in the barn, Cade mowed the back yard. Claire filled the gasoline-powered weed-eater and trimmed along the sidewalk and the fence posts. A dry westerly breeze had been blowing all afternoon, and finally, as the sun dropped in the sky, the wind calmed.

Cade hurried inside the house to work on his homework as dusk fell, leaving Claire to put the equipment away. As soon as the clean-up was done, she stopped at the horse's stall. Gently, she stroked Blaze's face. Horse breath tickled her cheek.

"I know you miss Denver. I've got to convince the sheriff to consider other suspects. See you in the morning."

Claire turned off the light in the barn and closed the doors. Outside, she lifted her face toward the western horizon. A pair of crows flew overhead, heading east, cawing with each flap of their wings. She breathed deeply, pulling in all the smells of spring, and relaxed for a moment as the sun dropped below the horizon.

"Claire?"

Holt crossed the yard towards her. He reached for her hands as he stepped up, but she tucked them into her pockets. "I'm sorry I didn't help today like I promised. I drove to Oklahoma City to deal with an emergency."

"I wondered what had happened." She folded her arms and waited, expecting a more detailed explanation.

"I promise, if nothing intervenes, I'll be your slave tomorrow."

"No need, Holt. Cade and I worked all evening. We've cleaned the barn and Cade mowed the grass while I edged."

Holt surveyed the yard. "Well, grass grows and stalls get dirty. You can count on me in another couple of days."

"If it works out." She turned toward the house.

"In the meanwhile, I'll make dinner for you and Cade tomorrow."

"Not necessary. I need a shower. I smell like the barn, and I feel gross. See you later."

He walked with her to the back door. "I really am sorry, Claire."

She flashed him a small smile and stepped inside the house, leaving him on the back porch.

He owed her a better explanation. She didn't see any way they could ever be more than friends.

Claire headed for her room, intending to take a long, soaking bubble bath and let the scent of lavender empty her brain. Cade stepped out of his room.

"Mom? Is Ranger with you?"

"Haven't seen him for a while. Did you check outside?"

"I've been calling him. Izzy's here, but not Ranger."

"Maybe he caught the scent of a rabbit or something and is off hunting. He's a smart dog. He'll find his way back here."

Grumbling, Cade headed back to his room. He'd gotten attached to Ranger, and so had she. The dog was a protective animal, and affectionate, too. He'd probably be back in the morning, waiting outside to be fed.

Just before midnight, Claire's eyes flashed open to the blackness of her bedroom. Something had awakened her, and not the usual nightmare–killing Max.

She climbed out of bed, padded across the room to the window, and opened a crack in the drapes. The full moon illuminated the yard and wind-driven shadows became strange moving shapes beneath the oak trees. Then, one of the shadows moved. A figure with a familiar stride trekked away from the house.

Cade?

Claire dropped the drapes back into place and switched on a lamp. She pulled on jeans and a sweatshirt, socks and running shoes.

Where was he going?

Claire locked the house, pocketed her keys and jogged into the moonlight. A chorus of frogs blasted the damp night air with their croaks. Cade's shadow figure was now about an eighth of a mile in front of her. A great horned owl hooted to her left and as she crossed the bridge over the creek, three bats swooped c.

Twenty minutes later, her heart pounded, and not just from the lengthy jog. Cade had slipped through the gate to Cimarron Valley Rescue Ranch.

Claire paused to catch her breath before she shimmied through the barbed wire fence a block from the gate. She'd stepped into the middle of a grove of fragrant sumac. The bushes rustled as a creature–a rabbit?–startled from its sleep and leapt away.

What was Cade doing? Someone was probably staying at the ranch. They might call the police. Cade could be arrested for trespassing, or, depending on his intent, something even worse.

Why hadn't Cade told her what he was planning? She'd have found some way to make it happen legally, without trespassing in the dead of night.

She pushed through the bushes and farther into the ranch.

Chapter 48

Claire circled a grove of persimmon trees and trudged through ankle-high weeds on the ridgeline that rimmed the valley. Below, Cade's shadowy figure jogged across the headquarters plaza. She picked her way past small trees and plowed through last year's waist-high grass.

A coyote yipped to her left by the river's oxbow; another howled in response a half-mile away. Neighboring dogs serenaded the moon, their voices splitting the quiet night like bugles playing Reveille. She scanned the shadows and listened for movement.

The headquarters compound lay in the valley below her. She watched and waited for a sign as to where Cade had gone.

The house's dark windows remained black.

A light on a pole near a barn shimmered on the long metallic husk of a horse trailer that had been backed against the gate of the biggest corral.

On the other side of the courtyard, Cade darted beneath a mercury vapor security light. Seconds later, a light flicked on in a building at the east end of the compound.

Claire picked her way down the rutted road to the river rock plaza. Crime tape still flapped around the central flagpole. A horse neighed in one of the barns.

The side door of the small barn gaped open; light streamed into the black night. Claire stepped inside and made her way around equipment placed haphazardly throughout the long room. At the barn's far end, another door stood open. A padlock dangled from its broken latch.

Drawers slid open and snapped shut.

She trod softly toward the open door and eased into the room. On the far side of the space, Cade peered into the bottom drawer of a gray file cabinet. The upper drawers hung open, empty. Other office furniture remained, but everything else–pencil holders, pens, staplers and the other accoutrements of an office–was gone.

Claire breathed in the stale, musty air. "Cade?"

The teenager's body jerked and he looked up. "What are you doing here, Mom?" He glared.

"What are *you* doing here?" Claire fired back as she crossed the room.

"Looking for Ranger. He had to have come back here, but he's not here."

"You think he'd be in this office?"

"You said Floren had a silent partner. I thought something might have the partner's name on it."

"You broke in, Cade. You should have talked to the sheriff first. And to me."

"The sheriff is convinced Denver did it." He slammed a desk drawer. "We're too late. They've cleaned everything out."

Tiny feet scurried in the corner of the office, behind one of the filing cabinets.

Mice.

Cade was right, there could be something here that would indicate a partnership. Claire wandered the room, looking behind the furniture, under the desk, beneath the file cabinet for scraps of paper, receipts, anything.

"There's nothing here," Cade said, scowling. "And there's no sign of Ranger, either."

Claire glanced over at the copy machine in the corner. How many times had she left an original on the machine at work and had to go back to retrieve it? She crossed the room and lifted the top of the copier. A sheet of paper lay face down on the glass. She read the receipt, dated a week ago, the day before J.B. Floren had been murdered.

"To CB Processing." She read the top section of the page aloud, and scanned the accounting columns below. "This statement is stamped 'paid' for twenty-five horses and seven burros, dated two months ago. What's CB Processing?"

The itemized list of horses and seven burros included descriptions of each animal—bay, black and white pinto, chestnut, gray, roan—and each animal's approximate age. The notation 'sold to a good home' followed each entry.

Claire peered closely at the signature on the paper. It seemed familiar. Then, she knew. She'd seen this signature before on the sales contract for her grandfather's farm. *Corbin Brook.*

Cade read the page over her shoulder. "Denver thought J.B. was sending the horses to slaughter, Mom. He wasn't rescuing them. If we hadn't bought Smoky when we did, he'd have been in the next trailer, shipped out to a dog food plant in Missouri. CB Processing must be the place he was sending them to."

"Or else it's the middle man–the transporter," Claire suggested. Her mind whirled. *Corbin Brook.* He'd bought her grandfather's farm. And abandoned it, leaving a gully full of animal bones. *Mustang bones?*

"Denver was so mad. He came in here to get a piece of equipment. J.B. must have been in this office on the phone, probably laughing about 'making glue' and dog food." Cade's voice trembled as he spoke. "He was a liar and a crook. 'Rescue ranch.' Some rescue."

Pair an animal lover with a scammer who delivered his 'rescued' horses to slaughter, and what did you get? Murder? *Denver?*

"We need to go, son. The police have been here, maybe they recovered some files before the place was cleaned out. If they found this information it might seem to prove Denver's guilt. This could give him a motive." Claire folded the paper and stuffed it into the pocket of her jeans. "This won't help him or us."

"But Mom, Floren was a liar. We should tell people. And we have to find Ranger."

Claire thought of Lucia and Cassandra Winchell. Did both women know the rancher's true purpose for bringing the mustangs and burros here? Had the farce started all those years ago before Cassandra divorced J.B.?

At the office door, Claire picked up the broken padlock. It was irreparable. She hoped Cade had found it already broken. If so, someone had been here before. Looking for what?

Claire and Cade hurried across the grounds of the compound. Claire thought of all the crime novels she had ever read. Neither she nor Cade had worn gloves tonight; their fingerprints were everywhere. It would be easy for the police to determine who had been in the office, if the sheriff cared.

Claire scanned the deserted ranch. No lights anywhere. The place appeared empty, but that didn't mean it was. The hair on the back of her neck raised. Someone could be here, watching them from inside a building.

Floren's silent partner?

Back in bed at home, Claire tossed, twisting the bed sheets and tumbling her pillows to the floor. She and Cade could be charged with trespassing, possibly even with breaking and entering. They had both left fingerprints in the office. No way could she help Denver if she was in jail, too. And forget raising bail. All her funds were tied up in Denver's original bail bond.

'We weren't really breaking and entering, Sheriff,' she imagined saying. 'Floren told Cade to stay out of the office. His curiosity got the best of him. Besides, there was nothing there to find except one receipt on the copier.' Mentally, she prepared her speech, hoping she would sound contrite when she delivered it. And there was the kicker, the truth about the true purpose of Floren's 'rescue' ranch. That truth could cement Denver's guilt in the eyes of the law.

Ranger had not been home when they returned. Her stomach knotted with worry. The dog had been so good about staying close to home in the time he'd been with them. Why would he run off now?

Had something happened to Ranger? She didn't want to think about the stick horse head in Lucia's shed. If it had been a warning, and it was meant for her, too, had someone done something to Ranger?

She scooted across the bed to where the sheets were cool and jammed a pillow over her head. Sleep was unlikely, but she had no desire to read or watch late-night television. As painful as it was, she wanted the evidence she'd found on the copier to recirculate in her mind. She wanted to think about Corbin Brook and his connection to the Cimarron Valley Rescue Ranch.

Could Corbin have bought her family property to build a slaughterhouse? She'd seen no evidence of one during her last visit, or any of the previous ones. But there were portions of the farm–like the southwest corner–where she never went.

She knew that the existence of wild pigs on the farm was not a lie. But had Corbin perpetuated that myth to keep her away from the area? Was that where the slaughterhouse had been built?

Her mind spun with the possibilities as well as the coincidence that she had been the one to write the article about the Rescue Ranch, made J.B. out to be a hero, and then found him, murdered, at the ranch headquarters. And all the while, her former land was being used to slaughter the very animals she'd lauded him for saving.

Sleep would not come.

This hand is killing me. Bad enough to have bruised it on her face last night, but then the damn dog took a chunk out of it. Should have killed the beast. Would have, if that witch hadn't stepped in to stop me.

She can't be out of my life soon enough. Complete opposite of Claire.

I'd be off my rocker if I didn't know what was coming when this was all over. That sweet smile. That body. All mine.

Nothing to stand in the way. No dogs. No son. No 'maybe' boyfriends.

Just her and me.

For as long as I can make it last.

Surely that animal had his rabies shot this year. Floren wouldn't have neglected that, would he?

A good splash of hydrogen peroxide ought to help. Dad's cure-all for anything and everything. Stuff still brings tears to my eyes.

But it'll all be worth it.

She's worth the pain. And worth the wait.

Chapter 49

Hours later, Claire squeezed lubricant drops into her eyes to eliminate the reddened blood vessels crisscrossing them. The cool liquid briefly eased the discomfort. She dabbed concealer on the gray pouches beneath her eyes. *What a nightmare night.* She and Cade *had* been at the ranch office; it hadn't been a dream.

She trekked into the kitchen and peeked out the window, hoping to see Ranger curled up asleep near the back porch. She stepped outside. "Ranger?"

No dog.

Cade emerged from his bedroom, and Izzy raced to where Claire stood in the kitchen drinking coffee.

"Is Ranger back?" Cade yawned.

She shook her head. He sighed and headed to shower.

Claire broke the speed limit on the way to work, keeping a wary eye out for the police or the sheriff's department. She did not want to test Manny's patience again.

At her desk, she flipped on her computer and focused. When the internet search engine opened, she typed in 'CB Processing,' and clicked on the first link provided. Photos of a factory appeared. An aerial view showed stockyards behind the factory, as far from the road—and the public eye—as they could be located.

Claire rubbed her forehead and closed her itching eyes. *This is horrible. And to think I wrote an article praising the man. I gave him national publicity.* She could imagine the silent partner–was it Corbin Brook?–laughing, as well as anybody else familiar with Floren's 'real' business.

She stewed over this new knowledge. Mentally, she revisited the murder scene, replayed finding J.B. Floren at the flagpole. A deputy had opened the barn door and Ranger had raced out growling. Growling at who? Strangers in general, or someone specific? Ranger knew the killer. But did the killer know she'd given Ranger a new home? Had they come to her place and taken Ranger away?

Claire phoned Reed at the bank. "J.B. Floren did his banking with you, didn't he? Did he have a partner?"

After a pause, Reed said, "Claire, that information is bound by a confidentiality clause. I can't discuss our depositors without a subpoena."

"I'm not going to publish it," she insisted. "I need to know. Who's taken over operations, watering the stock, feeding the animals? Those mustangs and burros can't care for themselves."

"Those animals did it on the western free range, didn't they?" he scoffed.

"And they were starving." She waited, hoping he would give in and tell her what she wanted to know.

"Why are you asking this? Why does it matter?"

Her mind raced to come up with a logical explanation. "Surely someone–his partner–wants to know what's happened to Ranger?" She wouldn't tell him Ranger had disappeared.

"The dog?" Something buzzed in the background. "Sorry, but I've got another call on hold. We'll talk later, Claire." The banker disconnected.

Claire traipsed to the newspaper morgue. The lights were off but the door stood open. Claire scooted in at Maggie's desk. She flicked on the computer. When the machine had booted up, she searched again for articles about J.B. Floren or the Cimarron Valley Rescue Ranch. The search of the paper's archives provided nothing she had not already seen. She typed in 'horse rescue.' The search engine reported no results. She typed in 'starving animal.' Five stories popped up, all about puppy mills or animal hoarders. She typed in 'horse slaughter.' She got the message 'no files found.'

The idea of the rancher having a silent partner had seemed unlikely when Lucia first mentioned it. But now she knew what the ranch's true purpose was, it seemed logical. The partner would have been protected if J.B. Floren's real intent was discovered. What if her upcoming article had caused the rancher's death because someone feared the publicity would result in an investigation? Maybe the partner had killed him to protect his–or her–identity.

What was it she'd said in the article, 100 mustangs and burros on the place? With so many animals, shouldn't she have seen or heard a few of them last night?

Maybe their carcasses are scattered across the ranch. Maybe they are all already dead.

A long horse trailer had been parked close to the corral last night. Maybe someone–the partner–had moved the livestock under cover of darkness.

"Claire? What's happening?"

Claire flinched when Manny stepped into the morgue. "Crap, Manny. Quit sneaking around."

"You're deep into something. New investigative article?"

"No. I can't get past Floren's murder. And Jenny's assault."

"And it doesn't help that Denver is in jail and the primary suspect for both crimes, does it?"

She didn't need to be reminded about Denver's current stay in jail. The police still had 24 hours to officially charge him in Jenny's case. "I wonder what's happened to those mustangs and burros since the murder. Are they being fed and cared for? Do you think he had a partner?"

"Wouldn't he have told you if he did? I'd think his partner would want the same kudos Floren expected after the article came out."

"But what if the partner didn't want kudos? What if he didn't want the article printed at all?"

"So, tell me—what do you think that rancher was up to? And how come you just got a whiff of it after the story went national?" He held out a copy of the Denver Post, featuring her story and her by-line on a story from the Associated Press, *Oklahoma Rancher Praised for Rescue Efforts.* A small box at the bottom of the article noted J.B. Floren's unsolved murder.

By 3 p.m., the headache she had been trying to ignore all day exploded. She'd been arguing with herself about calling the sheriff and telling him what she suspected, but that meant admitting that she and Cade had been trespassing, opening the possibility of a charge of breaking and entering.

Her vision swam; her head pounded. Even the soft swoosh of the now-computerized printing press sounded like a jackhammer. She raided the medicine cabinet in the ladies' room for pain meds, took three of them and dragged herself into Manny's office.

"I've got to call it a day. I'm leaving early; you're not going to get anymore work out of me when my head feels like a vise is clamped on it. I'll make up the time."

"Go home," Manny said without looking up. "We'll talk about it tomorrow.

Chapter 50

In a roundabout way, the Cimarron Valley Ranch lay in the direction of home, or so Claire told herself. The worry about the horses had exacerbated her headache. And as much as she knew she should go by to see Jenny and Casey, she would not have been good company for either. The empty ranch weighed heavy on her mind, and so did Ranger. What had happened to the dog?

As she neared the ranch, Claire watched for the change in the fence line indicating J.B. Floren's property. When she drew alongside his red pipe fence, she slowed and looked for burros or mustangs. The oak trees and eastern red cedars grew so thick in some placed it was impossible to tell if animals grazed among or beyond the trees. She pulled into the short, graveled entry.

The red gate swung back and forth in the southwesterly breeze. The lock and chain hung from a nearby post. Claire pushed the gate all the way open, and drove over the rise to view the headquarters area.

The horse trailer was gone and the ranch headquarters looked even more deserted in daylight than it had last night. A lone hawk soared overhead, and a trio of grasshopper sparrows whistled nearby in the green grasses. She let out a sigh of relief when she saw no vultures soaring in the skies above the ranch.

No vultures meant the mustangs and burros weren't lying dead anywhere on the acreage. But her mind raced on to their alternative location: a processing plant.

Claire drove the few miles back to her house, her brain jumping from Brook to Floren to the ranch and to her grandfather's farm. The bones she had seen in the ravine had a new meaning. They could have been the bones of Corbin's personal farm animals, as she had first thought, or they might have been the bones of mustangs from J.B.'s ranch. That brought up another question. Had Corbin been the rancher's silent partner or only assisted in the disposal of the animals?

A quick check around her little acreage didn't turn up any sign of Ranger. Inside the house, Claire locked the front door and headed to her bedroom, kicking off her shoes, unbuttoning her shirt and unzipping her jeans as she walked. A shower followed by a nap in the cool sheets of her bed sounded a little like heaven; her head boomed. She could nap for a good two hours or more before Cade got home from soccer practice. She ignored Izzy's yips and howls from the back porch; the dog would settle down if she didn't let her into the house.

A delicious aroma wafted from the kitchen. Claire smiled. Holt had kept his promise and had dinner in the oven.

At the bedroom doorway, she paused. The drapes were closed, the room dark, with only a shaft of light shining across the bedroom from the master bathroom. She closed the door, dropped her blouse on the chair and shimmied out of her jeans. Forget the shower. She took an aspirin and crawled between the sheets.

Thirty minutes later when she woke up, the headache was gone. It had been replaced by a racetrack of galloping thoughts. Claire bolted out of bed and dressed, her desire for a shower gone. She stalked through the house to the kitchen and peeked inside the hot oven. Savory smells rose from a foil-covered casserole dish. A prepared Caesar salad cooled in the refrigerator, and a loaf of French bread waited on the countertop.

She glanced at the wall clock again. Possibly two hours until Cade came home. She could drive to the farm and return before Cade came home expecting dinner.

There had to be something there that would confirm what she suspected about Corbin Brook.

Chapter 51

The cross timber forest, with its characteristic scrubby blackjack oaks, flew by her window as she drove highway 77 toward Perkins and her grandpa's farm. Unlike the previous Saturday, when her mind had been full of memories of weeks spent there as a child, her mind spun with thoughts of Corbin Brook and the bones at the bottom of the gully.

She tried to remember what Corbin looked like, but when she thought of the sale closing at the realtor's office in Stillwater, all she could picture was a man wearing a hat with a wide brim hiding straggly blond hair badly in need of a cut. Had she even seen his face?

Did Corbin work for J.B. Floren? Had Corbin bought her grandfather's farm to use as a slaughterhouse for mustangs? If so, heavy trucks had entered and traversed the property. Paved roads must exist as well as the slaughterhouse. She'd seen no signs of either last weekend.

This time, when she arrived at the gate, she parked the Explorer and got out. The acres her grandfather had lived on for fifty years had not all been farmed. Native Oklahoma trees–persimmon, elm, ash, and the ubiquitous eastern red cedar–covered over half the acreage.

She paced the fence line from the farm's main gate to the gate on the neighboring property. An asphalt road began at that gate and disappeared in the tall undergrowth only a few yards inside the fence. Heavy vehicles could easily have entered that property and driven over the hill into the center of the farm, unseen from the road.

For all she knew, Corbin Brook owned the adjacent property or had purchased an easement to access the back section of his own acreage.

Claire climbed over the neighbor's gate and followed the asphalt through tall grass and oaks. Meadowlarks and field sparrows twittered, and an occasional critter rustled in the grasses. Several hundred yards in, the road angled through trees toward the property line of her grandfather's former farm.

She passed through an opening in the trees. Ahead, the ground had been cleared, and a hundred yards farther on, behind a finger of thick blackjacks, stood another wide gate and a cattle guard. Beyond that, on the back portion of the land that Claire's grandfather had owned, a group of buildings were clustered.

Claire stopped at the cattle guard. The breeze carried the heavy, putrid odor of offal and death. Nothing moved in the small complex of buildings ahead. The asphalt road connected the structures and nearby stock pens.

Gullies bisected this section of the property. In the spring, the ravines ran with water. The rest of the year, they offered dry, secluded pathways for wild critters–coyotes, deer and even an occasional mountain lion–to cross the land. She felt certain that none of those gullies were empty any more. They were probably full of bones, bleaching in the sun.

Claire approached the largest building. A padlock on a thick metal chain secured the wide doorway. She circled the building and found a second padlocked door.

She rounded each of the buildings in turn and found the same thing at each, a chained and locked entrance. There was no evidence of living animals or humans, but the stench of death hung in the air.

Unbelievable. All this had been going on right here, practically under her nose. No wonder Floren always wore a sly grin when he talked to her. Questions fluttered in her mind. Did he know the slaughterhouse was located on property formerly owned by her family?

She thought back to the time when she had first received the purchase offer for the farm. Reed had told her he had a potential buyer and facilitated the sale, knowing she needed the money to buy her own tiny acreage outside of town.

Just this morning, Reed had dodged her question about J.B. Floren's partner, claiming to have a call holding. He'd been stalling, not wanting to answer. Did he know that Corbin Brook and the rancher were working together?

Claire surveyed the area again before she struck out through the surrounding trees in the direction of the old farmhouse, nauseated by the stench hanging over the area and by the new knowledge of what Brook had been doing.

A trampled trail led through the interlocking fingers of forest and meadows. To a casual observer, the trail would look like an animal path, but she suspected Corbin Brook had used it to get from the farmhouse to the slaughterhouse. Sure enough, a few minutes later, after ducking under or pushing through hundreds of blackjack trees, she reached the old farmhouse.

Claire stopped and waited, watching for signs of activity. Once satisfied she was alone, she climbed the steps to the back porch and rattled the locked door. She backed away, grabbed a rock from the yard and threw it at the door, shattering the window. Back on the porch, she used a stick to clear away the glass before she reached in to unlock the door.

The air stunk of garbage. She wandered through the vacant house. Only an occasional worn-out piece of furniture remained–a chair or a side table pushed against a wall. The stairs creaked as she climbed to the second floor. Dim light beamed through the grimy glass panes of the windows in the two empty bedrooms. A mattress lay on the floor of one of the rooms. An old dresser held a few articles of clothing.

Back downstairs, she rummaged through the drawers of the side table and checked the kitchen cabinets. Nothing. The smell of rotted garbage turned her stomach. She pulled the trashcan from the curtained space beneath the kitchen sink.

Remnants of what might have been a chicken breast, a mashed potato container and used napkins were now molded and infested with maggots. She held her breath and dumped the garbage out onto the warped linoleum floor.

An assortment of trash, including stained envelopes stuck together with some unidentifiable liquid, plopped out on top of the rotted food. With the toe of her shoe, she moved the envelopes away from the rest of the garbage. One envelope bore her bank's logo in the upper left corner.

She picked the envelope up by the edge and slid the contents out. The letter was a thank you from the bank, and said only, "I've enjoyed doing business with you."

Reed Morgan had signed the letter.

Claire pried the other paper items apart. An electric bill. An AT&T bill for cell phone service. So much for living off the grid. She separated a receipt from the envelope behind it. *For services rendered in partnership with Cimarron Valley Ranch.* Liquids had smeared the ink, but she could decipher the initials written at the bottom, next to the typed name of J.B. Floren. By *R.M.*

Reed Morgan? She compared the handwritten initials with the signature on the letter. Claire didn't want to believe it. She compared the handwriting again. It was true. Reed Morgan had signed both.

Claire hurried away from the house toward the front gate of the property. Every step jolted her. *Reed.* She had not known him at all.

She shook her head, forcing herself out of the fog of disbelief. What was her next step?

Reed. Should she call the sheriff?

She pulled her phone out and checked the time. Cade might be home by now. She needed to hurry.

The gate came into view. Beside the parked Explorer, blocking the road, sat a black sedan, its engine rumbling.

Claire dropped to the ground, blood pounded in her ears. She lifted her head and peered between the grass stalks at the road.

No one had known she was coming here. But Holt could have seen her leave from his porch or his second story windows. Had he followed her? Someone did.

Her stalker? The rapist?

Either way, someone was waiting for her on the road.

Chapter 52

Another motor whined. An old farm truck hauling a dented horse trailer clattered over the ruts as it made its way south on the road past the farm. The black car blocking the road revved its engine and crept north as the rattletrap truck came closer.

Claire ran in a stooped position toward the Explorer, only straightening when the old truck blocked the line of vision between her and the black vehicle. She threw herself over the gate and dashed to the SUV. Once inside, with the doors locked, she checked the road. The black sedan had passed over the far north hill.

Claire pulled the SUV onto the road and gunned the engine, heading south. Seconds later, she caught up with the farmer in the old truck. She accelerated and passed his vehicle and the horse trailer, barely keeping her SUV out of the bar ditch on the opposite side of the narrow road. Behind her, the ancient truck rumbled along, engulfed by the Explorer's plume of dust. No sign of the black sedan.

Eventually, she negotiated enough turns that the dirt roads took her back to the highway. During the remainder of the twenty-minute drive home, she checked each side road and driveway she passed for the black vehicle.

At home, Claire pulled into her garage. The back door opened and Izzy raced out of the house.

"Mom? Where've you been? I'm starving. If you'd been another five minutes, I'd have eaten without you." Cade snapped his fingers and Izzy trotted to his side.

"I thought I'd be back before you got home." She cleared her throat. "Holt fixed dinner, and it looks great."

"Is he coming over?"

"Not sure, I thought so, but ..." What if it had been Holt in the black car, waiting outside of the old farm? She didn't want to believe it. But he wasn't here, even after fixing dinner for them. What excuse would he give this time? "Let's get supper on the table."

As she set out the food, her thoughts churned. Corbin Brook had been working with J.B. Floren; Reed was his associate at the bank. Reed could have been the silent partner.

Could Lucia Valdez confirm her suspicion?

"Mom? About last night ..." Cade scooted his chair up to the table.

Claire blinked. Last night? Her mind was so overwhelmed with what she'd found at the old property that it took several seconds for her to register what he meant. She nodded. "Yes, let's talk about last night. What were you thinking going to the ranch alone in the dead of night? It was dangerous, and not smart."

"I get that. First, I was thinking about Ranger, that he might have gone back. When he wasn't there, I decided something in the office might clear Denver."

Claire had to admit her mind had run down that same path.

"And you were right there with me. You didn't drag me out of there, you dug around, too. And you were the one that thought to check under the copier lid."

She couldn't argue with that.

"How are we going to convince them Denver is innocent of everything? And what are we going to do about Ranger?" Cade picked up his fork and cut into the pork tenderloin and mashed potatoes.

Claire didn't want to tell him about the possible connection between Corbin Brook and Floren. And as far as Ranger, all she could do was report him missing. Meanwhile, she'd pray they didn't find the dog out in the yard, dead. Inwardly, she shivered as she thought of the stuffed horse's head on the floor of Lucia's shed.

Cade laid his fork across his clean plate and rose from the table. "Jeremy's coming to pick me up, Mom. I need to go to the library to look at this book my teacher wants me to quote in my paper. She wants something besides internet sources in the bibliography. I'll be back by ten. Okay?"

"I guess so." She followed him into the kitchen with her plate, the food on it barely touched. "I wish you would have checked with me earlier, though." A nervous twinge pinched her stomach at the thought of spending the evening alone. The black car had followed her to the farm. And her stalker knew where she lived, and had a set of keys.

Do locksmiths work 24/7?

"Why? You don't usually care. What's different about tonight?" He went back to the dining room to carry the rest of the dishes to the kitchen.

He didn't need to know that their family property had gotten caught up in the rancher's hideous enterprise. Hopefully, it would never become common knowledge.

A horn sounded out on the driveway. Izzy barked. Cade shushed the dog as he grabbed his backpack and headed out the door. "Be back later, Mom. Lock the doors."

Claire finished rinsing the dinner dishes and placed them in the dishwasher. She wandered to the front window to peer out in search of the black sedan. A neighbor scurried down the street, pulled by her dog on a leash, and a boy zipped past on his scooter, making wide arcs from side to side. A normal night in the neighborhood.

From the kitchen window, she studied the streaks of pink and orange edging the clouds. Outside, the beautiful sunset would be a 360-degree show, with the thin cloud smears in the eastern sky also glowing with fuchsia and gold.

Claire grabbed her jean jacket and her phone, let Izzy out and cautiously followed her into the backyard, after scanning the nearby properties for activity. The dog raced off, scooted under the fence at the back of the property and dashed for the creek. Outside the barn, she paused for a better look at the sunset. The breeze that licked her face smelled of fresh grass and earth. Smoky brayed in the barn.

She dug into the pockets of her jacket, searching for a leftover sugar cube or piece of carrot, anything to give the animals. Her pockets were empty except for her cell phone.

As she watched, the sunset display and the clouds faded to blue-gray. Claire could no longer hear Izzy barking. She glanced over her shoulder toward the house. She shouldn't be out here alone. With Ranger gone, and Izzy off somewhere, she had no alarm system to warn of an intruder. Should she go get the gun?

It was not yet dark, and there were people about on the nearby street. She would be fine.

Get the gun, her brain urged. She shook off the sudden fear, telling herself that nothing would happen.

Claire shoved the barn door open and walked into the cool interior. Dusky horse scent and acrid manure smell filled her head as her eyes adjusted to the dim light. The animals greeted her, their necks extended over the tops of the half-doors.

"Hey, you two." She reached one hand to each animal, scratched behind their ears and stroked their soft muzzles. "What a day."

Blaze blew air out of her nostrils in agreement. Smoky jerked his head up and down.

For a moment, she relaxed in the quiet. Blaze nudged her hand with her head. "I know, I know. It's getting late, Cade isn't home, and you haven't been exercised." She pulled out her cell phone and glanced at the time. A short ride would do the horse good and maybe relax her a little. The muscles across her back ached.

Claire grabbed her saddle, blanket and halter from the tack area and hauled them to the stall. As she saddled the horse, her mind shifted to Holt. He'd pulled another disappearing act today. Cooked dinner for them but didn't show up to eat it himself. Where was he?

Blaze tossed her head. Claire threw on the saddle blanket and hoisted the saddle onto the horse's back. She cinched the girth and slid on the bridle. Blaze rolled her tongue around the bit.

"Okay, okay. One more minute and we'll go. Let me give your little buddy something to keep him happy while we're away." She scooped oats from the barrel into a metal bucket, poured them into Smoky's feed bin and set the bucket on the floor.

Blaze stomped her foot and swished her tail at a buzzing horsefly.

Outside the barn, Claire swung into the saddle. She circled Blaze in the yard, and then led her toward the house. Her stomach tightened when her thoughts returned to the black sedan.

Her cell phone rang. She checked the ID screen. *Lucia?* She punched the button to accept the call.

"Lucia? What's up?"

"I need to see you, Claire. Can you come here, first thing tomorrow?" The woman's voice was strained.

"I can stop by on my way to work, if that's not too early." Claire guided Blaze toward the east property line.

"The earlier the better."

"See you about eight." Claire disconnected.

Now what was that all about? She needs me to stop by, and I need her to confirm that Reed was Floren's partner.

As she shifted her weight to slide her cell phone back in her pocket, Blaze side-stepped, startled by movement in the grass, real or imagined. Claire tightened the reins and clutched her phone.

Blaze shied again, ducked to the left and bucked, kicking out her hind legs.

Claire catapulted from the saddle and landed on her bottom; the phone flew from her hand.

"Oof." The hard landing pushed the breath from her lungs. She tried to pull in air for a half-minute before she could breathe again.

Ignoring a pain from her backside, she scrambled to her feet and lunged unsuccessfully for the horse's dangling reins. "Whoa, girl. It's okay."

The horse's wild eyes rolled. She backed away and lifted on her hind legs, thrashing her front hooves dangerously close to where Claire stood.

"Calm down, Blaze."

The horse neighed and tossed her head, the muscles in her withers quivered. Legs stiff and apart, she watched Claire approach.

"You're okay. It's all right." Claire eased toward the animal, repeating the words in a quiet, low voice until she could grab the reins and step closer. She stroked the animal's neck and Blaze whinnied, still unsettled. Claire glanced back to where the mare had bucked her off. In the deepening gloom, she couldn't see her cell phone in the yard. Blaze pulled against her lead.

"Okay. That's my girl. Let's walk back to the barn." She would look for the phone in a few minutes, on the way back to the house.

Claire stroked the frightened animal with one hand as she led her toward the barn. Crickets and frogs croaked and peeped. A great horned owl hooted.

The horse's steps quickened.

"Time for a good brushing and oats, okay?"

The horse nickered as if she understood. With one hand, Claire rubbed her hip, where she'd slammed into the ground. *Ouch.* She'd have a good-sized bruise come morning, on the opposite hip from the bruise she'd gotten when the horse bucked her off last Sunday.

Inside the barn, Smoky brayed; Blaze neighed in response.

When Claire led Blaze to her stall, the mare tossed her head and snorted.

"We've had enough of an adventure for tonight." Inside the stall, she stood close to the horse's head and stroked her velvety nose. Claire loosened the girth, pulled off the saddle and the saddle blanket. She worked the bridle off the horse's head, and slipped on the halter.

"Let me put away your saddle, and we'll walk the ring a bit. Easy. One minute, Blaze." Claire lifted the saddle from the ground and backed out of the stall.

A hand clamped over her mouth and an arm circled her waist.

Her body stiffened and panic closed her throat as she struggled against the tight grip.

Chapter 53

"Shhh. You can comfort the horse, why not me?" A voice whispered in her ear. "Give me a little of what you've got. Come on, Claire."

A moist tongue licked her ear lobe. She kicked back with one leg and her blow landed on a knee cap. The arm and hand dropped.

"You hurt me," the man groaned.

Claire whirled, dropped the saddle and faced her assailant, her hands fisted. Adrenaline raced through her body.

"Purdue?"

The deputy grabbed her again. He cinched her waist tightly with both arms and straddled her legs with his own. She kicked out, lost her balance and fell against him.

He nuzzled her neck, holding her fast against his solid body.

She jerked her head. The hardest part of her skull smashed into his nose.

His arms released her and he staggered away. Blood dripped down his chin. "Is this how you want to play it?" He swiped at his chin and glared.

"Get off my property."

The man chuckled. "You really are something. I like your fire. It'll be good, honey. I promise."

"Leave. Now."

"It's not over until I say it's over." Purdue leapt and grabbed her, his arms squeezing, his legs spread to avoid her kick. They wrestled and slammed into the side of the barn. Claire scrambled for a foothold, but the deputy held her above the floor. Her feet flailed uselessly. He threw her to the ground and straddled her, pinning each of her arms at the wrist.

Claire stopped struggling. He leaned over her, grinned and kissed her closed mouth. He shifted, crushing himself against her, his hardness pressing her pelvic bone.

She jerked her head but he found her mouth again, nipped her lips, licked them. "Like that, baby?"

The big man held her immobile, his body stretched to cover her torso, his full weight pressing her down into the hard earth floor.

"I can't breathe," she croaked into his open mouth.

"Hmmm." He nibbled at her lips. "You taste so good. Tell me you like this."

Every inch of her screamed *No*, but she didn't have the breath to scream. She groaned, and when he lifted for an instant to look at her, she sucked in a quick, shallow breath.

"You like it. Hmmm." He shoved himself against her again and again, each time harder than the previous. His breath grew hot and fast.

His full weight pinned her. He pushed her wrists together above her head and locked them with one hand. With the other, he unbuckled his belt.

She twisted her body, trying to ease the pressure and pull air into her lungs.

The light from the overhead bulbs began to dim.

Behind them, in the stall, Blaze screamed. Her hooves slammed into the board walls.

Purdue's weight shifted. Claire sucked in a breath, arched her back and squirmed. His weight slid partially to one side.

She quickly folded her body and jammed both knees into the soft tissues of the man's midsection.

"Ugh," he groaned. He covered his crotch as he rolled on the ground.

Claire staggered to her feet, gulping air.

Purdue glared, still holding himself. "I should beat you half to death like I did Jenny. You girls are all the same."

Claire's blood chilled.

He clambered to his feet.

Blaze thrashed in her stall, lashing out with her hind legs, pounding them into the walls. Claire grabbed the pitchfork that rested against the end of the narrow barn. She lifted the implement and pointed it at Purdue. "Don't come any closer."

His fists clenched and unclenched. "You've ruined the atmosphere. I've been dreaming about this—" He kicked the empty oat bucket, sending it flying across the barn. "You're too smart for your own good, Claire."

"Stop." She tightened her grip on the pitchfork.

"Stop," he mimicked.

Blaze burst through the open door of her stall.

The 1200-pound horse slammed into the man and raced out of the barn.

Kent Purdue lost his balance and pitched toward Claire.

The pitchfork jerked from her hands.

Chapter 54

Purdue fell to the floor, the tines of the pitchfork half-buried in his torso. Uneven circles of deep red bloomed on his shirt.

"Claire?" someone shouted. Outside the barn, Blaze whinnied.

Claire backed away. Her ears buzzed.

Blood. So much blood.

When arms encircled her, she batted them away. "No."

"Claire, it's me. You're okay." Holt's voice spoke clearly in her ear.

Purdue tried to sit up. He fell back and groaned.

"Blaze rammed him into the pitchfork," Claire whispered. She rubbed at her wrists; her hands tingled from lack of blood flow. "He attacked me."

"Help. Please," her attacker moaned.

"Go in the house, Claire. Call the Sheriff," Holt said.

"Purdue beat up Jenny and framed Denver. I think he planted the drugs."

"Go inside, sweetheart. I've got this."

Holt turned her around and urged her through the barn door. She pulled in a shaky breath and marched to the house, a sob hitching in her throat and tears swimming in her eyes.

Mary Coley

"*Now let me* get this straight," Sheriff Anderson said. Red and blue lights swirled in the blackness outside the front windows. An ambulance rumbled away from the house and into the neighborhood. "Purdue attacked you, and during the process he admitted he beat Jenny and framed Denver to break the two of them up?"

"Yes." Claire sat beside Holt on the sofa, his arm snug around her shoulders.

He peered at Holt. "Tell me why you got here, just in time."

"The media mentioned the owner of a black car wanted as a possible witness in the rape cases," Holt explained. "Tonight, as I drove home, I noticed a black car parked in a neighborhood alley. No one ever parks there. When I stopped to check on the closest neighbor, I heard Claire scream. But I was too late, it was over when I got here." He pulled Claire closer, and frowned. "Thank God that pitchfork was handy."

"You didn't see what happened?"

"No, but it was clearly self-defense."

"Purdue said she attacked him."

"That's crazy. The man is a rapist. He's been stalking her."

"I want him arrested, Sheriff." Claire pulled away from Holt to sit forward on the edge of the sofa cushion. "I'm filing charges. Purdue is lying. The man would have raped me. And he admitted that he assaulted Jenny."

The sheriff shook his head. "We'll have a guard on his room at the hospital, and he'll face charges for the assault. And about Jenny," the sheriff added. "I had word from the hospital about her condition. Her vital signs are strong and she could wake any time. Once she does, signs point to a complete recovery."

"And what about Denver? You'll release him immediately, won't you, based on Purdue's confession?" Claire insisted.

"You're the only one who heard his so-called confession. I'll talk to the judge. But there's still the matter of the drugs. And as for J.B. Floren's murder, the way I see it, nothing's changed. Denver is still our primary suspect."

"Purdue framed Denver for one crime, he may have framed him for the murder, too."

"Ms. Northcutt, he may have planted the drugs and beat Jenny Prather, but nothing tells me he killed that rancher. He had no motive. In fact, the more we've learned about Floren, thanks in part to his ex-wife, the more I believe it likely Denver Streeter *did* kill that rancher."

"I don't care what Cassandra said. What about the silent partner? What about the shadow slaughterhouse they were running? Have you questioned Reed Morgan?" Claire grabbed her purse and dug out the correspondence she'd found earlier that afternoon in the trash at the farmhouse. She handed the soiled papers to the sheriff.

"Quite a jump from banker to silent partner and slaughterhouse operator." He glanced at the receipts and then laid them on the coffee table. "Where did you get these, anyway?"

"Sheriff, I'm sure Claire would agree with me the important thing is to gather the evidence that your former deputy was the man terrorizing and raping Stillwater women and stalking Claire," Holt said. "My first priority is to see him behind bars for a good long while."

The sheriff lowered his head and stared at Holt. "We're on the same page, Mr. Braden. The investigation into J.B. Floren's murder will continue. Meanwhile, I'll leave you two to ponder what else you think you know. Let's have this conversation tomorrow morning, in my office."

The sheriff headed for the front door, but the door burst open before he reached it. Cade pushed past the sheriff and into the house. "Mom? What happened? Why are the police here?"

"It's okay, Cade. I'm okay."

"What happened?" His look bounced from Claire to Holt Braden.

Claire rubbed her forehead.

"One of the sheriff's deputies attacked your mother," Holt said. "He'd apparently been stalking her."

"Someone really was stalking her?" Cade rushed across the room. "Mom?" Cade's forehead furrowed with worry.

"The man you met at the Hideaway, the same man who arrested Denver. Deputy Purdue." Claire took a deep breath, and forged on. "He admitted to stalking Jenny and framing Denver to get him out of the way. After she and Denver spent Tuesday together, he broke into the apartment and beat her. And he's been after me, too."

"I should have been here tonight, Mom. None of this would have happened."

"It would have happened, Cade, if not tonight, another night."

"I'll leave you to talk with your son, Ms. Northcutt. And I'll see you in the morning." Sheriff Anderson closed the door as he left the house.

Cade pushed his hair off his forehead. "So what about Denver? If that deputy admitted he framed him, won't he be set free?"

Claire managed a smile. "The charges for Jenny's assault will be dropped and possibly the drug charges. But he's still a suspect in J.B. Floren's murder."

"You'll get the bail money back."

"I will. But Denver is still a suspect, Cade. The sheriff intends to solve the murder. As much as we'd all like this to be over, it isn't yet."

Cade's expression darkened. "What about the ranch office? Totally cleaned out. That's suspicious. Did you tell the sheriff?"

Clare smiled wryly at her son. "I can't do that, Cade, without admitting that we were there."

"When were you two at the ranch?" Holt asked.

"It doesn't matter." Claire shook her head and sent Cade a warning glance. She stood, rubbing her forehead. "And I'd like to take a bath and relax. I'm exhausted, and I've got an early appointment in the morning."

"My cue to go." Holt scratched his head as he headed for the front door. "Goodnight, Claire." He made no effort to hug or kiss her.

"G'night, Holt." She closed and locked the door behind him.

"I'm not a little kid, Mom. You should have told me you thought someone was stalking you." Cade dropped onto the sofa. "That was why you were so freaked out about that phone call the other night."

Claire looked at her son, inches taller than she, all arms and legs and red acne bumps on his face. He *wasn't* a little kid anymore. "I should have, son. Next time–and hopefully there's not a next time–I will let you know."

As water poured into the tub, she added two capfuls of her favorite bubble bath. Her muscles ached and the back of her head hurt where she had slammed Purdue's chin. The fight–the whole evening–didn't seem real.

And Holt had left her tonight without even a kiss on the cheek.

After what she went through with Purdue, it would have been nice to have had a hug.

Chapter 55

Claire rolled out of bed. Every muscle in her body cried out, from her neck to her ankles. And the bruise on her butt hurt. She thought about calling in sick to give her muscles time to heal from last night's attack.

"Mom?" Cade knocked and threw the door open. "Ranger's still not back. Did you call the dog pound?"

She nodded. "And I'll call again today from work. They have no dogs at the shelter that fit his description, and no one has called about a stray. Maybe he'll show up today."

"What if someone shot him, thinking he was a coyote or something?"

Claire didn't tell him that she'd been thinking even worse things. Ranger knew who killed Floren. Would the murderer have 'taken care' of Ranger, to be sure he was not identified by the dog? Another possibility was that Ranger had gone to the ranch, found it empty, and gone to Lucia's. But wouldn't she have let Claire know that the dog was there? Was that why Lucia wanted her to come to her ranch?

She could be all wrong. Who knew what went on in a dog's head, or a human's.

If the murderer had lured Ranger away, they'd never see the dog again.

Claire drove directly through Lucia's open gate and onto the ranch. During the drive, she'd watched the countryside between the ranch and her neighborhood for Ranger, but had seen no stray animals.

She walked the flagstone path to the front door. The day was already humid, with the southern wind carrying moisture from the Gulf of Mexico 600 miles to the south.

Flowering vines covered the lattice of the portico, buds ready to open. She concentrated on the blue morning glories, bright against a green background. Cushions on a chaise lounge matched the Talavera tiles on a nearby wrought iron table. Despite the festive air, Claire's mood remained somber.

Her body wasn't the only thing that ached after last night's scuffle. Emotional bruises hurt, too. A second attack by a stalker in three years. What was it about her behavior that drew these men to her? Was she subconsciously asking for their attention?

Her thoughts returned to the counseling sessions she'd attended for months after she'd shot and killed her first attacker. The diagnosis had been extreme anxiety. She'd been afraid to socialize or be seen outside of the house. With the counselor's help, Claire had finally accepted that nothing she had done had drawn the man to her. She had simply been sought out by an unstable person.

She wondered, was that also true of Purdue? She hadn't met the man before Floren's death. But once he had made the connection between her and Denver, his plan must have quickly fallen into place. She shuddered at the thought of what could have happened last night if Blaze had not rushed out of her stall. Would she have killed him, or would the threat of the pitchfork have made him back off?

Claire lifted her hand to knock, but before her hand connected with the wood, Lucia opened the door. Behind her stood a much younger version of herself, with green eyes rather than brown. Deep dimples pitted the girl's cheeks even though she wasn't smiling. She peered behind Claire as if she'd expected someone else to arrive.

"Come in, please. Claire, this is Graciella. Gracie is what she wants to be called, but I love the old name, my mother's name."

Claire smiled at the young woman. The girl turned away and rushed through the living room toward the kitchen. Lucia's daughter, or a relative? She and Miguel looked enough alike to be brother and sister.

"We'll sit on the patio. Graciella will bring us coffee in a moment, and breakfast bread."

"What is it, Lucia? I'm on my way to a meeting, and then work. You sounded as if it was urgent that I come by, but I don't have time for breakfast and chit-chat."

Lucia continued toward the patio.

"Is Miguel here?" Claire asked.

"He's at school. Graciella is visiting."

The woman seemed subdued. Rather than appearing interested in talking with Claire, she didn't even look at her. Instead, she stared out at the pasture where three horses grazed halfway between the house and the Cimarron River.

"Are you all right, Lucia?" Claire asked as she dropped into one of the cushioned seats on the patio.

When Lucia finally looked at her, she stared at Claire's bruised cheek. "You've been hurt."

Claire saw worry in her eyes, and something else. "A man assaulted me last night. He was the man responsible for planting the drugs that led to Denver's arrest. He also beat up my friend, Jenny Prather, Denver's girlfriend."

"Where is this man?"

"Under guard in the hospital. And after he heals, he'll be in jail–for a long time."

"Denver has been cleared of the charges?"

"The sheriff told me the assault charges will be dropped, but Denver is still a suspect in J.B.'s murder. I don't think they have any other leads."

Lucia closed her eyes. "There is still so much no one knows."

"But you do. Please tell the sheriff about the silent partner. He could be the key to all of this."

"Go ahead and tell her all of it," a woman said from the patio doorway.

Claire recognized the voice. Cassandra Winchell stood with one hand on the doorframe and the other inside the pocket of a boxy cream-colored jacket.

"Tell her," Cassandra repeated.

Lucia cleared her throat. Her long fingers tapped on the table top. "I'm so sorry to have dragged you into this, Claire. I shouldn't have insinuated anything, and now . . . you'll pay the price like me." She looked at the other woman. "It doesn't have to be this way, Cass. You can solicit her silence, just as J.B. persuaded me to keep silent all these years."

"If you're talking about the truth of your ex-husband's so-called rescue operation, the secret is already out," Claire said, twisting in her chair to look at both Lucia and Cassandra. "I've told the sheriff. In fact, he's expecting me within the hour at his office to make a statement about what I found in a house in the country that used to belong to my family, the house on the acreage owned by Corbin Brook where J.B. sent the horses to be slaughtered."

A man pushed past Cassandra and onto the patio. "And how much credence will the sheriff pay to your information when he learns it was illegally obtained and unusable in court?" Reed Morgan asked. "Breaking and entering, Claire? I wouldn't have believed you capable."

"Reed? What are you—"

"I think you already got the drift, at least most of it," he interrupted. "I was Floren's banker. And despite their divorce, Cass has remained a shrewd, silent and absent partner. You met her second husband, Corbin Brook, several years ago when you sold him the family farm."

Another man sauntered through the doorway and onto the patio. His hair was short and neatly trimmed; she could not have identified him as the man who bought her grandfather's farm.

"Ms. Northcutt, so nice to see you again." He leered at her. "Purdue was certainly right about you."

"Be quiet," Cassandra hissed.

"So much for wanting to live off the grid," Claire said. "You two bought the property and created your own slaughterhouse."

Cassandra spoke up. "When J.B. agreed to your article, bringing him to the forefront of such 'heroic' work, he neglected to inform me. When he finally admitted what he had consented to, I knew our real enterprise might come under scrutiny. People might investigate, others might speak up. Corbin and I took care of that last week, but not in time to stop your ridiculous article."

A chill slid down Claire's back. "You killed J.B. because of my article?"

Cassandra smiled. "Paybacks are sweet. He wasn't the best partner, or the best lover." Her eyes narrowed as she looked at Lucia.

Lucia's stare was focused on the pasture and the river beyond.

Claire glared at Reed. "When we first met, I told you about my grandfather's property. Then, you connected me with 'the perfect buyer.' My farm was the perfect location to create a side operation for Floren. You had insider knowledge, and you used it."

"Nothing illegal about it. You told me about the farm. I helped Cass and Corbin secure the purchase. Everything was above-board."

"You didn't tell me what he wanted to do with the property."

"I was under no obligation to do so, and neither were they."

"He told me he was all about living off the grid. I assumed he would raise vegetables and have farm animals."

"But you didn't keep in touch, and you didn't ever consider anything out of the ordinary was going on, even when you and Cade visited," Reed persisted. "Imagine how surprised I was to learn you were writing the article about J.B.'s 'rescue' ranch." He chuckled.

"Enough," Cassandra Winchell interrupted. "We have pressing matters. Like your future, Claire." Smiling, she crossed the patio, and turned her back to the lush yard and the river bottom land beyond. "Denver has been the perfect decoy," Cassandra continued. "Too bad a soldier who fought for our country returned in such an angry state. In the absence of any concrete evidence to refute his guilt, I'm sure he will go to prison for killing my ex-husband."

"You can't really believe you will get away with this." Claire's mouth went dry.

"Here's how it will play out," Cassandra continued. "You came here this morning at Lucia's request. The two of you argued. Maybe about Denver's innocence. It doesn't matter. Lucia killed you in a rage before taking her own life, all witnessed by Graciella, Floren's daughter."

On cue, the girl appeared in the doorway. Eyes downcast, Graciella stepped onto the patio and stood, hands clasped in front of her, next to Reed Morgan.

Lucia gasped. "No. You will not involve Graciella. She is innocent. This is unfair."

"What is fair or not fair has nothing to do with anything." Cassandra shrugged. "Life is. You break it, or it breaks you." When she pulled her gloved hand out of her jacket pocket, her fingers clasped a small silver revolver.

Claire stiffened. Her mind raced. Was she going to be killed right here, in a set up that also resulted in Lucia's death?

"My news article stirred things up, but they won't calm down if Lucia and I end up dead. Everything will get worse, no matter how you make it appear. I've documented my suspicions. There's a trail to follow, and I'm sure the same conclusion will be reached by the police."

"Reed will smooth things over concerning J.B. And I suppose he could also hint that Lucia killed J.B. Maybe that's how it should go. What do you think, Reed?"

He shrugged. "We could clear Denver. Bound to be ways to cast blame on Lucia. And to make it appear Claire had figured out that Lucia was guilty. The intrepid investigative reporter, hot on the trail of the real murderer." Reed grinned.

Claire's stomach clenched. She had thought Reed interesting, intelligent and even caring. Why had she not seen how despicable he was?

"It is a shame she has to die, though. I've always had a crush on her, Cass." Reed smiled at Claire.

Her stomach clenched.

"I imagine you have," Cassandra drawled.

"She was always a challenge. And lately, following her around in my Charger has had some interesting results."

Claire shook her head. Reed in the black sedan. Reed, following her out to the farm.

"Please ... please don't kill my mother," Graciella pleaded. "I'll do whatever you want me to do, but don't kill her." Fat tears rolled down the girl's cheeks. Corbin Brook grabbed her, and held her tightly against him.

Claire chewed her lip and studied the group on the patio. Her thoughts raced.

"Ah, touching, Gracie, considering you didn't even know she *was* your mother until today," Cassandra Winchell sneered.

Lucia swiped her forehead with one finger and slumped. "Claire, she is Miguel's twin. I made a deal with Floren after the babies were born. Cassandra agreed to leave quietly with the baby girl she'd always wanted, while Miguel stayed here with me where he could see his father. Graciella only recently learned I am her mother, not Cassandra."

Claire looked at Cassandra with new horror. She was a ruthless woman, and she was holding a gun.

Lucia stiffened. "Cass, please?"

"Sweet Gracie, I've been your mother all these years. You don't need another one. You'll be gaining a brother, not losing a mother." Cassandra smiled a sick, sweet smile at Graciella.

A crashing sound came from the barn a hundred yards from the house, and everyone looked out at the yard as a black dog raced toward the patio.

Ranger.

Claire's world shifted into slow motion.

Chapter 56

A snarling blur of black fur vaulted over the hedge bordering the patio and straight into Cassandra. The gun slid across the tiled floor. Claire dove for it and snatched the gun before rolling to her feet. Ranger clamped his teeth onto Cassandra's arm and shook it, growling and snarling.

Corbin lunged toward his wife.

"Stop, Corbin. Reed, don't try anything." Claire clutched the gun with both hands, one finger on the trigger. She pointed it first at one man, and then the other.

"Ha. Like you could shoot somebody," Corbin scoffed. He took a step toward her.

"Try me," Claire said.

"I don't have any doubt she'll kill you, Corbin," Reed said. "I'd back down. She's killed men before."

Corbin straightened and stopped.

"Get off me, Ranger," Cassandra cried.

The dog shook her arm again and growled.

Claire held the gun securely in both hands. "Call the sheriff, Lucia. Graciella, go with your mother."

"Gracie, no. Help us. Get the gun from that woman," Corbin shouted, shaking his fist in the air as Gracie left the patio with Lucia. "You've been my daughter, too. How can you do this?"

"Corbin, do something," Cassandra shouted from the floor.

"Both of you be quiet. Ranger, drop it," Claire commanded.

Ranger released Cassandra's arm but stood close, a growl rumbling in his throat, his teeth bared. The hair on the back of his neck bristled.

Claire stepped back until she could see all three people, easily. Her heart skipped in her chest. She focused; her hand on the gun was steady. "Stay put, all of you. When I shot that other man, I was trembling. I'm not trembling now."

In the distance, sirens wailed.

"It sounds like the police are on the way. And there are a few things I want to know. I'll start with you, Reed."

"Claire, I really had no idea what J.B. had in mind when he sent Brook to me to buy property. And you and I had just talked about your family place the night before. It seemed a good option. You sell the family property, and this friend of J.B.'s has a nice place in the country to build a business."

"You knew they were going to slaughter the horses there?"

"I had no idea. But he came back to me with a request for a loan to build structures and a business plan. J.B. endorsed all of it, and co-signed the loan."

"You were another partner?"

"Only in a financial sense. It sounded like a lucrative business venture. And once the construction was done, the operation was almost immediately in the black."

"But I could have found out about it. Gone out there to visit while everything was being built."

"But you didn't. I remember how sad you were about the sale after you'd gotten over the initial relief of no longer owing the property taxes or worrying about trespassers, illegal hunting, and the hogs."

"I was worried about those things, but that doesn't mean I forgot about my family's heritage."

Reed shrugged. "And I let you tell me all about it, remember?"

The conversation came back to her in bits and pieces as she watched the three people, keeping the gun pointed and ready in case one of them made a move.

She and Reed had been having an Italian dinner at his condominium. He'd cooked his specialty, paella, the same dish that Lucia was so fond of. "I remember. You told me it was wonderful to have those memories, and that I should let them suffice for as long as I could before I went back out to the property. 'He might make changes,' you said. You advised me to stay away for at least a year, because when I went back it might look very different than I remembered."

"And it did, when you finally went back, but you still didn't find the slaughter house operation."

"No. It was hidden on the back acres, the areas where everyone knew the wild hogs lived."

"That was genius, actually. My suggestion," Corbin said. "First time I went out there and found those hogs, I said to myself, there's the cover. Nobody wanted to cross those hogs. Dangerous and unpredictable. Must've killed a good two dozen of them when we went in to clear the area before the buildings went up."

"Reed, how could you allow the killing of the mustangs and burros Floren was supposed to be saving?" Claire's arm was tiring from holding the gun. The siren sounded closer.

"It was about the money. Surely, you've learned that money talks. I had a nice little sideline business going. In fact, that enterprise provided Denver's bail money. It seemed appropriate to use some of those funds to help get your nephew out of jail for trumped up charges we'd arranged."

"That you arranged? I thought Kent Purdue was behind that."

"Kent was behind it. But who do you think our Deputy Purdue was working for?" Cassandra asked.

"He was working for you?"

"He was our insurance policy. Our ear on the force, you could say. But he had urges he couldn't control. We let him turn them to our advantage."

"You ordered him to plant the drugs, and to beat up Jenny?"

Cassandra smiled. "All part of making Denver the sheriff's number one suspect."

"You're horrible."

"And you're screwed." Corbin Brook threw himself across the room at her, a determined look on his face.

Claire pulled the trigger and sidestepped an instant later. When Corbin hit the ground, Ranger was on top of him.

The world went into a slow spin and turned black.

Chapter 57

"Claire." A familiar voice said in her ear. "Claire, can you hear me?"

Her eyes opened to a blurry world.

"You're okay. I'm here, and everything is fine. Trust me. Everything's fine."

Her vision cleared briefly, and then began to swim again. "Holt?"

"Yeah."

She tried to sit up. The movement made her want to retch.

"No, no, just lie here. You hit your head, an ambulance is on the way. Two ambulances, actually."

"Two?" Vaguely she remembered the blood. She'd shot someone, again. *Corbin Brook.*

"Everything's under control. Please, lie still until the paramedic gets here."

"Corbin?" She tried to sit up, to turn her head to see the other body. Pain boomed in her head.

"He's alive. You didn't kill him."

"I didn't?"

"You shot him, but he's not dead. I've cuffed him, and staunched the bleeding, but he's alive."

Somewhere nearby, Ranger whined.

"Ranger?"

"He's here. I guess they had him shut up in a barn."

"He disappeared. Days ago. Cassandra must have ..." The world began to swim again. Her head pounded.

"Here," another voice said. Cool water touched her lips and she took a sip. A dog's nose pushed against her cheek and his tongue licked her chin.

"Ranger. I got the gun because of him. He knocked it out of Cassandra's hands." She lay back, and this time something soft was beneath her. "Corbin? You cuffed him."

"Yes."

She could hear the siren, and it sounded like it was right outside the house.

"You have cuffs?"

"Yes. I haven't been entirely truthful about what I do for a living."

She squinted up at him. "What do you do?"

"I'll have to shoot you if I tell you." He smiled.

"Tell me, but don't shoot me. Okay?"

He squeezed her hand. "Later."

The siren stopped. Seconds later, the sheriff and three deputies burst out onto the patio.

"Braden? What are you doing here?" The sheriff stood beside Holt.

"Trying to make sure nobody gets killed on your watch. But I was almost too late. Hope you brought the ambulance. Claire hit her head, and that one over there has a bullet wound."

Behind the sheriff, Lucia and her daughter, Graciella, stood together holding hands in the doorway.

Claire saw concern on Holt's face, his furrowed brow, the fearful look.

"I think it's over, darlin'," Holt said, stroking her cheek with his fingertips.

"Give me a little time, Holt." She patted his hand.

About the Author

Mary Coley is a native Oklahoman. An award-winning novelist, she was nominated for the Oklahoma Book Award for her second mystery, Ant Dens, and received the Creative Woman of Oklahoma Award for both her first and second mysteries, **Cobwebs** and **Ant Dens**. She has been a finalist in the Arizona/New Mexico Book Awards twice.

Blood on the Cimarron is her fifth book.

An avid traveler and nature lover, Coley splits her time between Tulsa and Santa Fe.

www.marycoley.com
www.marycoley.me (blog)
www.facebook.com/MaryColeyAuthor
www.pinterest.com/mmcint2415
www.goodreads.com/MaryColey
www.amazon.com/MaryColey

Books by Mary Coley

<u>Cobwebs – A Suspense Novel.</u> Published by Wheatmark. 2013
A present-day mystery that delves into the tragic and troubled
history of the Osage Reign of Terror in the 1920s. Jamie Aldrich
scrambles to save her aunt's life, as well as her own. *Someone wants
the past to stay buried.* (Also available as an Audible audiobook.)

<u>Ant Dens – A Suspense Novel.</u> Published by Wheatmark. 2014
Slavery and human trafficking are real. In this sequel to <u>Cobwebs,</u>
Jamie Aldrich races against time to discover what happened to her
missing stepdaughter, and unleashes a madman responsible for
horrendous suffering.

<u>Beehives – A Suspense Novel</u>. Published by Wheatmark. 2015
A woman hermit living in Oklahoma's beautiful Osage Hills State
Park is found dead. Jamie must solve the puzzle of her mysterious
death and revisit a long ago 'suicide' to save the man she loves.

<u>The Ravine</u> – Published by Wild Rose Press. 2016. Katy Werling is
injured, lying at the bottom of a ravine. Only a stray black dog
knows she's there. Can the humans in her life look past their own
troubles and listen to the dog before it's too late to save the child?

And coming in 2018, Chrysalis – A Suspense Novel

Made in the USA
Columbia, SC
26 April 2019